HEARTSCAPE

Member	Due Date

HEARTSCAPE

GARRETT LEIGH

HeartEyes
Press

CHAPTER ONE

Tanner

"Special of the week is a red from Sparrow Farm." I zoom the bottle along the bar to the cluster of staff I've gathered together. "It's a Frontenac blend. Full-bodied, cherries and vanilla, and some other fruity stuff I can't remember. Have a taste if you want and check the board for the notes."

The spiel is about as good as it gets when it comes to me waxing lyrical about wine. And I'm fooling no one, not even my boss, who rolls his eyes on his way out the door. I don't give a shit about wine, and he knows it. A few months back, I couldn't tell one grape from another, or explain how tannin levels affect the palate. I still have trouble with both, but I'm getting better, because I want to be. Somewhere along the line in the last few months I've learned that matters—the will to be a better human, not just at wine, but at life.

It's a work in progress, but I care enough to keep at it.

Most days, at least. And today is one of those days. I slide more bottles on the bar and take my best shot at teaching my crew how to hawk them to the locals and tourists who patronize the inclusive wine bar I'm lucky enough to run. Vino and Veritas. Vino is me—dark leather, rich wood, and rainbows in the window. Veritas is the adjacent bookstore, but I know even less about books than I do about wine.

When the wine briefing is over, I clear away the empty wine boxes, turn the music on, and fetch the cash floats for the registers. The list of jobs in my head gets checked off, task by task, and I settle into the routine I need to keep my brain quiet. I'm good at organizing people. At checking they have everything they need to do the job my boss pays them to do. When I get it right, I can almost avoid the actual bar altogether, but the problem with "right" is that it's never too far from being catastrophically wrong. Dodging folks isn't good for me—even strangers who want ten-dollar glasses of Chablis to go with their hipster spiced nuts. They're nice people, and they want to talk to me, so I do my best to show up.

Smoky jazz music fills the bar, blending perfectly with the wood and leather interior. The space is the living room I'd have if I ever find the inclination to decorate my apartment. It's cozy, warm, and welcoming to anyone who ducks inside to seek shelter from the chilly fall days.

The rhythm of the night takes hold. Feeling weak, I keep my distance from the bar for the first hour of my shift, collecting glasses instead, and taking out the trash, all the shitty jobs no one else wants to do, but eventually it's time to rotate staff breaks, and I take my place with a suppressed sigh.

Regulars call my name. Lucky for me, one of them is my brother, checking in on his way out of town.

I bring him a soda. He doesn't drink wine either. "Heading out?"

Gabriel ignores the glass in front of him, letting me know his appearance has nothing to do with refreshment. "I'll be back before Christmas. Just wanted to let you know you could, you know, like, call me if you need anything. On the phone, Skype, whatever."

I snort out a laugh that feels hollow in my chest. My brother is a horrible communicator. He's saying this shit because I am too, but I never used to be, and he still doesn't know what to do with that. "I won't need anything. I've got six-day work weeks through the next month, and I sleep all day on Sundays."

His frown deepens. "You live a blessed life, bro, but do you have to be a dick when I'm trying to be nice? It's not easy to walk out on you for months at a time."

Guilt rattles me, a beast that can't be tamed. Nothing about being my brother should be this hard. My *kid* brother. Gabi is younger than me. It's eighteen months, but still. It burns that he feels so responsible for me. That I've given him every reason to worry, and it's not over. "All right, all right." I step away to pour fruity red wine for another customer and make change, hoping Gabi's expression will lighten by the time I get back.

It doesn't, and the sigh I swallowed when I shuffled behind the bar escapes. "Look, I'm sorry. But I'm fine, honest. I've got plenty to keep me busy around here, and I promised Eve I'd help her move into that girl-tastic yoga commune next week. She mentioned plumbing issues. I don't think she was kidding."

A bare hint of a smile warms Gabi's earnest features. Eve is his nearlygirlfriend and one true love, and I'm well known for avoiding her as much as I do him. I adore her, but…she's a lot. For me, at least. Typically, Gabriel has the decency to sigh and leave me alone. Eve stands her ground. She leaves me nowhere to hide, and I'm not always in the mood.

Scratch that, I'm never in the mood. It's only her kick-ass mac and cheese that pulls me in. That, and the house full of chicks she's about to move in with. I have zero interest in romance right now, but despite my best efforts to live a quiet life, I'm still a red-blooded bisexual.

I'm also weak enough to crave my brother's embrace, even if I'm not man enough to tell him I don't want him to go. That I'll miss him, like I always do.

I lean over the bar and hug him. He hugs me back and presses his forehead to mine like he did when we were kids and I was the one taking care of him. "Call me," he says. "Doesn't matter why, when, whatever. Just do it, okay? I need you as much as you need me."

He makes it sound like we're star-crossed lovers, but he's depressingly right. Our parents have been gone a long time. There's no one else, and the guilt in my gut kicks up a notch as I recall, unbidden, how close I've come to leaving him on his own.

Gabi leaves. I wish he hadn't, and I wish he hadn't stopped by at all. I keep moving, fighting shadows. The low lighting of the bar cloaks me, and I remember why I like working here. My team keeps me company even when I forget to speak, and it's past nine o'clock before I give in and take a minute upstairs in my office.

Silence envelops me, but it's not literal. As the night draws in, I can still hear the buzz of drinkers and the music. But up here on my own, the pressure of being "on" fades. I suck in a deep breath and drop into the chair at my desk. Wine notes and delivery schedules litter my workspace. Tidying it up has been on my list of things to do forever, but I like it messy. It reminds me I have something to occupy myself with if I need too many of these precious minutes. That I never need to be truly still, even if I've convinced myself I like the quiet.

My phone buzzes, breaking my dirge-like internal monologue.

I rummage around on my desk for it, then wish I hadn't as Eve fills my screen with her bright eyes and kind smile. I hate ignoring her, but I do it anyway, and that makes me feel like shit.

So call her back.

I don't. I bury my phone beneath more paperwork and go downstairs.

"Yo, Tanner." Rainn, my favorite part-time bartender, is looking for me. "There's a bunch of fire trucks outside. Looks like that hostel went up. You'd better check it out."

Rainn doesn't waste words, so I take him seriously, and duck under the bar to make my way to the front door.

Flashing lights greet me, along with the kind of milling crowds you always get around a disaster. Grief vultures. I sniff the air and smell smoke, and sure enough, Rainn was right. The backpacker hostel opposite V and V has gone up in flames.

Firefighters pile out of their trucks, running hoses across the street and dispersing the masses. It's a thrum of activity I don't enjoy, but the masochist in me remains on the street, gawking as much as the next dude, eyes peeled for casualties.

After a while, it becomes clear that the hostel had been evacuated before the fire took hold, leaving only fixtures and belongings inside. Relief makes me sag against V and V's old walls. I don't know anyone at the hostel, but I've learned the hard way you don't need to know a soul to grieve for them. Or feel responsible for the premature end of their life. I lean hard against the wall, dampening anxiety I haven't earned tonight. A shiver passes through me, but not from cold, and I let my attention wander, cataloguing my surroundings to anchor myself to the present.

The fire is still burning, but the fire crews have it under control. And the crowds have thinned out too; only a few distraught hostel guests remain at the barrier the first responders set out to keep people back. Some of them are arguing with the firefighters—pleading with men who've seen horrors they can't imagine—to go back into the burning building and rescue their gadgets and snowboarding gear they can't even use yet. It's irritating enough for me to look away and swing my gaze carelessly until it lands on a set of slumped shoulders. *Broad* shoulders, that belong to a lone figure crouched on the ground a few feet back from the rest of the hostel residents. He has his head in his hands, and for a moment appears so lost that an emotion I can't quite name stirs in me.

I straighten up. The man stands too, and seems to give himself an internal shake. Then he turns his back on the flames, shoulders a bag, and walks away, gifting me a perfect view of his face.

And man, what a face. With his golden hair and high cheekbones, the dude is gorgeous. I'm betting he has blue eyes, and long lashes—I can't see from here—and I'm digging the scruff on his chiseled jaw. I admire the determined set of his strong shoulders too. It's clear he's lost something to that fire, and he's forcing himself to make peace with it fast.

Making peace is a skill I've never had. I fester and brood, until the time for healing has passed, and old wounds become permanent scars that keep me awake. Until they don't and they haunt my dreams too.

But still. The man is beautiful. Perhaps I'll dream of him instead tonight, because he sure seems like a face I won't forget.

Jax

I walk away from the smoldering hostel, resigned to the fact that unless I want to kick it around Burlington in full hiking gear, the sweatpants and hoodie combo I'm sporting are my only clothes in the world. Fuck it. Maybe I'll go get drunk. At least my wallet is safe in my pocket, and most of my kit—save what I have in my bag—is stashed at work. If I'd lost that too…damn. I can't contemplate it without my eyes getting hot and my chest too tight.

The urge to head back to HQ and check on my collection of secondhand cameras, lenses, and rigs is strong. Only the reality that I need to find a bed for the night stops me. I don't fancy sleeping in the currently unheated offices of Wildfoot Adventure. I'm a summer child at heart.

Yeah? Shoulda stayed in California then, shouldn't you?

Scratch that. Maybe I should've stayed on my own side of the Atlantic. Maybe then I'd have more to my name than a couple of cameras and some kick-ass snow boots.

I keep walking with no clear idea of where I'm going. Aside from my boss, I have exactly one friend in Burlington, and she lives in a tiny studio apartment she's about to vacate. No couch. And a moody boyfriend-not boyfriend who won't take kindly to me snuggling up to his girl, even if he is rarely in town.

Besides, I'm not the kind of dude who rocks up on his BFF's

doorstep asking for help. I deal with my own shit. It's easier that way. And it's not that cold yet. Maybe I'll head up to HQ after all. My legs are already beat, but I can handle the walk.

As the thought processes, my phone buzzes. I fish it out of my pocket and answer with a sigh I can't quite help. "Let me guess. You saw the smoke from your window and you're checking I'm not bacon right now?"

Eve laughs a little. "I know you're not bacon because I can also *see you* from my window. Are you okay?"

"Course I am. Not bacon, remember?"

"What about your stuff? Your cameras weren't in there, were they?"

"No, I left them locked up at the office. They're safer there even without catastrophic fires. Pretty sure my iPad is dust, though. And I now have even less clothes for you to bag on."

"I don't bag on your clothes."

"Stop trying to get me to wear flannel shirts, then."

Eve laughs again, and despite the gloom settling over me, I chuckle too. But I must do it real badly, because Eve's laughter fades fast. "Right," she says. "Come over to my place. I'll fix you some dinner and you can have my bed for the night."

I snort. "As if I'm taking your bed. Where will you sleep?"

"I have a zillion girlfriends."

"Lucky you."

"Am I? Thought you'd sworn off the fairer sex for good?"

"I've sworn off all the sexes for good, but that's not really the point. I'm not taking your bed."

"Why not?"

"Because I don't want to. I'm not your problem. We went to the same uni for six months about a million years ago. We're not siblings." It comes out harsher than I mean it to, but I know she won't flinch. Despite every word that's just left my mouth, we were close enough once that I probably could sleep naked with her and not get wood. She's also the only person I can talk to without measuring my words a thousand times first. It's a habit

I'm trying to break, but life keeps getting in the way. And today my life has literally gone up in flames and I'm taking it out on the person who cared enough to pick up the phone. "Sorry I'm such a dick."

Eve is silent a moment, then she sighs. "You're not a dick, but I get why you don't want my help. Do you think I don't know you?"

"I don't know what I think right now. I might have to take you up on that flannel shirt, though."

"And what about a bed for the night? Jax, you can't wander around Burlington all night."

She's right about that, and if I don't want to turf her out of her bed, I'll have to spring for a hotel room. But seriously, fuck that noise. I can barely afford to eat as it is.

"Listen," she says when I fail to answer. "I know a guy who's got a couch you can probably surf for a few days. He works in a bar, so he's never home, and he needs the company as much as you do."

"How can someone who works in a bar need company?"

It's Eve's turn to snort. "Trust me, you'll see. Of course, that's if he says yes. He's a grouchy asshole if you catch him wrong. Good luck with that if you do land on his couch."

Awesome. If there's one thing less appealing than drowning in kindness, it's forced proximity with someone who'd rather you were anywhere else. But I've run out of energy to argue with Eve. I'd rather kip on a stranger's couch than rinse my bank account or put her out of her bed. "Okay. Ask him. But don't make him feel bad if he's not up for it. I'm not his problem either."

"Sunshine, you're not anyone's problem."

She hangs up without waiting for an answer. Mindful of the fact I'm getting closer and closer to her studio apartment, I spin around and head back the way I came. The fire trucks are still in the street and smoke lingers in the air. I find a bench outside the bakery and sit, gaze fixed on the damp remains of the hostel. Truth be told, it wasn't the nicest place to sleep anyway, and I've never been particularly attached to my cracked and ancient iPad. But losing my clothes hurts more than I want it to. Board shorts, and ten-year-old T-shirts that have no place when I'm camping in the Vermont wilderness. The jeans I wore on the flight I took from Heathrow to Cali all those years ago. They were all I had of the naive dude I was back then, and I don't know how I feel about that. I left enough of myself in California.

It's a while before Eve calls me back. I wrap my arms around myself and fatigue sets in. Even before the hostel fire it had been a hell of a long day. Tracking through the wilderness from dawn till dusk, then persuading my boss that we're not on a wild goose chase every time we put boots to dirt. He wants to capture the elusive Canadian lynx on film as badly as I do. But he doesn't want to waste his hard-earned bucks on footage I might not get before my contract runs out in the spring. And I don't blame him. *Stick to squirrels, man.*

I shiver. It really is fucking cold. I lean forward and blow on my hands. I'm still thinking about hoofing it back to the office to get my mountain coat and gloves. Or maybe giving in and sleeping under my boss's desk. It can't be colder than this, and at least I'd be out of the wind.

A booted foot nudges my leg. "You Jax?"

I blink and find myself lost in the darkest eyes I've ever seen. They're round, gold-flecked and grave, and attached to a hand-some face covered by the kind of beard I dream about when I'm not up to my neck in mud and snow. Huh. Maybe I *am* dreaming. It would make more sense than the inked tower of mountain man leaning over me. Though the irritation in his liquid gaze rings a bell. *"He's a grouchy asshole if you catch him wrong.* Okay, well fine. If this is my knight in shining armor, I'll take the grouchy part.

Too late, it dawns on me that I've left the guy hanging too long.

I uncurl my body faster than my cold-stiffened back really wants to and lurch unsteadily to my feet as Eve's friend starts to turn away. My hand lands on his arm by accident—his bare, inked arm. And just for a moment, there's nothing in the world but my fingers wrapped around solid flesh. Then I come to my senses and regain my equilibrium. I drop my hand. "Shit. Sorry. Yeah, that's me."

"Are you drunk?"

"No. I'm Jax."

Something flickers in the man's dark gaze, and it's not humor. He darts a rapid glance to where my hand had touched his arm as if he expects to find a mark, then he stares at me again and the exasperation in his eyes has gone. "I'm Tanner," he says. "Eve was worried about you. Said you need a bed for the night."

"A couch will do if you've got it, but I don't want to be any trouble."

"It's no trouble. Besides, I'm not gonna leave you out here with no fucking coat, am I?"

I don't see why not, as he doesn't know me from the next guy, but this dude has an intensity so compelling I can't look away. I can only stare as he picks up my bag and points across the street.

"My place is just over here."

I don't move, though I can't say why.

The man—*Tanner*—frowns, and a big hand appears at my back, splaying across the bottom of my spine. "Come on," he says. "Let's get you inside."

He gives me a gentle push. My legs finally connect with my brain, and lacking any better ideas, I do exactly what he says and let him tow me all the way to his place across the street.

CHAPTER TWO

Tanner

I shouldn't have answered the phone. But idiot that I am, I thought Eve might have been calling about Gabi, despite the fact he left only a few hours ago, and if anything happens to him, it will be me who gets the call, not her.

But I did answer the phone, and now I have one of her bum friends shivering on my couch. A bum friend who bears a striking resemblance—insert sarcasm—to the hot dude I spied earlier, though, if possible, the close up version of this guy is ten times more attractive. Only the fact that he's cold to the bone and pale enough to make my stomach churn is stopping me from cataloguing every facet of his handsome face that I missed the first time around.

I back away from him and head for the kitchen area of the open-plan apartment. My refrigerator is pretty bare, but I have sandwich fixings and water. I throw turkey and Swiss between slices of organic whole-wheat from the bakery next door, and take him a plate with a bag of chips.

He blinks, startled. "Thanks. You didn't have to do that."

His accent throws me. I need to get back to work and close the bar, but I sit on the coffee table in front of him instead. "Where are you from?"

"In general? Or tonight?"

"All of it."

A faint smile curls his full lips. Already, color is returning to his face, but still my heart won't stop racing. "I came from the hostel across the street," he says. "At least I would've done if it hadn't burned down."

"And in general?"

"St. Ives. Cornwall."

"You're British?"

"No, I'm Cornish."

"There's a difference?"

"Probably."

His faint smile fades, and I miss the effect it has on me. Even with his dazed expression, Jax is ridiculously gorgeous. But his smile is nuclear. It's hard to believe it's real. "I've gotta go back to work for a bit and close the bar. Are you going to be okay?"

"Hmm?" Jax blinks again. "Sorry. What?"

"Eat your sandwich," I say instead of repeating myself. "And get warm. I'll be back in a couple hours. Bathroom's down the hall."

He nods and I force myself to stand and back away from him. Common sense tells me he's cold from however long he's spent outside with no coat, and the shock of watching the hostel burn to the ground caught up with him while Eve was waiting for me to answer my damn phone.

Common sense hasn't been my friend for a long time.

Leaving Jax alone makes my skin itch.

I do it, though, because I have other responsibilities. I go downstairs and close the bar. Clear tables, mop floors, and send my guys home for the night. Then I cash out the registers, bypass my usual stop in my office, and take the cash bag to the third floor with me. As I let myself into my apartment, it occurs to me that the total stranger in my home is more of a risk for stealing the night's take than he is for dying on my watch, but that's not how my brain works. I don't do logic. I do fear and agitation, and I'm not ready for the sight of Jax sprawled out on my couch.

But as I shut the door behind me and glance into the living room, I see he's not asleep yet. He's exactly where I left him. All he's done is eat his sandwich and take his shoes off.

He's set them neatly next to the hiking boots I haven't touched in months. We have the same size feet. I can't say why I notice that, but I do. I file it away somewhere, and set the cash on the kitchen counter. "You're still up," I say for the sake of saying something.

Jax stands and approaches the counter. His gait is steady now, and his long legs hold him up instead of wobbling like they did earlier. He's as tall as me, and just as broad, but his build is hard to gauge beneath the thick So-Cal hoodie he's wearing.

I resent that hoodie, and I don't understand that either. He's down on his luck and needs a port in a storm, not a weirdo bartender mentally undressing him.

Jax leans on the counter, stretching out his back and his elegant neck. "I thought it was a dick move to pass out on your couch without having a proper conversation."

"I wouldn't have minded." At least, not for the reasons he's worried about. "How do you know Eve?"

"Uni. We were on the same course for a bit before I dropped out."

I dissect his Brit speak. He's talking about college, and somewhere in the back of my fractured mind I remember that Eve studied marine biology in the UK before she quit school to teach yoga to Burlington hipsters. "You've been friends a while, then?"

"Off and on. Before I came here, I hadn't seen her for a while. And her boyfriend doesn't like me, so I don't see her much now either."

"Why doesn't he like you?"

"No idea. He doesn't say."

A snort of laughter escapes me. "Don't take that personally. Gabi doesn't say much to anyone. Reid boys are wired that way."

"Reid boys?"

"He's my brother."

"Wow." Jax digests that, and I can tell he's measuring Gabriel's stone face against mine and wondering why he didn't figure it out sooner. We're exactly the same. The only difference is my ink covers most of my torso, while his is hidden on his chest. Oh, and he's nicer than me when you get to know him, but I'm guessing Jax didn't get that far.

"Eve loves him," Jax says.

"I know." I turn away from him and light the flame under the tea kettle on my stove, my brain tracking back to pinpoint how we wound up discussing my brother's love life. Or if the fact that Gabi has kept Eve dangling for the last two years is going to be a problem.

But when I glance at Jax again, it's clear he's moved on. He's staring wistfully at my battered steel kettle. "My nan had one like that."

"Your grandmother?"

"Yeah. She read tea leaves for tourists every summer and told them all they'd die of horrible diseases if they didn't take their trash home."

"Sounds like my kind of woman."

"She was pretty epic."

I find a genuine smile from somewhere, and open the drawer where I keep the tea that stands between me and the bottle of sleeping pills in the bathroom. I never knew my grandparents, so the fondness lighting his lovely face is a mystery to me. So is the fact that having a stranger in my kitchen is far easier than I'd anticipated when I'd agreed to scoop Eve's college buddy from the street. But it's late, and I'm tired, so I don't dwell on it too much. "You want tea? British people drink that, right?"

Jax leans even lower over the counter and peers into my magic drawer. "We drink builder's brew with milk and sugar, not green stuff that tastes like perfume."

"Is that a no?"

He laughs. And I like that too. "You pick," he says. "I don't mind."

I grab a peppermint teabag to go with the floral one that seems to horrify him so much. He watches me brew tea in companionable silence I enjoy as much as his conversation, and I take the time to dart surreptitious glances at him. If he's the same age as Eve, he's twenty-six, two years younger than me, but he has wise eyes that don't match his boyish good looks. And his golden scruff gives his face a maturity that sets me on fire. It's been a while since a dude turned my head like this. My sexuality is fluid enough that I can happily swing in any direction, but when a dude gets me, it's right in the gut. And Jax has gotten me so hard I forget to slide his tea mug across the counter until he reaches across and helps himself.

"Thank you. For this, the sandwich, and your couch. I really appreciate it."

"It's nothing," I say absently. I'm still studying the way his hair curls at his neck and fight hard to snap out of it. Now the fear that he's dead on my couch has eased off, I'm plagued by a staredown I can't break. I need to go to bed. And so does he, but I can't seem to make myself move.

At least get him a fucking pillow. And a blanket. It's warm up here, but it won't be if he's huddled on that couch in his boxers.

The thought makes *me* shiver, but I cover it by pushing abruptly away from the counter and ducking out of the kitchen. I grab a pillow from my bed and a blanket from the linen closet. It's thick Vermont wool, and it smells of wood smoke from the last time I used it. The scent makes me shiver again, but keeping Jax warm is more important than old ghosts.

I take the blanket and the pillow back and lay them on the couch.

Jax takes his cue and drifts to my side. "Thanks," he says again.

I wave the sentiment away. "I told you. It's fine. But I'm leaving tonight's take on the counter all night, so don't rob me, okay?"

"I'll try not to. Can't promise anything, though."

British people make bad jokes, so I take his sarcasm on the chin and force myself to walk away. After a pit stop in the bathroom, I shut my bedroom door and lean against it, alone at last, but so aware of Jax in the next room I know I'll never sleep.

And I left my tea behind. *Awesome.* I cross the small room to my bed and take my clothes off, swapping my dark jeans and T-shirt for flannel pants I don't usually bother with. But bad dreams make me sleepwalk sometimes, and I figure Jax has had a crappy enough night without me stumbling naked and crying into his makeshift bedroom.

I save that shit for my brother.

Jax

Tanner has huge eyes. I register this the moment I wake the next morning to find him leaning on his kitchen counter again, watching me sleep with an expression that doesn't sit right on his handsome face. He has a dark beard, inky hair, and warm, tattooed skin, but even the sight of him shirtless doesn't hide the worry in those enormous gold-flecked peepers.

It occurs to me that perhaps he wants me to leave. I sit up in a hurry. The tight skin on my hip protests, but before I can lurch to my feet, Tanner is in front of me. He's brandishing more tea, and his face has relaxed. "Sorry. Didn't mean to wake you so early."

"You didn't wake me." I take the tea. "What time is it?"

"Six. Eve told me you're shitty at getting up for work, but I was gonna let you sleep a little longer."

"When did Eve tell you that?"

"This morning. She sent me, like, seven messages while I was in the shower."

I belatedly notice Tanner's damp hair, and the faint sheen of moisture on his inked skin. At some point in the night I've kicked his cozy blanket to his battered hardwood floor. I bend to retrieve it, hoping the action conceals the effect he's having on me.

If he notices, it doesn't show. He sets the tea mug on the coffee table and backs up. "Do you need a ride to work?"

"Nah, my boss picks me up from the parking lot right behind this place."

"Nice boss."

"He's okay. There's a shower at HQ too, if I can make the generator work. Jerry's kind of a miser about getting it fixed."

"Jerry Coleman?"

I'm staring at a bead of water still running down Tanner's long neck. "Yeah. You know him?"

Tanner nods. "I used to work for him."

"At Wildfoot?"

"Yeah." Tanner turns into the kitchen, showing me his muscled back. The wide expanse is covered with ink too, and I find myself squinting to decipher it before I realize he's not doing anything. He's standing at the kitchen sink as if he's forgotten why he's there.

I wonder if he doesn't like my boss, but that doesn't seem possible. Jerry has good reasons for doubting my lynx aspirations, but in everything else, he's been sound as a pound. Salt of the earth. I can't imagine anyone not liking him.

The thought returns me to the logical reality that Tanner wants his space back. I roll from his couch. My bag is at my feet. I retrieve it and straighten slowly, easing my body back to life, grateful for the night I've spent on a sofa that's three times the size of my bunk at the hostel. I fold the blanket into a neat square and set it on the coffee table.

Tanner still isn't looking at me. I contemplate leaving him to it and slipping away, but as I near the kitchen, I can't make myself do it. I come up behind him and touch his shoulder.

He startles, and whirls around.

I give him what I hope is an easy grin. "I'm off. Just wanted to say thanks for putting me up."

A beat of silence stretches between us. Then he nods. "That's okay. You good for tonight?"

I shrug, because I have zero clue, and I'm not a liar. "Dunno. I'll talk to Jerry later. He might know somewhere I can stay. Or he might advance my paycheck so I can figure something out."

"What do you do for him? Are you a ranger?"

"Nope. Videographer. He hired me to spend the winter cataloguing the wildlife on the new trails he's opening up."

"The Black Claw trails?"

"Yeah. You know them?"

"A bit." Tanner's dark eyes seem to flash. "You aren't going up there dressed like that, are you?"

I laugh. "No. I lost all my casual clothes in the fire, but my gear is stashed at HQ. I'm good for hiking and sitting in the mud all day."

"Is Jerry still renovating the office?"

"Yeah. I heard he's been doing it for years, though."

"He has," Tanner says shortly. "Using the generator for power is a new one, though. You'd think it was a fucking treehouse, not a downtown premises. What are you going to do after work?"

"What do you mean?"

"You have no clothes at all?"

I can't help the sigh that whooshes out of me. "Only what I'm wearing, but I guess I'll figure that out later too."

It's time to go. I want to touch Tanner again. Shake his hand. Hug him. Fuck, even a fist bump would do. But I don't do it, because his shirtless self is already too much. And he seems lost in thought again.

I leave, shuffling out of the apartment, and shutting the heavy wooden door behind me. Dressed in the same clothes I was in when I got here, it feels like the walk of shame as I head down the stairs past the wine bar, but without the thrill of a damn good fuck. As if I even remember what that's like. And maybe it's just as well. I'm having a hard enough time dealing with Tanner's hotness without imagining all the shit we could do together if life was completely fucking different. If we'd hooked up instead of me being a hobo who'd kipped on his couch.

If. Only.

My boss is waiting for me on the street outside. He's gazing at the blackened shell where the hostel once stood, phone in his hand, as I come up behind him.

I clap him on the back. "Morning."

He jumps. "Jesus. I was just about to call you. Bad night, huh?"

"Could've been worse. I wasn't there when it went up."

Jerry whistles all the same. "What about your stuff?"

"Anything important is at the office. Just lost my clothes and an iPad."

"Dang. You need a ride somewhere to get new gear?"

Probably. At some point. But replacing my clothes is going to cost money I don't have till my first pay check comes in, and I don't feel like disclosing that to a man I need to respect me. "Nah. It's fine. I'll get it sorted next week. It's not like I'm going anywhere that doesn't involve waterproof pants and boots."

"Where are you gonna sleep?"

"Not sure yet. The bloke from the wine bar put me up last night."

"Tanner?"

"Yeah. He said he used to work for you too."

"That he did. Was my best ranger for a while. Truth be told, we wouldn't be standing here together if I still had him on my books. No one knows Black Claw better than him."

"How come he's working in a wine bar, then?"

Jerry gives me a look that's somehow fascinating and distraught at the same time. "You'd have to ask him that, son. But as long he's doing okay, I can live with dragging my own damn self around those trails."

I don't imagine I'll get the chance to ask Tanner anything. He lent me his couch because Eve asked him to. There's no reason for us to see each other again, but as we walk to the parking lot and set off for HQ, he's all I can think about. His hot bod is the most obvious distraction from the long day I have ahead of me, but his eyes haunt me the most. They're kind, but so troubled I can't help the shiver of disquiet in my gut. And I have a forty-five minute car ride to think about it. At least, I will if Jerry ever stops talking. Yesterday, I'd been enraptured by his best efforts to play tour guide, despite the fact we've driven the same route out of Burlington every day for the last month. Today, I just want him to shut the hell up so I can brood over the handsome stranger who saved me from a night on a street bench.

But getting what I want is a rare thing. Jerry talks, and I listen, then we spend the day mapping out safe spots to fix static cameras and set up campsites.

It's getting dark by the time we roll back into Burlington, and I still haven't answered Jerry's question about where I'm going to lay my head for the night.

He pulls the truck to a stop in the parking lot behind the wine bar, then turns to me with a wince. "Damn, sorry. Been so fixed on getting those spots just right I forgot about this. Do you want to—?"

I silence him with a wave of my hand. He's about to offer me a bed for the night that I know he doesn't have. Jerry has six foster kids and a four-bedroom house, and…he's my boss. I don't want to be the mope employee who can't get his shit together. "Don't worry about it. Same time tomorrow, yeah?"

"Jax, don't be proud, son."

I laugh, cos if there's one thing I'm not, it's fucking proud. "I'm good, mate. Honest. See you in the morning."

He doesn't believe me, but despite days and days out on the trails together, we're not close enough for him to argue with me.

He lets me go. I slide out of his truck and sling my bag on my back.

Jerry pulls away. I take a deep breath and turn to go who-the-fuck knows where.

Tanner Reid is right in front of me.

"Come on," he says. "I got you something."

CHAPTER THREE

Tanner

I wasn't expecting Jax to land on my doorstep again. The bag of clothes I've pulled together for him is behind the bar, waiting for Eve to pick up. Then I took the trash out to see him getting out of Jerry Coleman's truck in the parking lot, and I'd walked up on him before I knew what I was doing.

He seems relieved to see me, but it's a different vibe to the one Gabriel sends my way when he satisfies himself that I'm no longer on the brink of putting his gun in my mouth. And I dig it, so I gesture for him to follow me inside.

Jax seems bemused, but I don't look at him too closely, because I don't like it when people look too closely at me. I lead him to the far end of the bar and hand him the duffle bag. "We're about the same size."

He opens the bag and his fair brows shoot up. "You're lending me clothes? Man, you're my hero right now."

"Don't make that judgment until you get to the flannel shirts. Eve tells me you have feelings about them."

Jax's laugh is the glow of a warm summer evening. "Maybe I spent too much time in California."

"Oh yeah?"

His smile fades and he makes a noncommittal noise. "Actually, scratch that. I definitely spent too much time there. And thanks for the clothes. I'll bring them back when I get paid enough to buy new ones."

"I don't want them back."

Something in my tone strikes him. I don't know why. He tilts his head sideways and turns the volume up in his hypnotic eyes. Yeah, that's right. They're the bottomless blue I expected them to be. "What else did Eve say about me?"

A whole lot of nothing. But enough that I don't want him worrying about returning a duffle of old clothes I don't leave my apartment enough to justify keeping. "Not much. Why? Are you a wanted felon?"

"I'm not that interesting."

"Neither am I."

He snorts, and I remember he's spent the day with Jerry. Perhaps he knows more about me than I want him to. Or perhaps he doesn't, and my newfound curiosity about him is not only one-sided but massively unfair. "Do you want a drink?"

Jax jerks his head up from pawing through the stack of shirts and jeans I've stashed in Gabriel's old bag. "Hmm?"

"Booze," I clarify. "You've had a long day, huh?"

"Yours is just getting started. Did you go back to bed after I left?"

I want to lie to him and tell him I did. That I crawled back between the sheets and peacefully snoozed my day away instead of letting my short conversation with Eve agitate me enough to clean my closet out for him. But he has an honest face that doesn't deserve my bullshit, so I give him a rueful head shake. "No, but it's okay. I don't need much sleep."

"People who don't get enough always say that."

"Yeah, well. What are you going to say if I ask if you need to crash on my couch again?"

He treats me to another brief but wonderful laugh. "Get out of my head."

I take the win and fetch him a beer. He doesn't look like a wine dude, and I've seen enough of them over the past few months to make the call.

He's slouched on a barstool when I come back, poking at his phone. His face has settled into the worry mug I saw the last time I laid eyes on him. I don't like it as much as his magic smile, but I'm not good-humored enough to make it go away. I set the beer in front of him, then reach into my pocket for my apartment key and make another decision without thinking it through. "I wasn't kidding about the couch. I'm working every night through next week, so you'll have the place to yourself."

Jax blinks, both at the sudden appearance of a pint of craft beer in front of him, and an offer he was clearly expecting as much as a bag of my old clothes. "For real?"

Offering up my space is the last thing on earth yesterday's me would've contemplated. I wonder if I've had a personality transplant, but here we are. The key is in my outstretched hand, and I want him to take it. "I don't say things I don't mean. Drink your beer, get a shower, and chill for the night, unless you have grand plans your face is being real good at hiding right now."

"Am I that transparent?"

"Is anyone? Probably not, but take the key anyway."

I leave it on the bar next to his beer, and go back to serving wine to the hordes of drinkers who've descended on V and V for happy hour. It's a while before I glance up and take a breath, and by then, Jax is gone.

And so is the key.

It's the early hours of the morning when I crawl upstairs. Jax is asleep, so I barely glance at him. I go straight to my room and pretend he's not there. I'm tired enough that it works for a few hours, then it's five a.m., and I'm wide awake, pacing, and my room feels like a prison cell.

I work out on the floor, ignoring the cut of the hardwood

against my bones. The exertion is the only therapy I'm getting right now. Endorphins fight the black clouds hanging over me, and for as long as I punish my body, they win.

But there's only so many pushups a man can take, and eventually, a soul-deep craving for coffee wins out.

I slip out of my room and pad into the living space of the apartment with every intention of tiptoeing past the couch. But Jax is awake. He's wearing my old sweatpants and a T-shirt that hugs every ripple of muscle just right.

It's the first time I've seen him without his hoodie obscuring his body, and for a split second I'm caught in matching how strong he is with the chiseled good looks I've been distracted by for the last two nights.

I lose the power of speech.

He gives me a nervous grin. "Morning. You look like you forgot I was here."

I don't forget things. If I did, my life, and anyone's who's unfortunate enough to give a shit about me, would be a hell of a lot easier. "I didn't forget you. I just, uh, woke up."

There goes my streak of not lying to him, but there's zero chance of me telling him about the possessive growl building in my chest at the sight of him wearing my clothes. Gabriel gets like this when Eve wears his shirts, and they've been pretending they're not soulmates since they were fifteen years old. I've known Jax thirty-six hours.

Damn.

I back up and continue to the kitchen. The coffeemaker calls my name. I make a pot big enough for two and open the refrigerator for milk. But my mind goes blank, and I stare at the shelves until Jax comes up behind me. "Want a hand?"

"Hmm?"

He reaches around me and grabs the milk carton. "I spent an hour looking for my spare socks yesterday and you know where they were?"

"Where?"

"On my fucking feet."

He hands me the milk carton and steps back with a slight wince.

My frown is instant. "What's the matter?"

Jax frowns back. "What do you mean?"

"You're moving weird. Is the couch no good for you?"

My nosiness earns me another twitch of his fair eyebrows, but he doesn't seem offended. He shakes his head. "The couch is fine. I've got an old injury that takes a while to warm up in the mornings. Or if I get super cold."

"Was it serious?"

"As a shark attack." His epic grin returns and he steps away entirely, returning to the couch to fold the blanket and stack the pillow on the coffee table.

I watch him move, noting the stiffness in his lower back and left side. It eases with every stretch of his strong body, but I don't look away until I'm in danger of being caught, and the coffee machine beeps loud enough to snap me back to reality.

Two mugs find their way to the counter. I pour coffee and add milk to both on autopilot without asking Jax what he wants.

I offer it to him anyway. "Sorry. I forgot to ask how you take it."

"I'm not fussed."

"What does that mean?"

He claims the coffee. "That I can drink it however. Thank you, for this and the clean clothes. I meant to say it last night, but I passed out before you got back."

Jax sits down on the couch. Lacking any better ideas, I perch on the coffee table. "Jerry picking you up this morning?"

"Yeah. We're building a camp at Stunt Point, but I don't know how far we'll get with that weather front rolling in."

I take a breath before I respond. Force it down to smother whatever fuckery my brain is about to gift me. "You don't want to be caught up there in a storm," I say carefully. "That rock isn't stable."

"Jerry said that too. He also mentioned you know those trails better than him. You ever seen lynx up there?"

His question shouldn't surprise me. He's already told me his job is to catalogue wildlife for Jerry, and it makes sense that I've come up in conversation between the two of them, even without Jax sleeping on my couch. But it catches me off guard all the same. I don't think about the great outdoors anymore. My world has narrowed to staff schedules and glasses of red, white, and rosé, and I like it that way. I *need* it that way. And I can't handle the expectation in Jax's ocean gaze as he waits for me to answer him.

The coffee mug burns my palm. I ground myself in the pain and take a sip large enough to singe my throat too. The lump there clears a little and I force my brain to catch up with the perfectly normal conversation he's trying to have with me. *Lynx. Trails. Lynx. Trails.* "Only once," I say eventually. "And it was so fast I was never sure. I kind of wish I never told Jerry, because he's been excited about it ever since."

Jax's eyes glimmer with humor. "Excited? He seems more pissed off about getting his feet wet."

I can't help a low chuckle. I know that side of Jerry all too well. "Don't be fooled by his grouchy old man act. He loves the lynx, and he's been wanting to get a good map of those trails for years."

"Why hasn't he, then?"

Another cinderblock fills my throat. "Because they're too dangerous for noob hikers to take their chances on. And assholes like me keep telling him it's bad for the environment. Think about it. If there are lynx up there, do you really want to unleash the masses on them?"

Jax sips his coffee, contemplating my pessimism as he swallows.

The subject matter is making me more jittery than the coffee, but watching his throat work and his tongue dart out to lick his lips is a welcome distraction. So is his bed head. His hair is wavy and golden, and lighter at the ends where it's been touched by the sun. I want to run my fingers through it. Not to straighten it out, but to feel if it's as soft as it looks. I haven't had a dude's head in my lap for quite some time, but good hair is still my kryptonite, perhaps more than the rest of it—the rocking bod pressed hard against me, the scruffy jaw that would scratch mine just right.

"You okay?"

"Hmm?"

Jax tilts his head sideways. "You're even less of a morning person than me, huh?"

He's wrong. I like mornings just fine. But I'm not about to explain to a stranger—or anyone who's not a shrink—that his peaceful nights on my couch have made my teeth itch. "Managing a bar doesn't leave me much time for Zs, unless I want to be a vampire. And I tried that. No daylight doesn't work for me. I'd rather be tired."

It's a half-truth, but Jax accepts it. "You have amazing weather here," he says. "It's more real than back in Cali. It reminds me of home."

"Your English home?"

He grins. "My Cornish home. But yeah. I mean, it's grayer there, and we don't see as much snow or sub-zero temperatures, but we get storms and rain and wind, even in the summer, and it keeps you alive, you know? Smaller waves mean more when they're freezing cold."

"Waves?"

Jax's gaze flickers, and I feel an affinity I can't decipher. "I was a surfer once," he says. "Chasing waves was my whole fucking life."

"Then what?"

"Then it wasn't."

Those three words make more sense to me than if he'd told me his entire life story. I absorb them, and accept his answer at face value. Because really, what more do I need to know? Except how he looks in a wetsuit, obviously. That would keep me up all night in the very best way.

I don't ask him, though. Instead, I track his gaze as it darts to the horrible plastic clock Gabriel sent me from Texas, and figure he needs some space to get ready for work.

Taking a shower gives me an out.

When I come back, Jax is standing by the couch, his bag and my duffle slung on his back.

"You don't have to take it all with you every time you leave," I blurt before my brain has caught up with the fact he doesn't actually live on my sofa.

He turns slowly, and the first haze of early morning light catches his hair. It shimmers, and my fingers itch again to touch it. His frown distracts me. "I don't want to leave you a mess," he says.

I cast a pointed glance around my apartment. There's literally nothing in the living room except the couch, the coffee table, and the TV that's set up on the floor. I'm not exactly house-proud right now, and it shows. "Dude. Leave anything you don't need right here. It's safe, I promise."

"I'm not worried about that."

But he is worried, I can tell, and it makes no sense. He seems like the most chill guy ever, but abandoning his bag at the end of my couch is making him bite down hard on his full bottom lip.

He steps back, still mauling his lip. I want to rescue it, but I walk away, and hover in the kitchen as Jax gets his shit together enough to leave.

I try not to listen to him move around my apartment. I wake up every day thinking I want to be alone, but something about this dude taking up my space comforts me. He hasn't said for sure if he's coming back tonight, but I want him to, and the abrupt certainty makes me dizzy.

Breathing slow, I tune him out.

Then he comes up behind me and every sense I possess comes alive.

I don't turn around.

29

And he doesn't speak.

Just lays a blazing hand on my bare shoulder, then walks out the door.

CHAPTER FOUR

Jax

"It was a nice idea," Jerry says. "But do you really want to hoof up and down this incline every day? The snow is gonna set in soon and you haven't seen a real winter yet."

I swallow an impatient growl, mainly because I know he's right. The static cameras I've set up along the steepest path were always going to be a ball-ache to monitor, but I didn't count on how long it would take me to check them every day. The only option seems to set up a camp where I can dig in for a few days, but I have a million things to do before that can happen.

Jerry stomps back the way we came when we set out on our eight-hour hike. I linger a moment, fiddling with the last camera on the route, changing the memory card and swapping the batteries, then I follow him with leaden legs, cos you know what? He's right about this fucking hill.

We drive back to Burlington in near silence. Jerry is humming the big-band music he thinks annoys me, and I'm, naturally, thinking about Tanner. It's all I seem to do when I'm not fretting about coyotes and bobcats. I've been sleeping on his couch for a week now. Each day I come home from work and find him at the bar of Vino and Veritas. He gives me a beer and the key to his place, and then I spend the rest of the night waiting for him to come home. Some nights I'm even awake when it happens. Others, I have to wait till dawn when he appears like magic to brew coffee and make me so comfortable in his apartment that I never want to leave. In California, I lived in a beachside condo with a pool and five bedrooms. I hated it.

But I love Tanner's couch.

Burlington seems to come around fast tonight. I blink and we're back in the parking lot. I slide out of Jerry's truck on autopilot, and shuffle the short walk into the wine bar, glad I ditched my cold-weather gear in the truck and wrapped myself in Tanner's clothes again. I'm still underdressed for the cozy establishment, but I'm fast learning that no one seems to care. Besides, the T-shirt and flannel combo smell of Tanner, so what other peeps think of me can do one.

Habit takes me to the quiet end of the bar where Tanner seems to gravitate when he's not busy. But he's nowhere in sight and a girl I don't recognize swoops in on me.

"What can I get you, sir?"

I've never been called sir in my life, and the girl is kind of cute, but a major brain blank stops me appreciating her sweet smile and auburn curls. I scan the beer taps beyond her, searching for whatever it is Tanner usually brings me, before I realize he's never told me. "Um. I don't know. You pick."

"Okay. I'm going to need some more to go on, though. Do you like red, white, or rosé? Or we've got craft beers from Colebury, Shipley cider, or there's the mocktail menu too..."

She says more words. I try to take them all in, but they convolute until my head is spinning, and I have no idea what she wants me to say.

Her expectant stare makes it worse.

I suck in a sharp breath. "I don't mind. Whatever."

She can't deal with my answer any more than I can handle her questions. Her frown deepens and the impasse between us widens, but just as I'm about to point at whatever bullshit drink is nearest me, Tanner appears beside the poor girl who's just trying to do her damn job. "It's okay, Molly. I got this."

The girl drifts away. I stare at the mahogany bar, tracing the wood grains, trying to pull my brain back together. I hate it when this happens, and I hate the people who made me like this. At least, I want to hate them. And I despise myself more because I don't.

Tanner drops a warm hand on my forearm. He doesn't say anything, just waits for me to look up. Then he offers me an apologetic wince I don't deserve. "Sorry. Molly's kind of a horrible bartender. We're working on it."

"She didn't do anything wrong. It was all me."

Curiosity lightens Tanner's dark gaze. He leans forward on the bar, his shirt sleeves rolled back to reveal his inked skin, and his hand still covering my arm. "How so? You don't strike me as the type of guy who gives bartenders a hard time."

"Get a lot of those in here, do you?"

"What do you think?"

I think Burlington is too civilized for the blokes I remember from pub brawls back home, but I'm also fairly certain Tanner can handle any drunk idiot stupid enough to cross him. So I let that one go, and search for the words to explain what he really wants to know. "I didn't make any decisions for myself for a long time, so I'm still really bad at it when I'm not prepared for it."

It's as good as I've got, and makes no sense on its own. I wait for Tanner to prod me more, but he just rubs his thumb over my wrist and walks away.

I sink onto the bar stool and go back to staring at the rich, textured wood. It's my favorite aspect of the gorgeous wine bar. I like the smell. Merged with the leather scent that makes me think of Tanner, it grounds me enough to raise my head and search him out. And I don't have to look far. He's in front of me again with a box tucked under his arm.

"Come on," he says. "Let's go home."

I like the sound of that more than I care to admit, but embarrassment still runs hot in my veins, and it's hard to follow him without tracking the passage of my feet with every step. But I do follow him, and I force my gaze up in time to get a full view of his backside as he jogs upstairs in front of me.

Every cloud. Seriously. The dude fills a pair of jeans like a dream.

Safe in his apartment, I take my place on the couch while he moves around his place, turning on lamps, and opening and shutting the fridge. It's not his normal routine. Most days he doesn't come up with me, and I spend my evenings falling asleep over my laptop.

Tanner disappears into his bedroom. Bemused, I shed my borrowed flannel shirt and fish the memory cards I've taken from the static cameras out of my pocket. My laptop is protected by thick casing that makes it weigh a ton. I heave it out from my bag and set it on Tanner's coffee table.

It's a good machine, but it's old and overworked, so it takes a while to boot up. Tanner comes back while I'm waiting and drops onto the couch beside me.

He's never done that before, and it strikes me that he hasn't taken a comfortable seat in his own living room since I've taken up residence in his life. He's also no longer dressed for work. His dark jeans and shirt have gone, and he's wearing sweatpants and thick wool socks that make me want to squeeze his feet, cos I'm a weirdo like that.

Tanner frowns at my laptop screen.

I move to close it. "Sorry, I can do this in the bar if you want some space."

"I don't."

His tone gives me pause, but staring at him has become such a thing that I have to make myself not do it every time he's close. I settle for watching my laptop come to life until he gets up and slopes into the kitchen.

Tanner is my newfound obsession, but my static cameras are

my babies—my life's work, especially as I have nothing else going on in my life. I forget about him rooting through his fridge and sparking his stovetop alight, and zero in on the footage from the first memory card. This one is at the very top of the trail and the one I hold out the most hope for in terms of rare sightings. It's *cold* up there, and there's already an icy carpet of the kind of snow I've never seen back home. Real snow, not the wet slush that brings England to a halt.

I sit back on Tanner's couch and watch as the video software speeds through twenty-four hours of mountain life. For a good while, nothing happens that I haven't seen already. The red foxes are the most curious. They come right up to the lens and nose at the camera, leaving a streak that freezes until it drops off sometime later.

But as amusing as the playful foxes are, they're not what I'm looking for, and the first memory card lets me down. The second is corrupted, but I'm prepared for that—shit happens. I'm loading the third into the slot when Tanner comes back to the couch. He's carrying two mismatched tumblers and has mini bottles of wine stuffed into his pockets. He sets them on the coffee table, then reaches across me to tap the track pad on my battered MacBook. "Marten. That's a good spot. They don't usually venture out of the trees at this time of year."

I lean forward and squint at the screen. I'm unfamiliar with the American Marten, but they're on my list of creatures Jerry wants me to capture. And Tanner is right—I wasn't expecting to see one on open ground. "Wow. They're smaller than I thought. Why would it be out in the open like that?"

I'm talking mostly to myself. But Tanner answers, reminding me that he knows my job better than I do. "It's either a male who's still horny after mating season, or it's a female looking for a safe place to nest."

"They don't have their young till the spring, though, right? They have delayed implantation?"

Tanner nods. "They don't carry the pregnancy if they're too

weak after the winter. But regardless of what sex that one is, you should document exactly where you saw it. They're still on the endangered list."

I had that list on the iPad that didn't make it out of the hostel fire. I haven't got round to researching it all over again, so I make a note in the crumpled pad that lives in my pocket while Tanner watches.

Then he returns to the kitchen, leaving me with his random bottles of wine, and a burning shoulder where his skin touched mine.

The next time he comes back he's carrying two plates balanced on one inked arm and silverware in his fist. I focus, dazed from scowling at my laptop screen, to find him brandishing one of the plates in my face.

It smells like heaven and my stomach growls. I'm still a week away from my first paycheck, and most of my meals since I arrived in Burlington have been instant noodles and energy bars. The thick slices of ham and creamy potatoes Tanner offers me could've come from my nan's Cornish kitchen, and I'm too hungry to turn it away.

Tanner settles beside me again, watching the screen. I'm hoping that means I don't have to, as the dinner he's brought me is awesome enough to require my full attention. I clear my plate while he peers over my shoulder. It takes me a while to notice he's not looking at the screen anymore.

"Can I ask you something?" he says.

I set my plate down with undue care. "Sure."

"Do you like the beer I've brought you every day this week?"

It's not where I expected him to go. But it's a complicated question, because I don't like beer in general, but I love that it was him who placed it in front of me six nights on the trot, so I drank it anyway. "It's not my favorite."

"What would you drink if I'd given you the choice?"

I laugh. "I don't know. Molly gave me the choice, and it didn't pan out."

"Because you don't know what you like, or you're afraid to say so?"

"It's not fear. It's habit."

Tanner frowns, then seems to make an effort to stop. "Sorry. I don't mean to get up in your shit. I don't like it when people do it to me."

"Who gets up in your shit?"

"My brother when he's around. Eve when I pick up the phone. Jerry would too if I didn't cross the street every time I see him."

That surprises me. Aside from checking I still have a roof over my head, Jerry hasn't mentioned Tanner at all. They don't seem close enough to be up in each other's business. I'm not surprised about Eve, though. She blows up my phone every day, and I don't mind that any more than I do Tanner's attention. And I want to explain myself. The truth is no worse than whatever he's thinking.

Not that I ever know what Tanner Reid is thinking.

I reach forward and set my laptop into sleep mode. "I told you I was a surfer, right?"

Tanner nods.

I take a breath and go on. "It's the reason I'm here...I mean, in the US and not back home. I turned pro when I was nineteen and moved to California. I met someone there who swept me up in their life because they wanted a slice of mine. We got married and lived it for a while, then I got hurt, and everything changed."

"It's funny how that happens, huh? Like, a split second and everything's different. Or sometimes it takes years and you don't even notice it's all fucked." Tanner's not looking at me. He's captivated by my blank laptop screen.

I want to nudge him so I can see his face properly when he elaborates, but he doesn't. So I take my cue and continue. "Anyway, my girl was pretty set on the pro-surfer lifestyle, so she was all kinds of disappointed in me when I couldn't give it to her anymore, especially when she figured out being married to a rookie filmmaker had nothing to do with Hollywood and everything to do with lying in the dirt all day to get that magical shot."

"She got mean?"

"Yeah, but it wasn't that simple. She played on my guilt, you know? And I let her, and before I knew it, the whole thing was toxic. Her parents got involved with every facet of our lives. They're rich as fuck. Her father controlled everything—the house we lived in, the cars we drove. Cos I'm a naive fuckwit, I thought they were helping us, then my choices disappeared one by one, and suddenly I was living in a prison no other fucker could see."

"Didn't your wife see it?"

"Nah, she hated me by then, and she let her dad push me around because it saved her having to do it for herself."

"She sounds like a bitch."

Tanner's blunt assessment makes me smile. "Yeah, well. I don't want to paint the sad picture of a cartoon evil ex, but she's not a nice person. I see that now."

I stand and take our plates to the sink. His phone is on the kitchen counter. A message from Eve lights up the screen and I wonder if she's said something that prompted him to ask me those questions, or if I fritzed out so bad at the bar that he's the one asking her. Either way, I don't feel good about it. I tackle the dishes to keep my hands busy, and it pans out because Tanner is a messy cook and he doesn't own a dishwasher.

He's also the quietest person in the history of quiet people.

"Hey."

I jump a fucking mile, despite the fact that his deep voice wraps around me like velvet. "Hey there, ninja. What are you sneaking up on me for?"

"I didn't. You'd become one with the dish-soap bubbles."

"Nice." I drain the sink and wipe my hands. "Sorry about that. I'm usually a good listener."

Tanner grunts. I don't know it that means he has nothing to say, or if he's just tired of me being a fucking flake already. Either way, he takes the dishtowel out of my hands and jerks his head at the living room. "I need your help with something."

He could ask me for anything, and I'd say yes. But as I follow him back to the couch, he gestures to the wine bottles and glasses. "I have to test these and pick a couple for next week's specials. With tasting notes. Which is, like, the worst part of my job."

"Free booze is the worst part of your job?"

"Hey, I know it's a first-world problem, but I never know what to say about this shit. Wine is wine."

"Why the fuck are you managing a wine bar, then?"

"Same reason you're not a surfer anymore, I guess. Without the bitchtastic wife."

Unless he has scars to match mine, he can't mean literally. Once again, I find myself leaning toward him, waiting for more, but it doesn't come, and it feels like the end of the world. Or maybe I'm just tired. And fucking greedy. After all, I'm holed up in a warm, comfortable apartment with a hot dude who wants to drink wine with me. What more could I want?

I take my place on the couch. Tanner sits next to me. His knee brushes mine and he makes a sound I think I imagine—I *do* imagine, unless he felt the jolt of electricity too, and his face is too impassive for that.

He opens the nearest bottle of wine and empties it into the two glasses he set on the table a while ago.

I eye the bottle with trepidation. "I don't know jack about wine."

"Neither do I, really. Only what I've learned the last few months."

"That's how long you've managed the bar?"

"Yup."

He hasn't worked for Jerry since the end of last summer. I want to ask him what he did in between, but I don't. I told him my shit because I wanted to, not because I want him to owe me the same. Also, Tanner often seems tense, but he's pretty chill right now. I don't want to trash his mood.

I take the glass of straw-colored wine he hands me. It tastes how it looks—like wine. I drink some more, but nothing changes, so I drain the glass and set it back on the table.

Tanner does the same.

"Aren't we supposed to spit it out like they do on TV shows?"

He thinks for a moment, then shrugs. "Fuck it. Let's get drunk."

CHAPTER FIVE

Tanner

"Fuck it. Let's get drunk."

It's crazy talk, but I don't regret it. Jax is a fun drunk. The measured way he speaks—which I understand more than I want to now—fades, and he's funny and weird and kind, and everything I need in my life on a night I'd otherwise have spent alone.

We drink all the wine. Jax tells me what he thinks of each one, but I forget to write it down, because I don't give a fuck.

Actually, that's not true. I do give a fuck because I'm committed to the people who scraped me from the floor and gave me a job. But I don't care about grapes and fragrance and fruit right now. I just want to listen to Jax's melodic, gentle voice, and lose myself in his boyish grin.

So I jog downstairs and gather up more wine samples I haven't gotten around to tasting and take them back to my living room.

Jax laughs as I dump them onto the table. "Man, I don't know how I'm gonna do with all this. I haven't got pissed on wine in years."

I like how he speaks, and I have no trouble understanding him, even when he says things that are upside down to my American ears. I guess that's what happens when you study someone's face so much, and the set of their shoulders, and the way they move their hands.

Language is more than words.

I line up bottles on the table. "Pick one. I'm gonna get more food."

In the kitchen, I find a bag of Cheetos and upend it into a bowl. It's all I've got that doesn't involve trashing the kitchen Jax has just put back together for me. I carry them back to the living room.

Jax is still studying the wine bottles. I want to tell him that I couldn't care less which one he goes with, but I don't. I sit on the floor and wait.

After more long minutes of protracted staring, Jax slides down to join me. He dangles a bottle from his long fingers. "This one?"

I hand him my glass. "Load me up."

Jax pours red wine into my glass and his, then holds it up to the light. "Tell me about it."

"It's red."

"That's all you know?"

"Yup."

Jax laughs, like he has a few times tonight, and with each warm chuckle, I feel lighter than I can ever remember, and I know it's not the wine. I've drunk alone enough to know it doesn't have that effect on me without him close by. And he's definitely close now. If I shift an inch, our shoulders will touch, and I'm trying real hard not to make that happen.

I take a sip of the wine. It's…nice. If I wasn't already lit, I might've been able to tell Jax why, but I can't draw my thoughts together enough to figure it out.

And he's still laughing, so there's that.

I set my glass down and swivel to look at him. "What's so funny?"

"You are. You run a wine bar and you don't know shit about wine." His laughter bubbles up until he's doubled over and slapping his hand on the floor, and I don't know what's better, that he's sized me up so easily, or that he's laughing without a care in the world.

I choose the second, because he's not the only person to figure out the first. I'm pretty sure everyone connected to V and V knows I'm out of my depth when it comes to the wine, and I'm lucky that no one minds too much. If that means I'm a consistent source of amusement, I'll take it.

I'll take Jax laughing at me all night long.

"I'm not as bad as I was," I say when he's finally chill again. "Harrison's mom taught me a lot when I first started. She basically set up a wine bootcamp at her house and held me hostage for a week."

"Who's Harrison?"

"My boss. But he's my friend too. I went to school with his boyfriend Finn, once upon a time."

"Like me and Eve? Or do you mean actual school, like high school?"

"High school."

"In Burlington?"

"Yeah, though I ended up graduating from Colebury."

"But you've always lived in Vermont?"

"Mostly. I left for a while, then I came back, and here I am."

Jax tips more wine into his mouth and licks his lips. "I can't imagine ever going home."

"To England?" For once he doesn't correct me and assert his Cornish identity. He shrugs and his gaze goes distant. I nudge him, because I don't want him to go, even if it's just for a moment. "When did you last visit?"

"Four years ago."

I whistle. "That's a long time, man. Gabriel would hunt me down if I stayed away that long."

"Yeah, well. I don't have a brother like that. I have parents who believe in the healing powers of dandelions and free spirits, so they'll never chase me anywhere."

I can't decipher the emotion in his eyes. "Do you wish they were different?"

Another shrug. "I don't think so, I just..." Jax shakes his head. "Never mind."

"I don't mind. Just say it. It doesn't have to make sense."

Jax chews on his bottom lip. I've spent a lot of time wishing I could rescue it, but drunk me doesn't have the patience for wishes. I swipe it to safety with the pad of my thumb, then retract my hand as if it's a normal thing to do, and wait for him to make something coherent out of whatever's going on in his head.

He drinks more wine. So do I. Then he sighs and clatters his empty glass onto the coffee table. "My parents are good people, but they're hippies, you know? All tie-dye and campervans. No structure or direction. All my school mates thought they were the coolest fuckers out there, but it doesn't seem that way when you're the one going to school without the right uniform and no homework done because your mum doesn't believe in rules."

"Were you close to them when you were young?"

"Not really. I mean, I thought I was, but looking back, I was just kind of there while they drifted around never really doing much. Huh...maybe *that's* why I'm shit at making decisions."

"You decided to be a pro surfer and come to America, didn't you?"

Jax snorts. "What else was I gonna do? I'd already dropped out of uni because I didn't know how to manage my own life. If I didn't surf, I had nothing."

And then he lost that too. The wine I've drunk settles heavily in my stomach. The lightness his company gifts me fades a little, and I fight to keep it from disappearing. I want to know more about him, so much more. Even the stuff that makes my heart stutter and my gut clench.

But when I look at Jax again, his head is tipped back against the couch and his eyes are closed. He's done for the night, and perhaps that's for the best.

I wake with a headache, but hangovers don't bother me. I'm more concerned with the fact that I don't clearly remember crawling fully clothed into my bed. I've been blackout drunk before, but never with an audience. And I don't even remember drinking that much.

Huh. Maybe I was drunk on Jax.

Whatever. It's ten o'clock in the morning and isn't that something?

Damn.

I roll out of bed and into the shower. By the time I shuffle into the living room, Jax is nowhere to be seen and the only evidence of our wild night is the empty bottles on the kitchen counter and the full bowl of stale Cheetos that's still on the coffee table.

The sight of them makes me laugh, and it's unnaturally loud in the empty apartment. Or perhaps it's just I don't laugh that often, especially when I'm alone.

I tip the Cheetos into the garbage under the sink and rinse the bowl. Jax has already washed the glasses we used, and I wonder why he left the bowl. Then I wonder where he's gone and berate myself for obsessing over him. It's Sunday. He's not working, and neither am I, but I have other shit to do that I'm already late for.

And I'm never fucking late. A fact Eve throws in my face when I show up at her old apartment a half hour after I'm supposed to, driving my car for the first time in more than a week. Yeah, I'm that lucky. In a country where most people live in their vehicles, I've scored an atypical life where everything I need is within fifty feet of my apartment.

Everything except Eve, my brother, and the ability to appreciate it.

Eve is waiting for me on the street and wrenches my car door open before I've shut the engine off. "You said you'd be here at ten."

"I know. I'm sorry. I overslept."

"You don't do that."

"I know that too, but I got pretty lit with your boy Jax last night. Blame him."

I don't really want her to blame Jax, but I see Gabi's fear for me reflected in her gaze, and I need it gone. I can't look at her and see my brother staring back at me. Not if she wants me to spend the day carting her life from her old apartment to her new house.

Eve wins the stare-off, but she sighs when I look away. She tugs me out of the car and into a hug. "Sorry, T. It's been a long day already and I miss him, you know?"

Of course she does. Eve has been in love with my brother since high school, but he's never around to tell her he loves her back. He's a fool. Eve is the best girl in town. If she wasn't practically my sister, I'd probably love her that way too.

"He said he'd call tonight." As if that makes it any better. "Don't tell him I was late, though, okay? I don't need that aggravation."

Eve laughs. It sounds wet, but she's clear-eyed by the time she lets me go. "I won't say a word. How's Jax? Does he look as bad as you?"

"Dunno. He was gone when I got up."

"But you had fun, though, right?"

"Think so."

"Good. He needs some fun in his life, and so do you."

I roll my eyes because it's what she expects of me, but her words stick. If Jax needs fun in his life, he's not going to get it hanging out in my living room with me. And Eve knows that. She knows *me*.

Or at least, she knows my story. Is that enough to truly know a person? Does the sum total of their life events make them who they are? And why the hell am I thinking about it right now? Or ever, actually, because who the fuck cares?

I spend the day doing the heavy lifting for Eve's apartment move. I carry boxes, build furniture, and fix the refrigerator in her new house. The swarm of yoga chicks haven't arrived yet. I'm less disappointed than I might've been a couple of weeks ago. Hooking up has been the last thing on my mind for months, but now I have a head full of Jax, I think about it even less.

At six o'clock, Eve offers me a plate of her famous mac and cheese. I'm hungry enough that my stomach growls hard enough to hurt, but I'm in a hurry to get home. It's open-mic night at the bar and I need to check on my guys. *Liar. Rainn handles mic night just fine every month. You want to find Jax.*

True story, but it's not one I'm prepared to share with Eve, so I bullshit her, and even then, she doesn't let me leave right away. She disappears into her new bedroom and comes back with yet another box. "It's Jax's. I know he hasn't found a place yet, but he seems to like keeping this stuff around. Don't know why, it's morbid if you ask me."

"What is it?"

"His wetsuit from the shark attack—what's left of it, anyway—and a chunk of his board."

I blink. "What?"

"He didn't tell you? Oh shit. I thought he might've. He's pretty hilarious about it if you get him drunk."

I stare at her for a full minute, at least it feels that way, with Jax's lilting quip playing on a loop in my head. *"...an old injury takes a while to warm up in the mornings. Or if I get super cold."*

"Was it serious?"

"As a shark attack."

It never occurred to me for a fucking millisecond that he wasn't yanking my chain. "He mentioned it," I say slowly. "But I thought he was kidding."

Eve gives me the same look she treats me to when I put Gabi in a bad mood. "He's chill about it, to be fair, but don't let him fool you. He died that day. He's only still here because an army medic on the beach plugged his artery."

A full body shudder passes through me. I'm no doctor, but I'm well versed enough in horrible accidents to compute the gravity of a severed artery. That it happened to Jax? Man, I feel sick.

I shudder again, and Eve lays a soft hand on my arm. "Sorry. I forget you probably don't like talking about stuff like that anymore."

"Don't baby me, girl. I don't deserve it."

"I know. But Gabriel's not here to do it, so you're stuck with me."

"He shouldn't do it either. I'm older than him."

"By eighteen months. You're practically twins."

I roll my eyes and plaster a grouchy grin on my face. It's convincing enough for Eve to let me go, and I make my escape. My phone rings as I'm parking my car. It's Gabriel.

"You're too late," I say instead of hello. "I just left her."

Gabriel grunts. "Don't start. I'll call her after. It's you I want to talk to."

"Why?"

"Why not?"

He has me there. But I hate these check-in phone calls. We're both horrible at it and I'd rather he sent me dirty memes like he used to. "I fixed the refrigerator in Eve's new place. She's on her own there right now, but the other girls start moving in tomorrow."

"What about the plumbing?"

"It was fine. Kitchen sink leaked a bit, but I fixed that up too."

"Thanks."

"It's nothing. I love Eve, you know that."

I wait for him to tell me he loves her too.

Instead, he sighs. "Who's the dude sleeping on your couch?"

"Jax. I thought you knew him?"

Gabriel's silent a moment, leaving me his steady breaths for company. I lean back in my seat and stretch my neck, but it makes me think of how Jax moves stiffly most mornings and that I now know why.

I stop stretching and throw Gabriel a bone. "Blond dude. Went to school with Eve when she was in England."

"Surfer dude? Yeah, I remember him. I think."

"He said you don't like him?"

"Huh? Oh. Fuck. Yeah, that's my fault. Eve went screaming up to him when we saw him in Cali one time. I didn't know it was her college BFF so I gave him the stank eye and she punched me in the dick when we got home."

I snort, because it's so Gabi. Stank first, think later. He deserves that punch in the dick. "He's cool. You'd like him if you met him again."

"No doubt. Eve said he's a sweet guy, but his ex fucked him up real bad. Kept him prisoner in the basement or some shit. So messed up."

I add it to the pile of Jax information I've learned today, and rage burns me up. I'm even angry with that damn fucking shark for attacking him, despite the fact that I have no right to feel anything about the *lifetime* Jax lived before I met him.

But I cut Gabi short all the same. I tell him to call his girlfriend and hurry inside.

I don't go upstairs, though. I wasn't entirely lying when I told Eve I had to check on my troops. Open-mic night is big business at V and V. The only reason I'm not working is because my boss insists I don't front more than six shifts in a row.

The place is pumping in its own laid-back kinda way. It's not the thrum of a regular bar, more a gentle hum that gives the joint its rep as a place for everyone. Rainn is running the show. There's not a glass out of place until my gaze falls on Molly trying to open the register with a corkscrew.

Sighing, I shoulder my way to the end of the bar and duck beneath it. "What's cookin', sweetheart?"

Molly turns her round, red-rimmed eyes on me. "I can't get the register to open and I need to give that guy his change before he gets mad at me again."

I follow her gaze to the smartly dressed dude at the other end of the bar. He's a regular who wouldn't dream of giving my staff a hard time, so I'm pretty sure it's Molly's douchebag boyfriend who's upset her, but I don't tell Molly that. Instead, I walk her through the transaction she's trying to make and point out that she's forgotten to press the enter button to log the items and amount she's trying to process.

It isn't hard, but Molly's a singer, not a bar girl. Yelling at her isn't gonna change that. Also, I drank all the wine samples and forgot to write down a single thing about them, so who the fuck am I to tell someone they're doing a shitty job?

I shadow Molly through her next couple of customer interactions, then I pack her off to get ready for her mic set. If I'm not working, I don't usually hang out when V and V hosts special nights, but I've promised her I'll watch, which really interferes with my plans to rush upstairs and find Jax.

But it turns out not to matter. The thing about being quiet is that I hear conversations that don't involve me. And I'm not the only one fixated on the handsome blond sleeping on my couch. Secondhand bar gossip tells me Jax has gone out, so I park myself on a barstool and drink a pint of the non-hard cider we've just started carrying. It's fruity and restorative, and it kicks the headache I've carried all day to the curb. Someone brings me a plate of tiny maple-glazed sausages wrapped in bacon, and I snarf them while wondering what Jax is up to. If he's eaten dinner yet, wherever he is.

I'm willing to bet he hasn't. He doesn't talk about money, but I know he doesn't have any until he gets paid by Jerry at the end of the month, and I've seen the ramen wrappers in my garbage can. It bugs me that he might not be eating anything else, so I try to feed him whenever I see him. But it's hard to marry that with letting him make his own choices. He's a grown man. I don't get to fix his problems for him just because I want to.

Open-mic night kicks off. Most of the participants are terrible, then Molly comes on with a fiddle player from out in the sticks and they blow the place down. She's amazing and I'm glad I stuck around to find out.

I give her a wave as she flits off stage, but I'm suddenly distracted by a tingling in the back of my neck. It's the same fluttering sensation I get when I stumble into my living room and find Jax on my couch. When he's awake and I can kid myself that he's waiting for me.

He's home.

I don't know how I know it, but I do.

Work forgotten, I take my glass and plate to the bar's tiny kitchen, then I jog upstairs, the dancing in my belly increasing with every step. I feel like a lifetime has passed since we parted ways last night, and I have no idea what I'm going to say to him.

As it turns out, though, I don't say anything. I let myself into my apartment and follow my gut to the living room. Jax is by the couch, stripping for a shower. He's shirtless for the first time since I met him, and despite the vicious scars disappearing below his waistband—no, *because* of them—he's the most beautiful thing I've ever seen.

CHAPTER SIX

Jax

I don't hear Tanner come home until he's right behind me. I whirl around. His face is inches from mine and he's staring right at me, clutching a box I'd forgotten about.

Have still forgotten about, as long as Tanner's looking at me like this.

It's not unusual for him to be intense. Over the last week or so, I've learned there's no middle ground with this man. He's either engaged or he's totally not. And right now, his dark gaze is piercing holes into me.

I open my mouth. Shut it again when nothing comes out.

Tanner sucks in a breath, then the box is on the coffee table, and his hands are on me. He lays his blazing palms on my back and turns me around. "I thought you were kidding," he whispers.

It takes me a heart-pounding moment to realize he's zeroed in on the scars that litter my left side. I think back to the one and only time we've talked about them. The brief exchange echoes in my head and I can see how he might've come to the conclusion that I was taking the royal piss. Surfer or not, it's an unlikely story.

"I wasn't kidding. I'm not that funny."

"You're funny enough." His voice is still low enough to seem reverent. "How far down do they go?"

"You want to see?"

He nods. And I resign myself to pulling my pants down in front of him for all the wrong reasons.

I drop the towel and edge my waistband over my hips, revealing the mutant scars, inch by inch. The worst is on my thigh —it's the one with actual teeth marks, and usually the point where most people back away in horror, or leer enough to make me want to die.

Tanner does neither.

He leans forward and slides his hand from the small of my back, over my hip, and down my thigh, tracing the raised flesh, apparently oblivious to the effect his touch has on me. How he can't hear my thumping heart I have no fucking clue, but I'm glad he can't. My snatched breath is embarrassing enough.

"Does it still hurt?"

I force myself to face him. "Not more than I've already told you. It's just a bit tight sometimes."

"I'll bet. He really wanted to eat you, huh?"

"So I heard. I don't really remember."

Tanner still has his hands on me. He reclaims them and seems to return to his senses. He straightens, leaving me to cover myself and reel in silent turmoil at the invisible handprints he's left on my skin.

He steps away, and looks as though he wants to say something. But he doesn't speak. Just gives me a soft smile, and leaves the apartment again.

Jax

"He's not being mean to you, is he?" Eve slides a burger across the table of the hole-in-the-wall joint she's deemed an acceptable place for me to buy her dinner with the last few dollars in my checking account. I'm pretty sure she's chosen the cheapest place in Vermont, but if she's happy, so am I.

"Tanner's not mean to me. I don't see him much, and when I do he's pretty fucking sound."

That's one way of describing the charged encounters I've shared with Tanner. He works a lot, and so do I, so we tend to be ships that pass in the night, but I've come to live for the early morning coffees and late night snacks we share when both of us are awake. Tanner makes me feel things I can't recall ever feeling before, about myself as much as him. He listens to me, and I like it, which is the weirdest thing, cos I don't usually feel much like talking.

At least, I never used to.

He's also a massive help with the work I'm trying to do on the Black Claw trails. This morning I woke up to find he'd come home from work and circled the map with alternative spots to mount the static cameras that aren't picking much up. I haven't had a chance to thank him yet. Maybe later, if he comes upstairs before two a.m.

"So…" Eve says when we've both made short work of the Vermont cheddar cheese burgers this place is famous for. "If Tanner's being so nice to you, why did you tell me you were annoyed with me on the phone?"

I laugh. "I was taking the piss, mate. But you could've told me Tanner was your boyfriend's brother. Your boyfriend hates me. How did you know Tanner wouldn't too?"

Eve pinches my fries and eats half of them in three bites. "Number one, Gabriel doesn't hate you. He gave you one bad look a gazillion years ago. Number two, Tanner's not a giant man-child like his brother. If he was going to hate someone, it would be for a better reason than his brother told him to."

"So why are you in love with the moody brother, then?"

"They're both moody. Tanner's just more reasonable about it."

"They look alike," I muse as I contemplate stealing my fries back. "But they're not the same."

Eve hums. "You're so right and so wrong. They're both super bad at communicating and talking about their feelings, but Tanner's better with people. He's just forgotten it."

"Why?"

"You'd have to ask him that. You wouldn't want me telling him all your secrets, would you?"

"I don't want you telling anyone my secrets, but to be fair, most of them are on YouTube."

Eve shoots me a dark frown. She hates it when I'm flippant about what happened in Cali. But sometimes it's all I have. Gallows humor. It's a thing.

We spend the evening eating junk food and drinking cider at a bar in Winooski—well, I drink cider. Eve sticks to hot chocolate and laughing at me, then she drives us back to Burlington and I walk home to V and V from her new house, letting the brisk air sober me up.

It's not that late, but when I look for Tanner behind the bar, he's not there. Molly is, tapping stealthily at her phone with a pout on her pretty face. "He went up a while ago," she says. "He's coming back to cash out the registers."

That's a new one, but I'm hoping it means Tanner's taking some time for himself. In the short while I've known him, I've never seen him do it. Even on his infrequent days off, he's still downstairs taking care of his crew.

Or upstairs making me tea and talking me out of digging in higher up the Black Claw trails because he thinks what I'm looking for can be found lower down.

I buy two bottles of the belly-warming local cider and take them upstairs. I'm quiet as I let myself into Tanner's place in case he's in bed, but I find him in his kitchen, perched on the counter, poking at his phone. "All right, mate?"

He glances up and nods. "I will be if I can figure out a way to upload this video clip to the bar's Facebook page. It keeps crashing."

"Show me?"

Tanner hands me his phone. The clip he's working with is already grainy as fuck. "You know Facebook is gonna compress this, right? It's going to look terrible by the time they've finished with it."

"It looks terrible already. Molly filmed it on her phone."

"What's it supposed to be? Promo for the open-mic night?"

"Not specifically. My boss wants V and V's social media pages to be more dynamic, but I don't have the time to be running around with my phone all night."

"Sounds like you need a cameraman. I know one of those."

It takes Tanner a moment to connect the dots. Then his dark gaze sparks a light. "As it happens, so do I. You think he'd charge me a good rate?"

"He probably wouldn't charge you anything if you threw in some cider."

"I'd throw in the cider regardless of how much he charges. Man, don't work for free."

There isn't much I wouldn't do for him, including sweeping my camera around his bar a couple of times for nothing but his smile and a drop of free booze, but Tanner has a face you don't argue with, so I name my price for a night's work, and he taps into his calendar to figure out the best night of the week to use me. "Does next week work for you?"

"I'd imagine so."

Tanner grins a little. "You don't need to check?"

"Check what? I don't do anything except work and kip on your couch."

"I didn't know if you'd still be here then. It's payday soon, right?"

"Wednesday. But wherever I go, it won't be far. I can be here whenever you need me to be."

"That right?"

For a fleeting moment, a pause stretches between us, hot and loaded. Tanner stares hard at me, and I stare right back. I let myself imagine that he's seeing in me what I see in him. That the heat climbing inside me belongs to both of us. But he blinks first and goes back to his phone.

Lacking any better ideas, I retreat to the couch.

I'm not expecting him to follow, but after a while, he appears beside me, the ciders I've brought back clutched in each big fist. "I don't know if one of these was for me, but I'm stealing it anyway."

"I brought it for you."

"How many did you drink first?"

"A few. Eve's a bad influence, and she was driving, so I drank hers too."

"True that. Where did you go tonight?"

"Winooski. Some hole-in-the-wall burger place and bar in an old mill. It was nice."

"Winooski is nice," Tanner agrees absently. He's looking at the map I left spread on the table before I went out. The one he's already circled with better spots for my cameras. "You should put one in the woods."

"I thought of that." We lean forward in synch, and I tap a location I've already earmarked. "But I don't have the right lens for a place that dark—no moonlight, no sun. It wouldn't work."

"What kind of lens do you need?"

"The kind I can't afford yet. Jerry said we could split the cost, but that won't pan out when my contract is up. I'd rather have the lens than the money."

"There's a place in Montpelier where you can rent camera equipment. They might have one."

Tanner writes the name of the store on my map. His letters are pointed and slant to the right. My nan used to say that meant a person was the perfect contradiction of intense and open-minded, a free spirit who wouldn't let themselves fly. I don't know Tanner well enough to judge him by his handwriting, but my nan was a wise woman.

I drink my cider while Tanner scowls at my map. Another drink is probably a bad idea, but I can't get enough of this musky stuff. It reminds me of home, and…something else. Whatever. It makes me feel good, and being this close to Tanner makes me feel even better, despite the fact his face is folded into a deep frown. I nudge him. "What's up?"

"Hmm?"

"Have I fucked something up?"

"With what?"

"The map. You're looking at it like it tried to kill you, so I'm assuming I've done something wrong with it."

"Why would you think it was your fault?"

"Isn't it?"

He snorts. "No. This is all me."

I've had enough conversations with him by now to know that's all I'm going to get. Tanner doesn't want to talk about himself, and I don't want to make him. I want him to chill, like he did the night we sank all that wine. But I want it to be real, not forced by booze and my average company.

The map is still giving him a migraine. I fold it up and drop it into the bag I've brought home from work. For once I haven't spent my day tramping up and down the freezing trails. There's another wet weather front moving in that's kept me grounded, and I don't know how long it'll last.

I'm willing to bet Tanner does. I toy with asking him, but he turns to me before I can speak, and lays his blistering palm on my knee. "Can I ask you something?"

He can do anything he wants if he's going to touch me like that. "Sure."

"Do you really not remember getting attacked by that shark? I just…" He takes a breath. "I can't imagine not remembering the worst thing that ever happened to me."

"It's not the worst thing that ever happened to me."

"No?"

"I don't think so."

Tanner considers my answer. He takes a deep sip of his cider, and his frown is back.

I don't like it. Tanner has an ageless face, and he's gonna look exactly the same in ten years' time. But right now he looks older than the twenty-eight years I know him to be. "It's a weird thing," I say when he doesn't speak. "It literally tore me in two, but I didn't feel it until much later, and by then, it was all different."

"What was? Fuck, don't answer that if you don't want to. We don't have to talk about this."

We don't. And I know that. But sitting so close to him, half drunk on heady cider, I don't mind talking. My hand hovers over where his is still on my knee. I don't cover it, though. I settle for tracing a pattern on his knuckles as the recollection of him searching my body for scars sweeps over me. Even if I didn't have massive gaps in my memories of that fateful day on the beach, Tanner's scorching touch would win out. "I really don't remember it. One minute I was in the water, the next I was in the hospital. In between there's just…nothing. If I hadn't had teeth marks in me I'd have thought I was being punked."

"Eve said you died on the beach." Tanner speaks so softly I barely hear him.

I peel his fingers from my knee and lace them with mine as though I do it every day. "That's what they said, but it was after that I felt the worst. I didn't expect blood loss to make me so ill. Like, I was totally dismantled by it. I felt like I *had* died, and I couldn't find the space to come back from it."

"Why not?"

I shake my head. "The day I came home from hospital, Ka— my wife—sold the story to a magazine. And that kind of shit kept happening. I couldn't—" I gather myself before my emotions run away with me and I want to Hulk smash Tanner's living room. "I didn't feel better for a long time, and by then, my life was a train wreck I couldn't escape. It was so fucked up, man. These days it feels like it happened to someone else."

Tanner says nothing for a long time. Then he squeezes my hand and blesses me with the gaze I dream about when I sleep alone. "You're safe now. You know that, don't you?"

I do know it. I knew it the moment I left California and discovered the sweet-smelling state of Vermont. But every word that falls from Tanner's lips is a gift, and his hand wrapped around mine means the fucking world.

CHAPTER SEVEN

Tanner

I'm not cut out to be anyone's roommate. Jax makes me feel Zen, but he has his life, and I have mine. We don't get to hang out much, and it doesn't take me long to realize I'm some type of mess right now when he's not around. Logical me knows I've been like this since long before I met him, but I feel so profoundly better when he's close that I can't help connecting the two. Maybe that's why I can't stop touching him. And why I'm addicted to the fact that he doesn't seem to mind. That he touches me too, and now I can't brush past him without squeezing his hand, or rubbing his arm.

Jax has good arms. They're hard and strong, and more than that, I can feel his pulse thrumming through his warm skin, even when he's just come home from a day spent in the cold. He's so fucking alive. Everything about him—his easy smile, his glittery eyes. Some days he doesn't seem real, and I'm not ready to deal with the reality that he's going to move out soon.

So I don't. I ignore it and pretend he'll be on my couch forever.

The day after Jax gets paid, I come home to find he's left a roll of bills on my kitchen counter. There's a note too.

For all the food and booze you've spotted me.

Thanks mate, J

I stare at the note as if the words will somehow rearrange themselves to say something else. Then I slowly turn and swing my gaze to the couch, bracing myself to find it empty, and Jax's tiny collection of personal effects gone. But the couch isn't empty. Jax is there, tapping away at his laptop, and I claim the few seconds it takes him to look up to fix my clattering heart rate. *Man, you need help.*

It's true, but my insurance company stopped funding that shit months ago, and I don't earn enough at the bar to pay for it myself.

"Hey." Jax appears in my personal space. I've missed him getting up and crossing the room. "You want a tea? I bought some Tetley from the store."

"Nice. Show me how you drink it?"

Jax grins and reaches around me for the kettle. He fills it at the sink and slings it onto the stove, and the sight of him moving around my kitchen makes up for the minor meltdown at the thought of him being gone. He looks good in my space. Like he's meant to be there.

I don't want him to be anywhere else.

So tell him. Right. Because that's how it works. I give a dude a bed for a couple of weeks then take him hostage for the rest of his life because I can't imagine a time when he won't be brewing his English tea in my apartment. It's a bad joke even without what Gabi told me about his ex echoing in my head. I watch him fix mugs of dark tea, then add sugar and milk.

He hands me a mug of rosy warmth and his grin turns shy. "You'll probably think it's weird as hell, but English people live on this shit."

"Even the Cornish ones?"

"Yup."

I take a sip. It's not coffee, but it's not bad, and not all that unfamiliar. Despite what Jax seems to think, lots of Americans drink tea. "I have to go to work. Are you going to be here tonight?"

Jax shifts his mug from one hand to the other. "Probably. Jerry's found a buddy with a studio I can get on a short-term lease until my contract runs out in the spring. I said I'd meet him tonight."

"Don't leave without getting drunk with me one last time."

"I won't."

I believe him. I knock my fist against his bicep and take my tea downstairs. Sometime later, I get the vibe that he's gone out, so I keep my head down all night waiting for the fluttering sensation that tells me he's back.

It doesn't come. I shut the bar down, buy my guys a drink, then make sure they all have a ride. After one last check of the building, I head upstairs, already knowing Jax isn't there.

The empty apartment still shocks me, though. I shake my head at myself and go straight to my room, leaving the door open so I'll hear Jax when he comes home.

I don't mean to fall asleep.

"I've never been up here without snow on the ground. I forget how green Vermont is."

I look up from the bag of information pamphlets I'm sorting through. Honestly, it's the worst part of my job, carting a shit ton of dead trees up a mountain to lecture city yuppies on the importance of preserving... yeah, you got it — the fucking trees.

But it's better than digging dead climbers out of avalanches every winter, so I'll take it. And I like this dude. He's a retired neurosurgeon with a childlike fascination for nature. It's cute enough that I don't mind ignoring the fact that he's flirting with me. At least, I think he is. My last job was testosterone central — it's been a while since a man last legitimately hit on me.

The presence of surgeon dude's long-suffering wife muddies the waters even more. She doesn't seem to mind the bromance he's trying to start with me, but as nice as the guy is, I haven't got time to humor him.

Besides, he's twice my age and then some. Wife or not, it's not happening.

I hand out the pamphlets and give the group time to read them while I make the rounds, checking that everyone's hydrated and eating their energy bars. Then we set off on the last hike of the day before we make camp for the night.

It's a long walk, but the terrain is pretty forgiving. The summer sun beats down on us, and after three years in mountains far fiercer than anything Vermont has to offer, I can dig it. I push the scratchy feelings in my brain aside and focus on my surroundings. Vermont is my home state and there's nowhere more beautiful. The air is fragrant and pure, and the romantic in me sucks in lungfuls of it, imagining it can heal a man from the inside out.

Perhaps it can. I came home with a gaping hole in myself I didn't know how to fix, but out here on the trails I walked as a kid, it hurts less. I breathe clean Vermont air, lead trail expeditions and teach survival skills, and somehow, I forget the hole is there.

We camp for the night at a spot I've laid my head more times than I can count. Surgeon dude's tent is nearby. He winks at me. I roll my eyes and turn my back on him, settling into my sleeping bag with my tent unzipped. Sleeping in the open is my jam. I like the smell of the earth and animal noises. It calms me, and I'm halfway to sleep when surgeon dude's wife comes to find me.

"Vic's sugar levels are down. He's taken his insulin and Gatorade, but they're not coming up."

I scramble out of my tent and follow her across the camp. For the first time ever, Vic doesn't seem pleased to see me. He's a doctor. He doesn't need me to tell him how to manage a condition he's lived with for half a damn century.

He adjusts his insulin dose. His levels begin to rise. I leave him and wife alone after making them promise to wake me if anything changes.

My sleeping bag welcomes me back. I fall asleep hard and dream of golden blond hair and strong hands. Of a voice that's somehow gruff and melodic at the same time. I dream of a smile too, one that makes my brain go quiet and my bones feel light.

The face the voice belongs to comes into focus. It's familiar and yet brand new. I lean forward, sucked in by killer blue eyes and a sunshine smile. I open my mouth to speak, but before I can draw breath, the face changes. Chiseled good looks become an older man with a gray beard. And his eyes don't sparkle. They're wide open and empty, and his wife's bloodcurdling scream wakes me up—

Jax

I don't know what wakes me, but suddenly I'm bolt upright on the couch, every sense on high alert.

Silence greets me. I shake my head to clear it, but the creeping feeling that something is wrong won't quit.

My heart thuds. I rub my chest, as if I can quiet it with the palm of my hand, but it jumps against my ribcage, and a sound I can't decipher swivels my head to the dark hallway.

Takes a moment, but I remember I'm not alone. Tanner's asleep in his bed down the hall. At least, that's where he was when I returned to the apartment after finally escaping the clutches of Jerry's fishing buddy, AKA the most talkative person in the entire world.

I start to relax, then I hear a muttered curse, and the raw pain lacing the single syllable drives me to my feet. Tanner's bedroom door is open, and in the darkness I expect to see him asleep, like I did earlier when I came home, curled up on his side with his back to the open door.

But he's not asleep. He's sitting on the far side of the bed, hunched over, with his head in his hands. Even from this distance I can see he's breathing heavily. That he's shaking.

Reason tells me that he probably wants to be alone with whatever this is, but I can't make myself do it. *I can't walk away.*

I get to him faster than I'm prepared for and sit on the bed beside him. He doesn't look up, and he's definitely shaking. I don't know what to say. So I don't say anything. I put my arm around his broad shoulders and hold him against me until he sighs.

"Sorry I woke you," he says.

"You didn't."

"Liar."

"Yup. You want me to chip so you can go back to sleep?"

"Chip?"

"Leave you alone."

"I don't want to go back to sleep."

Okay, then. I glance around. Tanner's bedroom is small, and as sparsely furnished as the rest of the apartment. It has nothing in it except a bed and a closet. It feels oppressive, but as if it's closing in on him, not me.

I find his hand and squeeze his palm against mine. "Come on. Let's watch TV."

He seems dazed as he gets to his feet, but he doesn't let go of my hand, even once we're settled on the couch.

I find the remote buried on the coffee table and flick the TV on. NHL highlights fill the screen. "This good?"

He nods and leans back, eyes already half closed again. I watch dudes fire the puck around the ice and try to keep up, all the while absorbing the scorching heat of Tanner's hand wrapped around mine. It's not the first time we've held hands like lovesick teenagers, but it feels different this time. Tanner's gripping me as though he's scared to let go, and I don't have the first clue why.

And I'm not going to ask him. How many times has he told me he hates it when people get up in his shit?

Too many to count. And I hate it too. So I don't ask him anything, or even speak, and before long he's asleep again, head tipped back, the arch of his inked neck exposed.

I want to kiss him there.

Shit.

The thought catches me off guard, but it shouldn't. Tanner is kind, gentle, and sexy as hell. Tonight, though, he's also a fucking mess. Thinking about laying my lips on his warm skin should be the last thing on my mind.

I push the thought aside and find the blanket that's slipped to the floor. I drape it over his long legs and try not to stare at his sculpted chest. And fail, obviously, because I'm only fucking human.

The hockey is still on. I turn it off so we're cloaked in darkness. Then I worry that it was the darkness that consumed Tanner in the first place and switch the TV back on.

I slide down the couch so I'm close enough that he can lay his head on my shoulder if he needs to. I have grand plans to stay awake and watch over him, but that goes as well as my vow not to ogle him. I have no idea what time it is when he shakes me awake.

"Bed," he slurs. "Come to bed."

"Wha—?"

Tanner is already pulling me off the couch. He fumbles his arm around my waist, holding me where my scarred body is weakest, though I don't need his help, even with my sleep-addled legs. I let him tow me toward his bedroom as I come to properly, then it dawns on me that his eyes are open but there's no one home.

He's sleepwalking.

Jesus. I've never seen it in real life.

We reach his bed and he pushes me onto it. I raise up on my knees and catch his shoulders. "Tanner, mate. You're not awake right now. Are you sure you want me in your bed?"

He shakes his head. It's not coherent enough to be an answer. Then he takes my hands from his shoulders and squeezes them. "I need you next to me. I need to know you're not dead."

"Why would you think I was dead?"

"Because you died. Because I went to sleep."

His gaze is unfocused and fixed on the wall behind me, but there's no mistaking the distress in his wild eyes. He grips my hands harder. "Don't die."

"I won't, I promise. You want me to stay with you?"

In answer, he pushes me down on the bed, and topples down next to me. He releases my hands and closes one around my wrist, his fingers pressed into my pulse point. Then he falls still. His eyes close, and his breathing evens out, leaving me the rest of the night to wonder what the fuck just happened.

CHAPTER EIGHT

Tanner

I know Jax is there before I open my eyes. My fingers clutching his wrist in a vise grip is one clue, the gentle sound of his breathing is another. Calmness settles over me. I roll over and find him wonderfully asleep, crashed out on his stomach, face turned toward me. His hair is a riot of gold. I want to touch it so bad my chest aches, but I haggle myself down to cataloguing the smooth expanse of his back and wishing I could dance my fingers along his spine to where the scars peek over his hip.

Yearning for something I haven't earned distracts me from wondering why he's in my bed, and from the stinging shame of knowing I've gifted him a broken night when he's got a full day out on the trails ahead of him. Black Claw isn't the place for a tired man. What if—

"Tanner."

My gaze drifts back into focus. Jax hasn't moved, but he's awake, and his eyes are wide and fixed on me. "Hey," he says quietly.

I'm still holding his wrist. I let go. "Hey."

"You doing okay?"

I'm not going to lie to him, but laying my bullshit on him isn't an option either. So I shrug and focus on the heat in my groin I hadn't noticed till his gaze locked on mine.

Jax doesn't ask me twice. He rolls over and sits up. For a moment I'm scared he's going to slide out of my bed and leave without looking at me again. Then he turns and reaches for my hand. "In case you're wondering how this happened, we fell asleep on the couch, then you decided we needed to sleepwalk ourselves in here."

I wince. "Really? That does sound like something I'd do."

"So I'm not the only one, then?"

"I meant the sleepwalking. I don't share my bed with anyone."

"It's not my business, mate."

It really isn't, but I don't want him to think there's anyone I want to wake up with that isn't him. That despite giving him a nuclear-level demonstration of how fucked up I am, I don't regret spending an entire night next to him.

I wrap my fingers around his, knowing he's about to tell me he has to go. There's a million things I want to say, but I don't say any of them. I don't say anything at all. I let him leave my bed and hold my breath until the shower turns on a moment later.

I'm frazzled enough to flop back onto my pillows and shut the world out a little while longer, but the need to make up for Jax's crappy night drives me out of bed and into the kitchen. I nuke him a breakfast burrito and wrap it in foil to go with the travel mug of hot sweet tea I know he prefers to coffee.

The shower shuts off. I take my chance and slip into the bathroom to wash up and brush my teeth. Apart from the steam, it's like he was never there. No wet towel on the floor and smears on the mirror. Is it fucked up that I want to drag him back in here so he can leave a wet footprint on the floor?

Probably.

I finish up and stick my head in the living room. Jax is covering his glorious body with too many clothes. "There's some breakfast on the counter. Take it with you. And sorry if I fucked the tea up. That shit is like sorcery."

I duck back to the bedroom before he responds and sit on the edge of my bed, scowling at the flurry of messages Gabriel has sent me overnight.

Gabi: *going dark*
Gabi: *look after eve*
Gabi: *love you*
Gabi: *mean it bro*

A fear that makes sense squeezes my heart. Gabriel's a private investigator. He works in Texas to keep his shit off his doorstep, and he's a pro at taking care of himself. But I hate when he disappears on me. He's all I have, and I love him.

I text him back and tell him so, then I resume my stare-down with the floorboards I promised my boss I'd get sanded by Christmas. It's November. Halloween has been and gone, and I'm running out of time, but all I can think about is another Thanksgiving without my brother, and the painful fucking irony that he was with me last year and I barely remember it.

Movement in the doorway rouses me. I glance up in time to see Jax walking away.

I frown and start to get up, but he's back before I can stand, dressed in his outdoor clothes, gloves stuffed in his pocket.

His gaze is fierce. Then it's not, and he steps back again.

Fuck that.

I grab his hand. Again. "Whatever you want to say, just say it. It can't be worse than anything Gabi and Eve have ever said to me."

"I don't want to say anything."

"Sure about that?"

Jax makes a sound low in his throat. He takes my face in his hands and leans down. "It's not something I want to say, it's something I want to do."

"So do it."

"I might not stop."

"I don't want you to stop—"

Jax kisses me. In my wildest dreams I'm expecting it, but it still catches me off guard. His lips are soft, but demanding, and there's nothing I don't want to give him.

So I kiss him back.

I slide my hands under his layers of winter clothing and pull him close, and we kiss and kiss and kiss as if it isn't the first time we've done it.

His lips feel like home.

His soft touch dances along my jaw.

I want to kiss him forever, but we run out of air.

Startled, I draw back and instantly find myself lost in Jax's blazing stare. His gaze usually calms me—it really is like the deepest, bluest ocean. But right now, his eyes are stormy and hot. I want to dive back in headfirst, and for once what I want makes sense.

And it's right here. I don't need words. I stand, cup a hand around the back of his neck, and kiss him again. Jax makes another low sound, and the fact that he's spent the night in my bed to babysit me stops mattering. Shadows fade. Heat draws us ever closer, and it's easy to pretend we spent all night doing this. I can't contemplate that it has to end.

But it does end.

Jax pulls back with a rueful smile, cheeks flushed, breathing hard. "I have to go. I promised Jerry I wouldn't be late again."

The mention of Jerry jars something in my brain enough to form a sentence that has nothing to do with how fast my heart is beating. "How did last night go?"

"Okay, I think." Jax steps away. "Dude talked so much I stopped listening, but the apartment was all right. I can move in whenever I want."

I should be happy for him. I *am* happy for him. He didn't deserve to lose all his things in the hostel fire, and it sucks he had to take help from a stranger when he needed so badly to depend on himself. But I'm still dazed from his kiss. I say the first thing that comes into my head. Raw. No filter. "I'm gonna miss you."

He gives me a soft grin. "I'll miss you too."

Then he leaves, and the reality that it might be the last time we do this hits me like a train. Jerry's buddy's apartment is probably outside of the city, closer to where Jax needs to be for his work. It isn't a million miles away—nothing in Vermont ever is—but it's not waking up to find Jax in my bed. It's not drinking his English tea together or eating dinner on the couch with him. It's not opening my eyes every morning to feel the comforting hum of his presence.

It's not being there to let him know, every day, that he fucking matters.

So tell him now.

I lurch from my bed and snag a T-shirt from the clean laundry pile I haven't even thought about putting away. My shoes are by the front door. I stamp into them and fish my keys from the dish. Then I make a run for it down the stairs and out into the morning gloom.

The sidewalk is icy from the plummeting temperatures that are starting to move in from the mountains. But I'm a Vermonter; I know how to handle that shit. I dash to the parking lot where Jax is waiting for Jerry, his broad back to me as he contemplates the ground.

I grab his arm. "You don't have to leave."

Jax startles and jerks around. "What?"

"You don't have to leave because you think I want you to. I don't."

"Don't what? Want me to leave?"

I search my brain for coherency. Nothing comes out.

Jax's frown deepens. "What are you trying to say?"

I have no idea. Am I asking him to crash on my couch for the rest of his life? Or do I want him in my bed every night for as long as he wants to be there? Either way, I'm standing here in a parking lot, dumping it on him first thing in the morning when he has other things to worry about. *You're an asshole.*

That's a sentiment I can articulate. But Jerry pulls up before I can speak.

73

Jax shoots a fractured glance over his shoulder. "I have to go."

"I know."

"Are you okay?"

I haven't been okay for a long time and for a million reasons that have nothing to do with Jax and everything to do with my inability to rip shit out of my head and lay it in the ground. But I've thrown too much at him already.

He deserves the world at his feet, not me on my knees.

I let go of his arm and start to back up.

Jax holds me firm. He doesn't say anything, still waiting for me to answer his question. But I can't. And he leaves anyway.

Jax

Today is long. I'm tired from a night of broken sleep, and my head is so full of Tanner I can't think straight. I stumble around the wilderness, marking abandoned cabins on the map, checking cameras, and setting up new look-out points, but I'm a fucking mess. Jerry calls time on our day when I walk into a low-hanging branch and bruise the shit out of my face.

"You look beat," he says to me on the way home. "And what was going down with you and Tanner this morning? Problems at home?"

"Hmm?"

Jerry gives me as long a look as he can while he's driving. Then turns his attention back to the road. "That kid has been through a lot," he says eventually. "If he's hard to live with, it isn't his fault."

"He's not hard to live with, he's just..." *No.* I'm not about to tell Jerry that Tanner is the perfect imperfect housemate. That he humors my rediscovered tea habit, cooks me dinner, and kisses like a wet dream. That he cries in his sleep and chases me down the street to throw wild eyes and aborted sentences in my face.

I don't tell Jerry anything. And his heavy sigh clues me into the fact that perhaps he understands.

He doesn't drive straight back to Burlington. We stop at the foot of another trail Wildfoot manages, and he hustles me out of the truck. "Gentle Deer. This is my easiest trail. The one we take corporate groups out on in the warmer months. We show 'em the views and birds. The moose at dawn and the geese arriving for the spring. It's not high-adrenaline, but some people don't need it that way. Simple things make simple folk happy. I like that."

Jerry sets off along the trail. Lacking any better ideas, I follow him to a lookout point on a raised ridge. He's right. The view is simple, but glorious. The mountains, the trees, and the late afternoon sky. It's a clean slate of beauty. Cleansing. Pure. The glimpses of Lake Champlain make me miss the sea. Perhaps. Or maybe I miss being underwater where the world is somewhere else.

I make myself look at Jerry.

He's watching me with a shrewd frown on his weathered face. "You know, both Reid boys worked for me once, back in high school. After their mama passed, Tanner was working hard to keep Gabriel out of the system. He did it too. Stuck around till Gabriel graduated, then they both jumped ship to do wild things."

"'Wild things', eh?" I wonder why he's telling me this, but I can't deny I'm fascinated. Even before I met Tanner, his brother intrigued me. "Where did they go?"

"One to the military, the other to mountain rescue in Alaska. I thought they were gone for good, but every year or so one of them would come back for a while. Never thought I'd get them on my payroll again, though, and I was sad about that. Those boys raised themselves on these trails when their ma was working. No one knew them better than they did."

I've heard an incarnation of this story before. And I already know Gabriel Reid was a military man once upon a time. That leaves the Alaskan mountain rescue to Tanner, but it doesn't come anywhere close to explaining why he's running a wine bar now and shouting in his sleep.

"Tanner did come back to work for you, though, right? You've both told me that."

Jerry leans heavily on the stone lectern that has a route map carved into it. "That he did, but he wasn't the same kid who ran these trails a decade ago. He was a man who'd seen too much, so I sent him up here to give him a break from that. Gave him the easy groups and the soft routes. I thought I was doing him right, but you know the trouble with the simplest of things, son?"

I tear my gaze from the horizon. His tale scares me, but I need to know the ending. I need just a single puzzle piece of the man who chased me down the street this morning. "Go on."

"They aren't ever what they seem. I sent Tanner up here without knowing he was already too close to the edge, and I'll regret that forever."

"What happened?"

"Up here?" Jerry casts his own glance at the Vermont wilderness. "Tanner took a group booking on an overnight last year. It was summertime, the weather was great. None of us had anything to worry about. So we didn't worry, and a man died in his sleep from a diabetic crisis."

The puzzle piece has jagged edges. I process what Jerry is saying and match it with the Tanner I'm getting to know. "That doesn't sound like it was anyone's fault."

"It wasn't anyone's fault, least of all Tanner's. But he wasn't doing so well already, and waking up to a dead body pushed him over. He hasn't worked for me since."

Jerry doesn't look at me again. Like, at all. We descend the light trail in silence and I don't say anything to him when I get out of his truck in Burlington. I have no idea why he's told me those stories, and it feels like he's broken an omertà, but I'm glad he did. Tanner is beautiful and complex and so fucking human. I'm not anywhere close to understanding him, but I'm closer than I was this morning.

I slip inside the wine bar, searching for him before the door closes behind me.

The bartender—Rainn—tips his head to the stairs. I wonder when I became so transparent to dudes I've never spoken to, but if it gets me to Tanner quicker, I don't actually care.

I jog up to the second floor where Tanner keeps his office. I've never been in there, and the door is closed, but I open it right up and barge inside.

Tanner is at the computer, frowning at the screen. He turns as I come up on him and I kiss him in such a perfect reenactment of this morning that I almost laugh.

But there's nothing funny about his lips pressed to mine. It's hot and brutal, and a shining example of why I can't do what we both want me to do.

I kiss him until my lips hurt. Then I pull back and press my forehead to his. "I can't stay here."

CHAPTER NINE

Tanner

I can't stay here.

His words don't surprise me. They make sense. Why the hell would he want to live on my couch when he could have an entire apartment to himself? And a bed where he can sleep undisturbed by my bullshit?

But as reasons he wouldn't want to fill my mind, Jax holds my face tight and forces me to look at him. "Don't do that."

"Do what?"

"Be thinking I'm doing this because I don't want you, or that what happened last night made me stop wanting you. It's not about that—it's not about you."

...made me stop wanting you. My brain chooses to fixate on those words and not on the fear that he wants to have an actual conversation about me waking him up and sleepwalking him to my bed. *He wants me.* Present tense. It doesn't fix the noise in my head, but I can't help the thrill in my gut, because *fuck* I want him too.

It would be so easy to kiss him right now. But I don't do it. I grasp his wrists and take his hands from my face. I study his earnest gaze, then my own falls on a fresh bruise forming on his cheekbone and my anxiety ramps up a notch. "What happened to your face?"

Jax rolls his eyes. "Walked into a tree. Swear down, I was a fucking liability up there today."

"Why?"

"Tired, I guess."

"I'm sorry."

"What the fuck for?"

"For waking you up? For being a—"

Jax cuts me off with another kiss. It's softer than the ones he arrived with, but takes my breath away all the same. "I need to take this apartment and learn to live with myself. I can't need anyone else, or depend on them; it fucks me up too much right now. But don't ever be thinking I don't want to spend every night with you wrapped around me like you were last night. It scares me, but it's everything, you know?"

I don't know anything. But I'm listening, and I don't want him to be scared of anything, least of all how he feels about sharing a bed with me. I'm having a hard time dealing with the bruise on his face too. With the scruff on his jaw and his wild hair, it's kinda hot, but the idea of him being hurt makes me nauseous.

We're still holding onto each other. I let my thumb graze over the mark on his cheek, then I let him go and put some distance between us. "This has gotten intense real fast, huh?"

Jax gives me a wry smile that does nothing to make me calm the fuck down. "Yeah. It's not a bad thing, though. I...really fucking like you. I just can't do that and live on your couch at the same time."

I don't want him to live on my couch. I want him in my bed. But I also want him to be happy and feel safe, and not wake up every day worrying that whatever plays out between us will make him homeless again.

He's right. He can't stay here.

But, man, I don't want him to go. "Where is this apartment anyway? It's Old Man Joe's, right?"

Jax smirks. "Right. It's three blocks away."

"Oh."

"I know, right? It's not so bad."

It really isn't. My treacherous imagination had already moved him out of Burlington. Three blocks is a five-minute walk. We can still eat together, chill, sleep, whatever, but we can breathe too. Despite the squeeze in my chest at the thought of him leaving, I know we both need that.

I have to get back to work. I don't ask Jax if he's leaving tonight because his face already says that he is. Instead, I crowd him against the office door and reach into his back pocket where I know he keeps the key I gave him to my place. The metal is warm where it's been pressed against his body. It grounds me. I pull the key out and press it into his palm. "Keep this and use it anytime you want, day or night."

It's as close to a goodbye as I can manage.

Jax

I'm still wearing Tanner's clothes. I have the money to buy more, but he doesn't want his bag of tricks back, and I don't care about how I look enough to replace them. Not that I look bad in Tanner's clothes. He's one of those blokes who makes being cool seem effortless, and his faded jeans and warm shirts make me feel good.

And they still smell of him too, of wood and smoke. As if I don't already know he's not a city boy.

Jerry hasn't mentioned him since our round-table talk at the lookout point. He knows I moved out, though, and I can tell he doesn't like it, even though renting his buddy's place was his idea.

We come home early on Friday and he drops me off in the parking lot behind V and V instead of the one by my apartment three streets away. "I want a beer," he says by way of explanation.

"Yeah, well. I need a shower, so you have fun with that."

I leave Jerry in his truck and walk away. It's cute that he's probably noticed I'm moping over the lack of tall, inked mountain men in my everyday life, but I can't handle being maneuvered. So I go home and take my shower before I head straight back to the bar on my own fucking terms.

By then, Jerry is nowhere to be seen, and it feels strange to be coming into the bar for no other reason than I want to drink cider and lay eyes on Tanner.

I try not to make it too obvious that he's all I want to see, but Molly clocks me as soon as I walk in. She grabs my arm and drags me to a quiet corner. "Where've you *been*? Tanner told me you were going to film the next open-mic night and then you disappeared for *days*."

"Only two." I take her hand off my arm. Not because I mind being touched by chicks I barely know, but her nails are *sharp*. "Did you miss me?"

"Of course. You're my favorite customer."

"You've served me once and I made you cry. What do you actually want from me?"

Rumbled, Molly lets her smile shine brighter. "I want to ask if you'll shoot my whole set, not just the bar stuff Tanner asked you for."

"He didn't ask me for anything in particular."

"Eh, he never does. But I know what he needs, and it's not ten minutes of me warbling my best impression of a Nashville reject."

"Warbling? That's not what I've heard people say about you."

Molly snorts. "Whatever. Will you help me? I need the footage for my performance class and my boyfriend bailed on me."

"Nice boyfriend."

"He's an asshole."

"Fair enough." I shake my head to clear it. "I can record your set for you. I'll set up a tripod at the front to get it all, and I'll give you anything I get with the gimbal."

"The what?"

"Never mind. I've got it, okay? I'll do you a solid."

"Does that mean I don't have to pay you?"

"Unless you want to bake me a cake or some shit, we're good."

"Works for me." Molly gives me a hug I'm not expecting. I don't hate the sensation of her soft arms around me, but they're definitely the wrong ones, and I get the feeling she knows it. She backs away with a wink and inclines her head to the right. "He's over there."

I glance right and instantly forget her. Tanner is weaving through the crowded bar with a tray balanced on one hand. It's piled high with empty glasses—too many for most people, but he makes it look easy. He's wearing his standard jeans and black shirt with the sleeves rolled up and he hasn't trimmed his beard for a few days. It's thick and dark and I want to run my fingers through it. I've missed him more than I can say. Is it weird that I've missed the inky scruff on his jaw just as much?

Beside me, Molly sighs. Startled, I spare her a glance. I thought she'd gone.

She sighs again. "He's so dreamy, isn't he?"

"Uh, if you say so."

"Oh, be serious, honey. I've seen how you look at him."

"That right?"

Molly snorts in a way that doesn't match her dainty beauty. "Yes, that's right. If you don't hook up with him soon, I'm going home to write some lemony fan fic about you to calm myself down."

She walks away before I learn what that even means, and I'm not sure I want to. She makes me laugh, though, and when Tanner finally looks up, I'm grinning.

A slow smile warms his handsome face. Then he's right there, standing so close his body heat warms me from the inside out. "You came back."

"Course I did. Told you I wouldn't go far."

"I know, I just…"

"What?"

He shakes his head. "Nothing. Just worried I'd scared you off."

The only thing that scares me about Tanner is how hard my heart beats when he's anywhere within a mile radius of me, but I'd be a liar if I didn't admit that I've stayed away for two days on purpose. Testing myself? Maybe. But I can't decide if searching him out tonight means I've passed or failed. Whatever. I don't care. I missed him, and I want him to know it.

He disappears with his tray. I expect him to pop up again behind the bar, but he comes back wearing his coat. "Wanna walk?"

"I thought you were working?"

"My shift finished an hour ago. I was only here to keep from knocking on your door."

"You could've done that. Or, you know, like, called me or something."

"I know." Tanner inclines his head toward the door.

I shrug. "Okay, then."

We leave the bar. Outside, he grips my shoulders and turns me to face him. "You finally bought a coat?"

"I guess. I gave a bloke in the office twenty bucks for his spare one."

Tanner snorts out a laugh that reminds me of Molly. "Whatever. It looks good on you."

He lets me go and we start walking in the general direction of my apartment. I'm not sure if he meant to walk me straight back home, but I'm not going to complain about strolling through the cinnamon-scented night with him. I knew Vermont was a nice place to be when I landed here all those months ago, but being with Tanner amplifies every sight and sound. The clean air and bright stars. The contented hum of people who live well. I could stay here forever.

I drift closer to Tanner. Our elbows bump and he gifts me another soft smile.

Jesus. He's so fucking beautiful. I want to spend another night with him, for real this time. Long, dark hours where we roll around a bed—his or mine, I'm not fussed—and get to know each other a different way.

The fun way. Cos I dreamt about that while we were apart, and the bed I've claimed as my own for the next few months was too big and cold to be without him. I *want* him. And I know he wants me. Maybe—

"Man, you're thinking so hard you're gonna have a stroke."

Tanner has stopped walking. Somehow, I have too, and I haven't even noticed. We're halfway to my place. The sea child in me can smell Lake Champlain, but we're still surrounded by shops and restaurants. Bright colors. Happy people. Even Tanner looks cheerful. Amused. And I dig that so fucking much that I forget myself and close the three inches of space between us.

My face finds a home in his neck. He makes a rough sound that welcomes me in, and wraps his arms around me. It's more than a hug. His body fits to mine and heat ripples through me. I want to kiss him. I *need* to kiss him. But we're out on the street, so I settle for hiding in his neck and breathing him in while he holds me tight and ghosts his hand beneath my secondhand coat.

His palm finds the base of my spine, and it reminds me of the night we met, how he seemed to know exactly where I needed him to keep myself upright. I'm in no danger of falling down right now, but I need his touch more now than I did then. It anchors me. And if his deep, measured breaths are anything to go by, maybe, just maybe, it anchors him too.

Shame we can't stand here all night. Tanner's soft sigh tells me he feels the same, then he pulls back, and we keep walking. There's a food cart outside my building. It's a vintage tea truck that sells hot drinks and thick toast with local butter and jam. It's an ex-pat's dream. I sit Tanner on a bench and fetch him a mug of the flowery tea he drinks in the evenings and a plate of strawberry jam-topped toast. He looks at it and laughs. "Sweet tooth?"

"Not as bad as I used to be, but yeah, I like desserts."

"This is breakfast, though, right?"

"Breakfast for dinner. Love that shit."

Tanner laughs again. I go back for a second plate of toast and the strong, sweet tea I'm rebuilding my addiction to now that I can afford to eat again. As far as I'm concerned, it's the best dinner ever, and Tanner doesn't complain. He eats his toast, then watches me hoover up twice as much with his very best amused grin. "You know, for a rugged outdoorsman you're pretty fucking cute."

I lick jam from my middle finger, then slowly flip it to him. "I try."

"That's the thing, though. You don't need to." He leans forward and does something to my hair. It's takes him a protracted second to pull his hand back, and me even longer to get over the fact that he does it at all. And by then we're nose to nose again and the urge to kiss him is so strong I fucking choke on it.

I bang my head on his shoulder and groan.

He says nothing when I draw back. Just stares at me with eyes that never end.

I don't want *this* to end, but I know if I ask him to come inside, something will change between us that we're not quite ready for. *But you want him. And he wants you.* But if that was enough I'd have stayed in his apartment.

Doesn't stop me wishing things were different, though. Wishing that I'd met him ten years ago when I wouldn't have thought twice about how I felt about him. I wouldn't have questioned it. I'd have just loved him, and maybe he'd have loved me too.

Tanner stands and tugs me to my feet. "I should go."

I nod, cos he's right, but fuck off if you think I'm saying that shit out loud. "I want to ask you to come inside."

"I know. I want to say yes, but I shouldn't. I'm still going cold turkey on you."

"That's a thing?"

Tanner tips my chin until I meet his gaze. "It's totally a thing, but I might have the cure."

"For real?"

"Maybe. You wanna go out tomorrow night?"

"Out?"

"Yeah. I miss eating with you as much as I miss ogling you when you're not looking, and you promised you wouldn't leave without getting drunk with me again, so I figure you owe me that." He's joking about me owing him, but I see the regret in his eyes as soon as the words leave his mouth. "I don't mean literally."

"I know. Damn, am I that fucking sensitive?"

"No, you just deserve clowns like me to choose their words better."

I will never, ever deserve him. And I don't need him to trip over his sentences to protect my fragile self-esteem. I've been hurt, but I'm not broken. Fuck that shit.

His hand fits in mine. I tow him away from the tea truck and into the shadows of my building. Tanner likes the dark. Away from the bustle of people, he relaxes. I push him against the wall and crowd him. "Don't be careful with me. I don't need it."

"I know."

"So stop second-guessing everything you say."

"It's not everything I say. It was one time."

"That's one time too many. You want me to tiptoe around every fucked-up thing that's ever happened to you?"

It's a low blow, but one he understands despite the fact he has no idea Jerry has run his mouth about what happened out on the trails last year. And the fact that he has no idea how bad I needed that single puzzle piece.

Tanner drops his hands on my tense shoulders. "I don't ever want you to tiptoe around me."

"Why not?"

"Because it makes me feel like a fuck-up."

I stare harder at him.

He concedes my point with a wry smile. "Yeah, okay. I get it.

But you should know I'm the king of putting my foot in my mouth."

"I don't believe you."

"Why not?"

Because Tanner is a thinker. If he fucks up it's a rare thing. But he doesn't want to hear that right now, so I take him throwing my question back at me and let it go. I kiss his cheek and step back. "So...I'll see you tomorrow then?"

"Sure. I'm working till the afternoon sometime, then we're good."

"Call me?"

"When?"

A laugh escapes me. Man, he's as bad at this as I am. "I don't know. Whenever you're free. I'm home all day."

"Why?"

"Because I'm camping out in a few days, so Jerry banned me from going out until then."

Tanner's gaze flickers. He covers it with a nod, but I see it all the same. "Okay. I'll call you."

He pushes off the wall and slips past me.

I don't watch him leave.

CHAPTER TEN

Tanner

I don't call him, because I don't call anyone if I can help it. I spend a long afternoon circling my phone as if it's an unexploded landmine, then I text him.

Tanner: *u wanna hang out later?*

Hey. I've never claimed to be articulate.

Jax doesn't respond for a while, but I figure he's enjoying his down time, so I leave my phone on the coffee table and head downstairs to check that my crew is ready for the evening shift.

They're not, and making it right takes longer than I'm in the mood for. But I don't take it out on them, because I'm a better man than I used to be. Some days. Maybe.

It's getting dark by the time I go back upstairs, though it's not that late. I'm hungry and agitated, a new combination I put down to skipping lunch and missing Jax, but the moment I see my phone flashing with a new message I forget about food and leap on it like a man possessed.

Jax: *I can hang…if you come with me to buy bed sheets. If I go on my own it'll take me all night.*

Interesting. For the life of me, I can't figure why it's a task that would take him so long, but when I meet him on the Church

Street mall a half hour later, I get it. He wasn't kidding when he said he doesn't do well with choices, and the overloaded store— seriously, there's a million and one types of crap I don't care about —has enough variety to give him a headache.

I stand behind him and try not to obsess over how good he looks in my jeans—though they're his jeans now, I guess. At least, I hope he sees it that way. "What size is your bed?"

"Dunno. This size?" Jax throws his hands out in a vague gesture.

"Erm…okay. Mine's a queen. Is it as big as that?"

"I don't know that either. Last time I was in it I wasn't paying attention to how big your mattress was."

He's not trying to be funny—he seems genuinely annoyed that he's finding this so difficult—but I smile all the same, and move closer to him, fitting my body to his from behind.

Jax leans back, tilting his head to frown at me. "I'm just gonna get the blue ones and hope for the best."

"You like blue?"

"Yeah, I think so."

I like blue too, but it has nothing to do with sheets and every- thing to do with his wide eyes. Also, the way he's looking at me has totally exposed his throat, and if he doesn't move soon, I'm going to kiss him there with no fucking care for whoever might see us.

He does move, and I can't decide if I'm relieved or bereft, but by the time he's paid for his sheets and we're outside again, I'm good with the world. With his grand purchase out of the way, Jax is as chill as I've ever seen him. His easy smile is back, and damn, I love that smile.

We meander aimlessly along the sidewalk. I want to ask him what he wants to do tonight, but figure he needs a minute before I drop that on him. Then the conversation we had less than twenty-four hours ago comes back to me, and I ask him anyway.

Predictably, Jax shrugs, but I see him catch the first answer that comes to him and swallow it down. "I'm hungry," he says instead. "Can we eat Vermont food somewhere and get drunk?"

Works for me. And if there's one thing I know in life it's, where to get good food in Burlington.

I take him to a family joint that serves breakfast all day long in diner-style booths. They light candles in the evening and serve Shipley cider with eggs, bacon, and waffles, and just about any other breakfast food you can think of. And I know Jax likes Shipley cider. Honestly, who doesn't?

And I love watching him eat. Maybe it's the shit ton of maple syrup I pour on my giant stack of pancakes, but it gets me feeling some type of way. When we're done with dinner, we stay in our booth and drink cider. Jax is opposite me, his legs tangled with mine, but as the fruity liquor settles in my belly, he's nowhere near close enough.

I lean back in my seat and tilt my head. "Come here?"

He smirks, slides out of his seat, and ducks around the table. His body feels good against mine. Too good. I want to take him home, but I settle for draping my arm across the back of the seat. "I keep meaning to tell you that you left your, uh, shark box behind my couch."

"I know. I'm good at that."

"At what?"

"At leaving it places. It's weird, I can't bring myself to get rid of it, but I don't want it too close."

"So you left it there on purpose?"

"Not consciously, but I'm not sad about it."

I process that. It doesn't make much in logical terms, but somehow I get it. "Well, it's still there whenever you want it. I'll keep it forever if you want."

Jax knocks his head on my shoulder. "I like the sound of that."

The server comes back with more cider before I can respond, and by the time she's gone, the moment has passed. And it's probably just as well. Jax makes my head spin just by existing. He doesn't need to know that every sweet thing he says to me robs me of coherent thought.

We drink more cider. Conversation is easy. Leaning ever closer to each other is even easier. By the time I'm comfortably lit, we're inches apart as we talk, and I've given up the pretense of not having my arm around him.

Jax is tracing the ink on my wrist.

It feels so fucking good. I cover my shiver by asking a question I don't mean to ask. "How did your wife feel about you being bi? She seems like she was an asshole about everything else."

"It never came up, so I don't think she knew."

"Seriously?"

Jax shrugs. "Yeah. I mean, I was committed to her, so I didn't think about other dudes any more than I thought about other women. It's not like that for me. I'm not torn between genders. I'm with who I'm with."

"Makes sense." I twirl my cider glass on the table. "It's like that for me too. At least, it is now. When I was younger I was all about the chicks. The dude thing came later for me. I was twenty-one before I hooked up with a guy."

"And you're what, twenty-eight now?"

"Yeah." I wonder how he knows that. If he's as interested in every detail about me as I am about him. I hope he's not. I can't be a details man anymore—unless it's about him because I apparently have rip-roaring double standards these days. "What about you? When did the dude thing come around?"

"I can't really pinpoint it. I guess it was always there." Jax smiles. "I lost my virginity to a boy in the back of a VW camper-van. It was a year before I took a girl up those cliffs."

"How old were you?"

"Sixteen. Just."

"You started young, huh?"

"Not really. This dude was just super nice. Easy to be around, you know? And it felt right. It took me longer to find a girl I felt that way about."

I shrug. "I never stopped to think about how I felt. I was just a horny teenager. And then with dudes...I was an adult, so it was different. I knew myself pretty well, so I had no fear."

"Good. It's not nice to be afraid of intimacy."

"Are you?" I throw a pointed glance to where he's still drawing pictures on my skin. "You don't seem to be."

"I'm not scared of intimacy with *you*, but I was scared of myself for a while. It's hard to explain, but when you've let someone make you feel inadequate in every way for such a long time, it fucks with your head in ways you can't predict. I mean, I didn't have a sexual relationship with my ex for years before we split, but she still fucking haunts me."

I hate his ex. Rage flares in my gut and I want to tell him so, but what good would that do him? My anger is selfish and all about me. Besides, he's talking, and I want to listen, not get caught in my own feelings. "When did you split?"

"A year ago."

"You've been in Burlington for a year? No fucking way. I'd have seen you."

Jax laughs. "I didn't come to Vermont until four months back. Before that, I was literally hiding in a tent so my in-laws couldn't find me and sue me or something. Sad, huh?"

It is sad, but not for the reasons he probably thinks. "Tell me about this tent. Where was it?"

"In the desert. I was off-grid and filming kit foxes for a startup YouTube channel. It was as much fun as I've ever had."

"Why did you come to Vermont, then?"

"The YouTube channel bombed, and they never paid me, and Eve said I needed to learn how to people again, so I reconnected to the matrix and answered Jerry's ad to come here."

"She says that peopling bullshit to you too? Man, I thought it was just me who got that lecture on a weekly basis."

"You people every day. And you're good at it."

It's cute that he thinks that. I don't correct him. What's the point?

Jax

Tanner is a fun date. If that's what we're calling it. And if we're just two mates out for some touchy-feely drinks, I'm okay with that. He wants to know how I got into filming wildlife for a living, so I give him the Cliff notes version. I want to know how he wound up working mountain rescue in Alaska, and why he came home, but I don't ask, and he doesn't tell me. He doesn't tell me anything, he just listens, so I guess I'm okay with that too.

It's late when we roll out of the forever breakfast joint. I've sunk enough cider that I'm warmly buzzed, but I'm not drunk, and I'm glad of it. I don't want to forget a minute of being with Tanner like this, even if he won't let me pay for his dinner.

"You let me live with you for free. It's the least I can do."

Tanner hustles me onto the street. "It wasn't free. You left a ridiculous amount of cash in my kitchen."

"It was fifty bucks."

"Yeah, for what? A couple of sandwiches and a teabag?"

"It was, like, twenty teabags."

He shrugs. "Bite me."

"Don't say things you don't mean."

Tanner shoots me a hot grin, and I take it as my cue to lead him to my front door. Last night he wouldn't come in, but it's a new day. The world is a different place, and this time, I don't give him the chance to say no.

He follows me inside and upstairs to the studio apartment I'm renting from Jerry's friend. It's tiny, and Tanner seems ridiculously tall in the room that doubles as my bedroom and my living space. I have to stand close to him to remember we're the same size. That his lips are exactly where I need them to be. That I could lick his instead of my own and I wouldn't have to move that much.

Tanner slides his hands over my hips. His thumbs ghost

beneath my clothes and find bare skin. "Should we put your new sheets on your bed?"

"Sheets?"

"Yeah. Seems an awful shame to leave them in the store bag after you spent so long picking them out."

"I spent three minutes picking them out."

"Yeah, I don't care about the sheets."

I don't either, but I want him in my bed, and tumbling him to my sleeping bag doesn't quite have the same appeal.

Tanner finds the store bag I've dropped by the door, while I pack my sleeping bag away and find the comforter my friendly landlord left in the linen closet for me. It doesn't take long to fix my bed—thanks to Tanner, the sheets fit—but it definitely looks like two drunk blokes made it in the dark.

I fall onto it, laughing.

Tanner flops down beside me. His coat is gone and his boots are with mine by the door. He's still wearing too many clothes, though. I don't know how naked I can take him right now, but his shirt needs to go. I need his skin against mine.

My pulse kicks up a notch just thinking about it. There's no way he can't hear it. I roll over and dig my phone from my pocket. The apartment came with a Bluetooth speaker built into the wall. I poke at my phone until it connects and cue up the first playlist I can find. Larrikin Love filters out. It's naughties punk, and it's not the worst soundtrack to push Tanner down and kiss the shit out of him. And he lets me, so it's not long before music and the fact that I forgot to turn the lights on are the last things on my mind.

I kiss Tanner on my clumsily made bed, pushing him into the sheets that smell brand-new. He's wearing a flannel shirt—obviously—and a T-shirt. The flannel goes first, then I yank his T-shirt up his hard body and drink in his inked chest as if I've never seen it before.

He's patient with my kid-in-a-sweet-shop impression. I straddle him and kiss him everywhere while he watches me with coal-dark eyes, his long fingers threaded into my hair. "You said you'd bite me," he says.

"No, you asked me to. Are you asking me again?"

"Maybe."

I can't tell if he's taking the piss, but his relaxed pose makes me want to dig my teeth into his unyielding flesh.

So I do. And he *moans*.

Wow. Okay. That's a sound I can live with, but before I can drag it from him again, strong hands grip me, and I'm on my back. Tanner claims the space above me. His muscles pop where he's holding himself up and I have to give myself a mental pinch to check I'm actually awake. That this is my life right now. *He's so fucking hot*. And he's smiling too, just to top off my wildest fantasies. Scratch that, he's *smirking*. I know I'm in trouble, and for once in my life it's the good kind.

Tanner eases his hand under my clothes. His palm blazes with heat and a whole-body shiver rocks me. "You need to lose this." He jerks his head at my shirt. "It's only fair."

Nothing about how he makes me feel is fair. But I ditch the shirt anyway and lay back down.

Tanner nudges my legs apart and makes a cradle for himself between them. His abs press down on mine, and fuck if I don't feel every part of him.

I suck in a breath.

He frowns. "Am I hurting you?"

It takes me a moment to compute that he's worried about my scars. "Nah. I'm good. I told you they don't hurt anymore."

"That's not what you said."

I know it isn't, but at the time I hadn't anticipated a scenario where we'd be having this conversation. And I don't want to be talking right now. We've talked all night long. I'm done with words.

Tanner takes his time exploring me. He has rough, work-hardened hands that don't belong in a wine bar, but his touch is soft. His fingertips are ghosts on my bare skin, and I feel it more than if he threw me down and clawed at me. He makes me tremble. And as he slowly unbuttons my jeans—his jeans, whatever—I realize that perhaps he always has. That I've been shaking since the very first time he put his hands on me.

He deepens his kiss and eases my dick free. His fist closes around my length and any composure I had left is long gone. Pleasure surges in my gut. I groan and tip my head back, ripping my mouth from his. "Fuck yeah."

Tanner hums and bites my neck with perfect pressure. Perfect *pain*. Another groan rips out of me, and I'm so fucking undone.

He watches me with rapt attention as I come. His liquid gaze catches every shudder and gasp, but I don't feel self-conscious. I know he wants me like this. That my pleasure makes him feel good. And I want him to feel good. I want him to feel dizzy and boneless like I do right now.

It takes me a minute to catch my breath, then I'm on him.

I roll him over and reach for his fly.

He shudders. "You don't have to—"

I cover his mouth with my hand. He bites my fingers. I press down harder and his eyes flash with an extra shot of heat I'm unprepared for. *Interesting.* I file it away for later brooding and undo his fly. His cock is hard and straining against his underwear. I set him free and wrap my fingers around his heavy length. After so long without a man's touch, it should feel strange to be with Tanner like this, but it doesn't. It feels so right my chest gets hot, my breaths short, and it's me who's gasping again instead of him.

"Hey." Tanner pulls me close and presses his lips to the fading bruise on my cheekbone. "Stay with me."

I'm not going anywhere. I kiss him back and zero in on his hot pants of breath against my skin. His shaking hands and straining muscles. I jack him until he's bucking into my hand. Then he comes with a deep groan, and his blunt nails dig into my shoulder before he catches himself and pulls them away.

I mourn the sharp, grounding scratch, and I hate the fact that he's careful with me in a moment where he should only think of himself. But there's nothing in the world right now that can take me away from the bliss on his face. Tanner's enchanting in any light, but in the dark of the unfamiliar apartment, splayed out on my brand-new sheets, he's everything.

We return to earth still kissing, but eventually, I force myself to roll out of bed and find a wash cloth to clean us both up. I leave again to throw it into the laundry hamper in the bathroom.

I come back to find Tanner hasn't moved. He's still sprawled out with heavy eyes. "I should go," he says.

"No." I find the covers we've kicked aside and drag them over us. "Stay."

CHAPTER ELEVEN

Tanner

Jax's alarm goes off before dawn. I'm ready for it, but he's not. He groans and rolls forward, burying his face in the pillow. A heartbeat passes between us. Then he reaches back for me and pulls my arm around his waist.

Chuckling, I fit myself closer to his spine and run my fingers through his hair. He sighs, and for precious moments everything is perfect. But nothing is perfect forever. He has to leave, and so do I.

Jax gets up and stumbles into the shower. I stay where I am to keep out of his way in the tiny apartment and try not to stare as he drifts around in a towel, dripping water on the floor, and gathering his clothes for the day. "When are you camping out?"

"Tomorrow." Jax tugs insulated pants up his long legs and covers his torso with a T-shirt emblazoned with the Wildfoot logo. "We're setting it up today, so it's not brand new for the forest critters."

"You know they might tear it all down overnight, don't you? That happened to me and Gabi once. We had grand plans to spend a week camping out, but a moose trampled our tent, and then the foxes came and stole all our supplies."

"How old were you?"

"Fourteen."

"Still not over it?"

"Not even close. It was a year before we could afford a new tent."

"Was your mum still alive then?"

"Yeah. But she worked six days a week to make rent on our shitty apartment, so me and Gabs were basically feral."

"I can relate to the feral part of that. Can't imagine anyone calling your brother 'Gabs' though."

"He's really not that bad."

"He's a dick to Eve."

"Not because he wants to be."

Jax gives me a look that tells me we're not going to agree on this unless I'm prepared to dissect my brother's entire life for him so he can pass judgement on actual facts. That ain't happening, and Jax is astute enough to know it. He lets it go and wanders off again.

He comes back with coffee. "You don't have to leave just because I am. Why don't you rest for a while?"

"Because I have zero interest in being here without you."

"I won't be in your apartment either, or the bar, or your office."

Touché.

Sensing victory, he ditches the coffee, crawls back onto the bed, and kisses me with lips that taste of toothpaste and Jax. I pull him on top of me and instantly resent every stitch of fabric between us—the underwear I've slept in, and the layers and layers he needs to keep him safe from the encroaching winter. He flexes his hips. I cant mine, and we need to stop before Jerry shows up and we have to tell him Jax isn't going anywhere with him today.

Jax draws back enough to fix me with eyes that are still half asleep, despite the fact he's been up and showered already. "I don't want to leave you, but I'll feel a lot better about it if I know you're getting some more kip before your shift. Why don't you hang out here a while? My laptop's right there. Watch Netflix if you can't sleep."

"What makes you think I can't sleep?"

"I don't think anything, mate. Just want you to rest."

His gaze turns beseeching enough for me to consider spending a few hours in a bed where we've kissed each other senseless, and made each other come. I've had worse offers. And I don't want him worrying about ridiculous things when he's out on the trails. "I'll stay for a while...at least until my Riesling delivery. How's that?"

Jax smirks. "It'll do. But I want you to tell me about that Riesling later."

"Why?"

"Because it's hilarious."

No one's ever accused me of being hilarious before, but if it makes Jax's eyes shine like they are right now, I'll take it.

He kisses me again and then he leaves. I lie back on his bed with every intention of staring at the ceiling for the next two hours, but Jax's spell on me is absolute, and I fall asleep.

I don't dream.

I seem to barely blink and my phone vibrates on the nightstand sometime later.

Dazed, I fumble for it, and take the call without looking at the screen. "'Lo?"

"Where the hell are you?"

Eve's voice is sharp, like it was when I showed up late to help her move, and I already know she's standing in my empty apartment freaking out that I'm not there. "Relax. I'm at Jax's new place. Why are you in mine?"

"I brought you breakfast. Why are you and Jax hanging out so early?"

"We're not hanging out. He's at work."

"And you're just chilling in his apartment?"

"Something like that." *Shit*. This is why I don't sleep. So I don't get caught out with truth bombs before I'm awake enough for diplomacy. "What do you care why I'm in his apartment?"

Silence.

Then Eve sighs. "I suppose it helps me out if I can track you both down in one place, but Tanner?"

"Yeah?"

"If you hurt each other, I'll have no problem killing you both."

She ends the call, and I'm bemused enough to be wide awake —mentally, at least. My body seems stuck in place. I drop my phone. I want to go back to sleep. But I feel guilty about upsetting Eve. I know she worries about me, and her dry parting shot reminds me I'm not the only one on her list. I've never seen her and Jax together. Sometimes I forget how close they are. That my friend Eve is his friend too.

A yawn escapes me as I consider my options. I should go home, shower, and get ready for work. More than that, I should find Eve and buy her lunch. But Jax's bed sucks me back in, and for reasons I can't explain, I fall asleep again.

It's midday when I next wake up, and I'm so confused by life I walk home in a daze.

The Riesling delivery has already arrived. Rainn is putting it away. I shoot him an apologetic glance, but he has his headphones in and waves me off without complaint, and I remember why he's my favorite bartender.

I shoot upstairs for the quickest shower known to man. Rainn is done by the time I get downstairs, so I pack him off to the bakery to take a break and get something to eat. With him gone, I'm alone again, and for the first time since I took the lifeline job at the bar, I don't like it. Rainn doesn't say much when he's into his audiobooks, but even his silence is company.

I'm ridiculously pleased to see Molly when she shows up early for her shift. Pleased enough that I let her hug me and don't comment on the fact that she's clearly been crying.

"Wow." She regards me over the top of oversized gold-framed glasses. "Did you get laid or something?"

"Watch your mouth."

Her watery grin turns impish. She flits away to replace the tea lights on the tables and because I'm in the strangest mood ever, I follow her around. "What are you singing on Sunday?"

Molly scrapes wax from spent candles into the tin container colloquially known as the "melt bucket." "I don't know. My dorm mate was supposed to be playing fiddle for me again, but he's rain-checked me until next month, so I'm stuck with my boyfriend playing guitar, and he's flaky as hell."

"I thought you played guitar?"

"I do, but I can't sing at the same time because I'm a freak who likes to wave her hands around."

"When you sing?"

"All the time, actually. It's why I keep flinging napkins across the bar. I'm not just doing it to annoy you."

"You don't annoy me."

"Yeah, well. I annoy everyone else. Ask my boyfriend. How's Jax?"

"Why are you asking me that?"

"Because he was staying with you all that time, so I figured you were friends."

"We are."

"So…?"

It dawns on me that she really does want to know how he is, and that she expects me to know the answer. More than that, she expects me to tell her, and there's no logical reason why I shouldn't. But when I open my mouth to speak, nothing comes out. I want her to know that Jax was smiling when he left his apartment this morning, and I don't care that she'll know I was there with him, but giving voice to what's between us feels dangerous. As if talking about it makes it real enough to break it.

"He's good as far as I know," I say eventually. "He's going to shoot the open-mic night, so you'll see him then."

Molly rolls her eyes. "I know that, you silly man. He told me last time he was here."

She wanders off. I watch her go with too much Jax on my mind to decipher how I managed to screw up such a simple conversation. I miss him, and not knowing when I'll see him again makes my stomach clench. I'm worried about Gabi too. I haven't heard from him since he went dark and neither has Eve. It's not an unusual situation—he's been gone for six months at a time before—but my brain has forgotten how to think reasonably. I've seen the worst happen too many times to imagine the best, and even the sinful image of Jax coming in my hand isn't enough to stop me from spending a perfectly chill shift stuck in my own head.

And you know what? It's hella boring being a terminal drama queen.

It's hungry work too. I take a break and go upstairs to raid my refrigerator. Eve has left enough mac and cheese for a small army, and there's a note on the dish.

Find someone to share it with x

It's a note she's left before, too many times to count, but this time I don't throw it away and eat the entire dish myself. I leave both where they are and make myself a sandwich.

I eat standing up while texting Jax.

Tanner: *did u eat dinner yet?*

Jax: *nope, still out*

Tanner: *it's getting dark, be safe*

Jax: *always am x*

I believe him. Jax doesn't know the trails as well as I do, but he knows his shit when it comes to staying safe out there. There's no reason for me to worry about him, or Gabi, but I do it anyway and wish they'd both come home already before it occurs to me that they both live somewhere else.

Idiot. Back in the bar, things are starting to buzz. Happy hour stretches out and doesn't seem to end. Molly cranks the music, and I don't make her turn it down again. I crave quiet, but noise suits me better. I weave through the crowd, gathering glasses and nodding at the regular faces who call my name. Somehow, I still find myself looking for Jax and my brother, even though neither of them have ever taken a seat in the comfy booths or the round tables, and the sinking feeling in the pit of my stomach makes no sense until it's abruptly not there anymore.

Skin tingling, I glance up from my loaded tray.

Jax is right there, a few feet away. The face that grins at me is tired, but he's *right there.*

I abandon the tray and thread my way to him. It's hard not to drag him into my arms, but I manage it.

Just.

He's still dressed in his outdoor gear.

"Damn. You just got back?"

He gives me a weary shrug. "We had to make a detour."

"Where to?"

"The hospital. Got snagged on a branch. Jerry made me get stitches and a tetanus shot."

"Where?"

"Which bit?"

"The stitches."

"My leg and there's, like, three of them, so it looks like a tiny mouse tried to finish what the shark started."

His scowl is so genuinely aggrieved that the bloom of concern in my gut turns to laughter. It bubbles out of me before I can stop it, and surprises me as much as Jax. I mean, I'm not laughing at him for getting hurt, but man, he knows how to tell a story. "Please tell me it wasn't the same branch you face-checked last week?"

"Can't confirm," Jax says. "And don't you go asking Jerry either; he already thinks I'm a trainwreck."

I won't be asking Jerry anything. Guilt threatens the light Jax has gifted me just by walking in the door, but I push it back. Jerry's the nicest guy in the world, and I'm a selfish fuck who needs space between my new life and the one I had with him.

Besides, Jax is leaning tiredly on the bar and nothing else matters right now.

Rainn is nearby. I point upstairs and he nods; then I take Jax's arm and steer him out of the bar. "Did you ever get your dinner?"

"Hmm?"

"Dinner," I repeat. "You hungry?"

Jax follows me through the doors and up the stairs. He doesn't answer until we're at my front door. "I could eat," he says. "But I should probably go home. I told them I didn't need the shot, but they gave it to me anyway and now I need a nap."

He isn't going home, at least not until I can go with him. I know better than to tell him what to do, but those are the facts.

I open my door and tug him inside. "Show me your leg."

"Is that your best chat-up line?"

"Top ten. Show me the leg."

Jax unties his boots and yanks them off. Then he rolls up his pant leg to reveal a dressed wound on his calf. It's small, clean, and beneath the bandage, neatly stitched. In fact, it's tiny. I lean closer, frowning. "That's it?"

"I know, right?" Jax lets his pant leg drop and resets his balance. "I'd have stuck a Band-Aid on it, but Jerry flipped when he saw it and drove like a maniac to the hospital. I mean, that was more likely to kill me than this is."

He yawns and gives me a searching look I don't understand. Or maybe I don't want to understand. Lord knows what Jerry has told him about me. Most days I'm convinced it's absolutely nothing; then others, when Jax peers at me like he's trying to see beneath my skin, I'm convinced he knows every weakness and flaw I have. And maybe I want him to, so he never turns that piercing gaze on me for real.

Whatever. He needs to eat, and I have to be pretty fucked up to turn down Eve's mac and cheese.

I direct Jax to the couch and fix two plates of loaded macaroni. Bacon, green onions, Vermont cheddar. While it's heating, I fetch Jax sweatpants to chill in.

He laughs. "If you give me any more of your clothes you'll be walking around naked."

"That a problem for you?"

He snorts. "What do you think?"

I think about a lot of things that involve being naked with him. But I remember the hint of panic in his gaze when he lit the fire beneath us last night, and so I douse the heat rising in me. I leave him to change and fetch the plates from the kitchen.

Jax falls on his like he does most meals we share, but Eve's macaroni is good enough that I don't stare. I snarf mine in record time, then wait for him in the path of a serious carb coma. Half my mind is still downstairs, trailing Molly around as she wreaks havoc on the bar that Rainn will have to handle in my absence, and I'm still worried about Gabi, but mainly I think of Jax. Of how good he looks in a pair of sweatpants, and how sleepy he clearly is now that his belly is full.

"I should go home," he says again.

But he doesn't move, and neither do I, except to put our plates on the table and lift my arm so he can lean against me. If anyone needs to be somewhere else, it's me, but his hair smells of the forest and of Jax, and I can't tear myself away. I close my eyes and imagine a world where my hair smells of wood and leaves too. It's a nice world, but it's not real.

I open my eyes and pull myself back. Jax is drowsing. I kiss his temple. "I've got to go back to work. You wanna hang here and I'll walk back with you later?"

"You don't have to do that. I'll head off in a bit."

He won't. I don't know Jax as well as I want to, but I'm ninety-nine percent certain he's gonna knock out the second I leave the apartment, and I want him close more than I want to do the freak dance with old ghosts.

I ease out from under him and leave him alone. Downstairs, the bar is still kicking, as if I never left, but I get a few curious stares from my staff. I don't often take a break; eating alone is no fun. Busy nights are, though, when I'm in the right mood. Time moves faster. I embrace the noise and let it carry me for the three hours it takes me to wind down the bar and send my crew home.

Molly gives me a wink as she leaves.

I try for a scowl, but a grin comes instead, and she walks away laughing.

Shaking my head, I lock the doors and head upstairs. On the landing, I watch her disappear to the parking lot. A few seconds later, the modified engine of her boyfriend's car pierces the air with an obnoxious roar, and I hate that douchebag a little bit more.

"Why do you look murderous?"

I spin around. Jax is behind me, leaning against the open door of my apartment. He looks sleepy and rumpled, and he's still wearing my sweatpants. "Murderous is probably a little strong, but Molly's boyfriend makes me fucking mad."

"Why?"

"Because he's a douche who makes her cry all the time."

"You've met him?"

"Nope. But did you hear his car just now? Anyone who drives like that is an asshat."

Jax shrugs his agreement.

I abandon the window and close the distance between us. "How are you doing? Did you sleep?"

"Think so. I fell off the couch, though, so I'm pretty sure Jerry is right about me being a liability. Maybe I should get a job in a library."

"But then I wouldn't get to see you covered in dirt with leaves in your hair, and I need that in my life."

"Yeah?"

"Yeah. It's a thing."

Jax snorts out a laugh. He holds out his hands and I take them, letting him tug me into my apartment. The door closes behind us. He pushes me against it and kisses me, and the sweatpants he's wearing do nothing to conceal how awake certain parts of him are.

My body's response is instant. I grip his hip and pull him closer so he can feel me where I want him most. He moans, and I kiss him harder, before I draw back and say the one word that's been on my mind all night. "Stay."

He doesn't answer with words.

CHAPTER TWELVE

Jax

Staying with Tanner is easy. So is rolling around his bed until the early hours getting naked enough for him to come all over my belly, then knocking out in his arms.

Leaving him is hard. I have every intention of slipping out while he's still sleeping, but when my alarm goes off, he's wide awake like he always is. I push him onto his back, splaying my hand across his broad chest. "Don't get up."

He opens his mouth to speak, but I seal it with my other palm. "Don't. I just need to go."

Tanner nods. His gaze is too dark to read, but he does what I ask and stays put while I find my outdoor clothes and put them on. I go back to his room and he's exactly where I left him, on his side, handsome face propped on his folded arm. I love and hate that he's naked beneath the crumpled sheets. The approaching dawn taunts me. If I stay, I'll get to see him as the winter sun streams through the open blinds. But I can't stay, and we both know it. Me and Jerry are camping out tonight for as long as it takes to get the marten footage Tanner thinks we'll find in the woods. I'll be back for open-mic night, but that's four days away, and I haven't been apart from Tanner that long since I met him.

The realization hits me like a stone.

He frowns, and I can't stand that he's so attuned to me. Or that I like it.

Because I don't like it. I don't want it.

Tanner lets me go. I back up and I can tell it's taking him a lot to let me. That he wants to reach for me, but he won't because he's Tanner, not the horrible people who made me scared of him wanting me.

You're not scared of him wanting you. He'd let you go in a heartbeat if you asked him to.

Of course he would. I *know* that. But it's too late to stop the flash of hurt in his dark gaze as he interprets whatever he sees in mine for exactly what it is.

"Jax."

He says my name like a prayer. A low, growling syllable that grounds me as much as it adds to the sudden disquiet raving in my nerves. My feet move of their own accord until I'm close enough to feel his body heat as he sits up to meet me.

The bedsheets drop to his waist. His inked skin calls to my treacherous hands and the dark blip in my brain starts to fade.

I let it happen, and slide my hands over his bare shoulders. His corded biceps fit against my palms like perfect, hard stress balls, and the bizarre imagery drives a sharp laugh from me.

Tanner doesn't blink.

I shake my head. "I feel wild this morning. I'm so fucking sorry."

"The fuck are you sorry for?" Tanner winds his strong arms around me. It's the perfect hug that makes me resent my clothes, but the kiss he brushes to my cheek is more comfort than heat. "Don't ever be sorry. Just be safe, okay?"

I am okay. Sometime I think I'm not, but I am.

My hands find their way to the nape of his neck, and I thread my fingers into his sleep-tousled hair. Another apology is on the tip of my tongue, but I swallow it down. I love seeing Tanner like this, so clear-eyed and earnest, and I don't want to waste it on words he doesn't want to hear. "I'll be safe. I'll have Jerry with me, and I think he's only coming so he can get a good night's sleep away from his kids."

Tanner snorts softly. "Sounds about right. Count on him pretending you don't have what you need so you have to spend another night."

"That's why I never let him look until we get back to the office." I kiss Tanner one last time. "And whatever happens, I'll be back for open-mic night. We've got a hot date after, right?"

"Of course. It's the only reason I'm going."

"You're not working?"

"Nope."

My mind immediately drops to the gutter. I was already looking forward to working on something that didn't involve getting cold and wet. Add in Tanner's free-agent status and I'm wishing the next four days away.

I kiss him one last time and leave him in bed. Every footstep away from him feels wrong, but it levels out as I walk to meet Jerry at the closest lot to my apartment. Tanner has his own life, and so do I. And despite missing him already, I'm eager to get outside and make the last month of hard work count. The elusive lynx footage is the Holy Grail, but even without it, Vermont is the gift that keeps on giving. Only Tanner by my side would make it better.

The thought is errant, but strong. He knows Black Claw better than Jerry. *What if—*

Jerry blasts his horn. He's waiting for me.

I hurry to where he's parked and fold myself into his truck.

He gives me a knowing look. "Slumber party?"

"Something like that. Can I ask you something?"

"As long as it's not where babies come from."

"It's really not. It's about Tanner."

"You didn't think to ask him?"

"Not yet. I want to ask him to come with me one night up the trail, but I don't want to upset him. You think it's a bad idea?"

Jerry says nothing for a long time.

He points the truck out of Burlington and his face is so unreadable I figure I've made a terrible mistake even voicing the question.

But eventually, he sighs and tears his gaze away from the road for a fleeting moment that makes my chest ache. "You can ask him, son. But don't get sore feelings if he runs a damn mile. This life is good for you, I can see it every day we're out here, but it hurt that boy more than I can ever explain."

CHAPTER THIRTEEN

Tanner

Jax is gone for three days. No contact because the spot he's camped out at might as well be on the moon as far as cell service is concerned. On the fourth day, he's resting at home, but any opportunity I might've had to see him is taken up by work, and Molly's drunk-ass, dickwad boyfriend who's apparently determined to ruin my life as well as hers.

I have no regrets as he hits the sidewalk the third time I tell him to get the fuck out of my bar. But I don't throw him far enough, and by the time Molly's shift is over, he's still loitering outside.

"Wait for me," I tell her. "I'll drive you home when I'm done."

She doesn't argue. As big a fool as she is for him, she isn't dumb enough to get in his car right now.

I leave her sniffling by the mocktail station and stomp around the bar for the rest of my shift, which is unfortunately all night long. It's late by the time I get a minute to text Jax, and he doesn't reply.

"I'm sorry," Molly says as I steer my car into the parking lot outside her dorm. "I know you'd rather be with Jax than with me."

"Doesn't matter where I'd rather be. You think I'd let you find your own way home at this time of night?"

"My shift finished four hours ago. I could've got an Uber."

True story, but Molly is strapped for cash, and I want to make sure she doesn't have a nasty surprise waiting for her at her door. "Why are you still with that asshat anyway?"

It's not what I meant to say, but I don't regret that either.

Molly sighs. "Because he isn't always an asshat. He's pretty sweet when he's in the right mood."

"How often is that? Every leap year?"

"More often than you were before Jax showed up and turned the sun on in your face."

I kill the engine and turn to face her. "Leave Jax out of it. I know I'm a grouchy bastard, and I'm sorry about that, but I still don't get why you want to be with someone who belittles and bullies you, on top of embarrassing you every time he shows up at your place of work out-of-his-mind drunk."

"You don't ever keep doing stuff that's bad for you?"

Molly's twenty-one. She has no business being so fucking astute. And perhaps I have no business lecturing her about how she treats herself. I let out a sigh that has nothing to do with her and everything to do with the unread message I've sent Jax. "Okay, fair point. I'm not that good at doing the best thing for myself either, but I'm worried about you, Molls. Brent is a massive pile of bad dick, and I'm scared he's going to hurt you when there's no one around to stop it."

"*I* can stop it. I don't need a white knight."

"Just the will, huh?"

"No, just the space to figure it out without being told what to do."

It occurs to me too late that maybe she'd be better off having this conversation with Jax, but I've already opened my big fat mouth, and as nice as Jax is, I doubt he wants to counsel my younger staff members through their tumultuous dating adventures. "Sorry, kiddo," I say after a beat of protracted silence. "I'm not telling you what to do. At least, I don't mean to. I just want you to be safe, okay? So I'm going to shut the fuck up and walk you to your door."

"Is that so I'll stop talking about Jax?"

"Partly."

"Why, though? Apart from all the reasons we just said. You two are so cute together."

"We're not together."

"Well, you should be."

"Yeah, okay." I roll my eyes and slide out of the car. Molly's dorm room is on the second floor and I walk her all the way in. There's no one around, save a few stoners who don't so much as glance up, and no sign of Captain Douche, but as I trudge back to the parking lot, I feel eyes on me all the same.

Back in the car, I shiver and open WhatsApp. Jax still hasn't been online, and neither has Gabi since the last time he messaged me. I feel adrift without both of them, and my thumbs hover to text Eve and tell her so, but my phone buzzes before I can send a message I'll regret.

It's Gabriel. He's online.

Gabi: *all safe. you doing okay?*

Tanner: *i'm good. was just starting to worry abt u*

Gabi: *no need. i'm all good. Eve okay?*

Tanner: *y don't u ask her?*

Gabi: *i did. i'm asking you too*

Tanner: *didn't like her answer?*

Gabi: *don't be a dick*

Tanner: *she's fine. missing you. we both are.*

Gabi: *not for long. this job is wrapping up early.*

Tanner: *how early?*

Gabi: *don't know yet*

Tanner: *helpful*

Gabi: *says you. i'm the one who's gotta crash at a yoga convention when i get back*

Tanner: *u can stay with me*

Gabi: *that what u really want bro?*

He goes offline before I can reply, and he doesn't come back, leaving me to contemplate the possibility that he'll be home sooner than expected. It feels too good to be true, and I wonder if that's how Jax felt the morning he left for his camping trip. If whatever he was feeling when he looked at me had felt like a cruel joke. Damn, he doesn't deserve that. I don't think anyone does.

I drive home and go to bed without letting myself dwell on it too much, and somehow I succeed.

My reward is a dawn text message from Jax.

Jax: *Sorry, I crashed. Missed you. You wanna have breakfast?*

Fresh relief tops up what Gabriel gave me when he came online last night, but it's laced with disappointment. I can't have breakfast with Jax—I have too much to do before I hand open mic night over to Rainn, including a meeting with my boss on a damn chicken farm. *Thanks, Harrison.*

Tanner: *i can't. work stuff. maybe later? lunch?*

Jax: *I can't do that either. Gotta go to HQ and review some stuff. Don't worry. I'll find you tonight x*

I don't want him to find me tonight. I want to knock on his door with breakfast and eat it in his bed with him. But my life doesn't work like that. I get up and drive to the chicken farm to have coffee and waffles with the best people on the planet, and the whole time they're being nicer to me than I deserve, I want to be somewhere else. *Hero.*

It's afternoon by the time I'm back in my car. I'd have missed lunch even if Jax had been free, but it doesn't make the pull to him any less, and I happen to know that Jerry shuts his Wildfoot office at three o'clock sharp on Sundays, whether his staff wants to work longer or not.

Somehow I find myself there. I park close by and kill the engine. People are still milling around inside. My view isn't clear enough to tell if Jax is one of them, but I hit the sidewalk anyway and find a bench across the street. My phone keeps me company for a little while. I have a million things to do on social media for the bar, including deleting the lewd comments Molly's boyfriend has left beneath the video clip of her singing last month.

I'm still going when a shadow looms over me a few minutes later. I'm stuck on Jax enough to assume it's him. "Can you block someone from a Facebook page?" I say without looking up.

"No idea. Ask someone younger."

Damn. I know that voice and it's far too Vermont to be anything like Jax's melodic Cornish brogue. I raise my gaze to meet Kai Fletcher's. He's taller than me, but lanky enough that the winter sun still makes me squint at him. "You're not that old."

"Maybe not, but I spend too much time without cell service to understand social media."

Of course he does. He used to be Jerry's head ranger before he joined the state's mountain rescue team. And seeing as we have nothing else in common, I'm guessing that's what he wants to talk to me about. *Awesome.*

Uninvited, Kai takes a seat next to me. He's dressed in the same clothes Jax wears to hike the trails, but despite his forest-man aesthetic, I don't dig it. I've only got eyes for my ocean boy. "What do you want, Kai?"

"A favor, obviously," Kai says with an easy grin. "Jerry told me to leave you alone, but I'm desperate enough to risk you kicking my ass."

"Why would I do that?"

"Because I'm about to ask you to take a spot on the volunteer rescue team. We're shorthanded till next summer. I know it's not your scene anymore, but you have more experience than the rest of my guys combined. Hell, I could probably even swing a paid spot if you'd consider a full-time move."

I stare at him as though he's speaking Greek, but my conscience knows I'm being unfair. It's not Kai's fault even thinking about my old life makes me want to jump in front of a truck. At least, it used to. These days I'm better at handling extreme thoughts, but I'm still all kinds of not ready for this conversation. "Thanks, but I have a job already."

"Dude, you work in a bar. That isn't a job for a bad-ass mountain man."

"Like I give a fuck what you think."

Kai doesn't flinch. He's genuinely confused, and I want to remind him that mountain rescue in Vermont is nothing like the five-year stretch I spent in Alaska, but...I don't care enough. Besides, people still die on the sweetest trails. If the last two years have taught me anything, it's that. "Look, thanks for thinking of me, but I'm not about that life anymore. You might not want my job, but I'm not a man you want doing yours."

"I don't believe that, Reid. You had a bad run. It doesn't mean—"

"Shut up, man." As I speak the words, Jax and Jerry step out of the Wildfoot offices. He doesn't see me at first, but Jerry does, and he looks like he wants to die. Or murder Kai. And I'm not okay with either of those things. I clap Kai on the shoulder and find an affable smile from the pit of my stomach. "Thanks for the chat."

I leave him on the bench and cross the street. Jerry has stopped dead in the doorway of Wildfoot HQ, but Jax is still drifting forward, poking at an iPad with a flush of excitement staining his chiseled cheeks. I wonder what he's squinting at, and he's cute enough that the forced grin on my face settles in enough to be real as he walks right into me.

"Fuck. Sorry—oh, hey. What are you doing here?"

"Just passing." I flick a glance at Jerry. "Figured I'd try my luck and see if you had time for pizza before the open-mic night."

"Pizza?"

"Yeah. You know me...always hungry, and you can bring Jerry too. He's got a boner for the Italian sausage at Titos."

Jax is already startled by my sudden appearance in front of him, but his eyes widen considerably more as he digests my invitation. He glances at Jerry, who's already shaking his head. "Don't mind me, boys. I have to get home. But thanks, Tanner. Maybe next time?"

"For sure." I find Jax's wrist and wrap my fingers around it, grounding myself in his flesh and bone. "See you around."

Jerry walks away whistling, but I know him well enough to call bullshit, and I feel bad that I've rattled him. He doesn't deserve it. Dude was like a father to me once upon a time, and now we can barely look at each other, and it's all my fault.

Guilt creeps in, bonding with the anxiety I'm never quite free of. My vision starts to darken, but Jax grips my hand before panic takes hold. He squeezes it hard enough to bend my bones and the shock of it turns me toward him with little conscious thought.

Jax searches my face. Lord know what he finds. "You okay?"

"Yup. You?"

He frowns, and it sucks away the exhilaration he was cloaked in when I set eyes on him across the street. That's my fault too, but I know if I sink into it, I'll make it worse.

His hand is still locked around mine. I focus on his warm palm and strong fingers. The bad shit ebbs away, and I'm left with the tingling sensation I get when Jax is anywhere near me. It feels amazing. I want to kiss him. More than that, I want to drag him home and get him naked.

But most of all, I want to know what's got him so excited. "Got time for that pizza?"

Jax blinks. His expression clears and he gives me a slow grin. "Sure. I need to get one with green shit on it, though. I'm carbed out."

"Death by energy bar, huh?"

"And then some. If you cut me open, I'd bleed oats."

I laugh, like I so often do when I'm with him, sudden and unexpected. Lighter than air. "That's some image."

"I know, right? But I forgot to grocery shop last night, so I'm still eating them."

"You didn't get dinner last night?"

"Nope. Fell asleep."

"Breakfast this morning?"

"On the run. More energy bars."

"That ain't healthy."

Jax shrugs. "It's not the worst thing in the world."

He's right about that. We slope to my car and drive back to the lot behind V and V. The pizza place isn't far and we're settled at a table ten minutes later. I'm pretty much done for the day except some mild supervision of the bar, so I order a beer. Jax gets the cider he seems to like so much, and I get a kick out of the way his Cornish tongue wraps around the word cider, so it's a win all around. There's even a pizza on the menu with enough green stuff on it that he won't get scurvy anytime soon.

When the server has gone, I lean forward and tap the iPad Jax has on the table. "What's cookin' on this? Something good come up on your trip? How did your leg hold up?"

Jax opens the tablet with his thumb and pushes it to me. "My leg is fine. The stitches dissolved already. As for the trip, it was kind of a bust as far as footage goes, but look what we found on the top static post this morning."

I take the iPad and press Play on the video already open on the screen. It's dark, and the weather hampers the powerful lens of the static camera, but I still can't miss the pointy-eared feline padding across the ground, its large paws hitting the icy crunch with a spreading toe motion that creates a natural snow shoe. "Wow." I let out a low whistle. "You got the lynx. That's fucking awesome. And high up too. That's what you get for listening to me, huh?"

Jax smiles like the sun. "Don't be so hard on yourself. If I hadn't listened to you, that camera would be on the other side of the ridge, and we'd have missed the whole thing."

I take that in as I watch the magnificent creature tread its way to wherever it's going off-shot. It's carrying dead prey—a squirrel, maybe? I can't be sure—but it feels good to see it with food in its mouth. It bodes well for future sightings and the survival of the species in general. "Can I snap that and send it to Gabi? He pretends he doesn't care about Vermont anymore, but he's lying."

"Sure."

Jax holds the tablet at just the right angle for me to take a picture on my phone without screen glare. Then he lays it back down on the table. "Jerry reckons we're gonna get a ton of conservationists wanting to head up there before long to track them. It means we have to map a safe route up there before spring that can take more footfall than just the two of us."

"That isn't going to be easy. I thought your job was videographer, not ranger."

"It is, but I know the trails pretty well now, so I said I'd help him, unless…"

"What?"

"I thought maybe you could help."

For a moment I feel so betrayed by him I want to flip the table and walk out. Then I remember it's a reasonable fucking question considering the cold hard facts. I *could* help if I wanted to. If I could drag my head out of my ass long enough.

"I can't go up there."

Jax drums his fingers on the table. "I know. I didn't go in the ocean for a year after the accident."

"Accident? That's what you call it? And whatever. I didn't nearly die on Black Claw, I just—"

"*What?*"

Jax's sudden frustration catches me off guard. I'm so used to being flippant about the mess in my head that I forget *he's* not used to it. He sees something in me no one else does, and it gives me less room to hide.

I blow out a long breath. The server brings two pizzas to the table and lays them in front of us, but I'm not hungry anymore. I'm trapped, and I need to get the fuck out of here, but I can't, because walking away from Jax is another mountain I can't climb.

Jax sighs too. He finds my leg under the table and rubs my

thigh. "Sorry, mate. I'm tired and talking shite. I get it, okay? Jerry told me about what happened last year. It just burns me to see you turn your back on your whole life because of it."

"You don't think the life I have now is good enough?"

"That's not what I said."

It isn't. And for a moment, the bubble of destructive reticence in my throat threatens to burst, but it holds firm at the last second, and all I have is a slow shake of my head.

Jax lets it go. He scoots his chair closer to mine and swipes a piece of sausage from my pizza. It's a peace offering I don't need —I can't imagine ever being angry with him—but I steal an olive from his plate all the same.

We go back to talking about pointy-eared cats. Food disappears. Then the empty plates. I wrap my leg around Jax's. He grins at me, and I forget that he's been gone for days and that I lived an entire lifetime before I met him. Jax is the happy I need right now.

The server brings the check. I let Jax take it without argument and study every facet of him as he pulls his battered wallet from his pocket and drops a card onto the bill tray. As if cataloguing the curl of hair at his collar will tell me everything about him. Questions surge. I swallow them down—it's only fair. I dodge most of his, and he lets me, giving me the space to talk if I want to, and the freedom to wallow in selfish silence. I owe him the same, but I'm not as selfless as him. "Can I ask you something?"

Jax shoots me a wary frown. "Um...okay. I'm guessing it's nothing to do with camera angles and lighting?"

"Gabi told me your ex's family kept you prisoner in California. Is that true?"

Jax has fair brows. They're lighter than his hair and soften his masculine features. He's way prettier than me, even as said brows disappear into his hairline. "Why the fuck would your brother tell you that?"

"He knows we were living together. You came up in conversation, and the only mutual we have is Eve, so I'm assuming it came from her."

"No, the assuming came from your brother. It wasn't like that. Not literally, anyway, and if Eve told him anything, he'd know that."

The server interrupts us. Again. Jax gives her a thirty percent tip and signs his name. Then he shoves his chair back and walks out. I follow, naturally, and reasonable me is weighted down with all kinds of regret. But the rest of me wants to push him and push him and push him until I understand him, and it's such a fucking unfair thing to want that I stop walking the moment I hit fresh air, and Jax gets away from me.

By the time I'm moving again, he's half a block ahead of me and on his way back to his own apartment. I trail him, keeping him in sight. He stops outside his building and doesn't turn round as I come up behind him.

He sighs. "You're a git, you know that, right?"

"Are you calling me an asshole?"

"Basically, yeah."

"I deserve that."

"Do you?"

"Yeah, I think so."

Jax unlocks his door and steps into his building, holding the door open for me to follow. Inside his apartment, he finally turns and kicks the door shut.

His kiss shocks me, like always. No dude before him ever kissed me like he does. As if we're two people at the end of the world and kissing me is all he has left.

Even the softest touch of his lips is like that. Blinding. Consuming.

Dizzying.

When he pulls away, though, my selfish question still hangs between us.

"I'm gonna answer you," he says. "Because I want to, and

because I hope you'll talk to me one day, and everything I know about you won't be secondhand."

"You know plenty about me."

"Like what?"

I watch him ditch his coat and shoes on the floor next to a guitar I haven't seen before, then I grab his shirt and pull him close again. "You know what makes me laugh. That I shout at myself in my sleep and worry about things that aren't real."

"Aren't real? What happened that night that wasn't real?"

"What I see in my sleep isn't always what happened."

"It doesn't have to be."

"No?"

"Reliving trauma isn't like that. It's not tangible, it's just a wicked piece of shit that steals your happiness until you think you don't deserve it anymore."

"You sound like a coarser version of the therapist I can't afford."

Jax cracks a wan smile. "Why do you think that is?"

"Because you think the shark was trying to save you."

"As fucked up as that sounds, you might be right." Jax tugs me to the couch. We sit facing each other. "But no one held me prisoner, so you need to get that image out of your head right now."

"Give me a new one."

He finds a thread in my shirt and pulls at it. "They took all my money and convinced me I didn't deserve it while I wasn't working to earn more. We moved to a house I didn't own, and I didn't have a car. Everything I thought I wanted disappeared. I wanted to die for the longest time, and I thought the shark attack was a sign from Mother Nature that I was meant to."

"What changed?"

"I remembered the cameras I kept at a lockup they didn't know about. I'd sold most of my good stuff after the accident, but I still had enough to get me moving. Then I realized it wasn't anyone else holding me hostage, it was me, and I left the next day."

There's more to the story than a suicidal epiphany, I can tell, but somehow it's enough. Jax possesses a quiet determination I've never seen in anyone else. I don't need a rundown of every second that made him that way. "I'm sorry I made you talk about it. I know it's not fair."

Jax's eyes have hazed over as he's talked. They sharpen now, but not with anger. "It's not fair...to *you*, not me. I don't need your life story to want you, Tanner. But this wall of fucking silence isn't sustainable. You know that, right? You know it's gonna fall when you least expect it, and that shit hurts if you don't have a safe place to land."

I can no longer tell if he's talking about me or himself. And we've run out of time. I need to get to the bar, and, actually, so does he. But neither of us make any move to leave.

Jax twines his fingers with mine, and I sit back on his couch, pulling him on top of me. He's wearing worn jeans and a Wildfoot T-shirt with the sleeves rolled up over his leanly cut biceps. I'm still wearing my coat. Jax unzips it and pushes it off my shoulders. I shrug out of it and kiss him, pressing up against him, reveling in the friction between us. I'm so fucking hot for him. My brain empties of all responsibility. I shove my tongue in his mouth and my hands into his silky hair. I want him naked, but this is enough.

Everything about him will always be enough.

I grip his shirt at the hem and inch it up his torso, my fingers gliding over his skin. He shivers and bites my bottom lip. A growl builds in my chest. I reach for his fly and—

My phone rings. "Motherfucker."

Jax laughs and lifts off me so I can fish it from my pocket.

It's the bar. I take a call about where to stack the chairs we have to move to make room for the cabling to the stage. By the time I'm done, Jax has his coat on again. He's bent over and messing with a camera bag on the floor. I come up behind him as he straightens. I press my face into his neck and breathe him in.

He reaches back and rubs my forearm with his spare hand. "Okay?"

I take one last lungful of him and press my lips to his warm skin. "Yeah, you just make me feel lucky sometimes, is all."

CHAPTER FOURTEEN

Jax

Tanner is much better at communicating without words. He helps me carry my gear back to V and V and leaves me alone to set up, but he's never far away, and he passes me often, every light hand on my back an apology for shit he doesn't need to apologize for. He's...complex, and he didn't ask for me to show up in his life and make him explain himself.

He didn't tell me that V and V has archaic electrics, though, and that shit *is* fucking criminal.

"It's an old building," he says with a wince. "It got refitted to be a bar, not a studio."

"Yeah, all right, mate." I'm grumbling and it amuses him enough for me to turn my back on him and try and figure out my cabling problem on my own. If it was just the cameras it would be no thing—they run on batteries. But if I'm going to catch Molly's best side, I'm gonna need more light.

Rainn finds an extra cable from Lord knows where. Tanner helps me run it along the wall where no one will trip over it. As a thank-you I tread on his hand by accident, but he doesn't seem to mind. "Where are you going to put the light?" He stares up at the wooden beam I'm taping the cable to. "In the corner?"

"Yup."

"You want a chair to stand on?"

"Nope." I find the variable LED I bought off eBay for filming tarantulas in the California desert. It's small enough to be incognito if I can get it high enough. I find another beam and lift myself from the ground with one arm, using the other to hang the light on a thick nail that was probably hammered in a hundred years ago.

It holds. I drop to the floor to find Tanner watching me from behind the bar with his lip caught in his teeth. "What?"

He rolls his eyes. "Nothing. Just keep doing shit like that all night long and see where you end up."

There's too many people around for me to respond. I wonder if he knows that watching him do the simplest of things has become my favorite activity. Like now, as he diverts his attention back to hefting trays of glasses from one end of the bar to the other. He's not officially working, so he's still wearing the gunmetal gray tee I wanted to tear from him an hour ago. His forearms are always on show; add his popping biceps and I need a fucking drink.

Shame I *am* working. The cider I had with our angsty lunch date seems a long time ago.

I finish my set-up. There isn't much to it, just my faithful spider light and a camera on a tripod pointing at the stage. I'll film the rest of the bar with a handheld on a gimbal and hope I'm not too out of practice at dynamic shooting. It's been a while.

"All set?" Tanner's hand on my back startles me. His lips at my neck, not so much.

Humming, I lean into his touch. "Think so. I'm trying to remember the last time I used the gimbal, though, so don't pay me until you've seen the finished result."

"Anything you produce will be better than the crap we already have."

"Hold that thought."

Tanner snorts. I can tell he wants to bitch me out for my pessimism, but he's called away again before he can comment.

The bar opens. Happy hour kicks off and I retreat to a side table to stand guard over my equipment and people-watch. Molly arrives. She looks tired and wet-eyed.

I frown. "What's the matter?"

"Nothing."

"Sure about that? Cos you look like you just got dumped."

Molly flops into the seat opposite and drops low on the table. "*I* didn't get dumped. He did. So he stole all my clothes, my guitar, and my laptop."

"He stole your clothes? That's fucked up."

"Yeah, well. He says he didn't…that I just left all my stuff at his apartment, but he won't bring it here because he's scared of Tanner, and I don't have a car to go and get it, so he says he's gonna take it all to Goodwill."

Molly has a habit of speaking too fast. I take a minute to dissect what she's telling me. "Okay. Roll back. Why is your boyfriend scared of Tanner?"

"Because he showed up here drunk a few days ago and called me a white trash ho. Tanner put him on his ass and drove me home. Brent saw him at my place and thinks he came in for a hook-up, so we fought, and here we are. He still thinks I'm a whore, and now I have no underwear, and he's threatening to burn my grandfather's Fender."

I can relate to that more than I want to. "What are you going to do?"

"About my underwear?"

"About all of it. I mean, I can't help you with the underwear thing, but I just brought my guitar back from the office to my place. I can go and get it for you if you need one for tonight."

"Can you play it for me?"

"On stage in front of a bar full of people? No fucking chance, even I didn't have my hands full already."

"Why not?"

"Because I'm a lousy hobby musician and you deserve better."

Molly sighs. It's a light sound, but carries the weight of the world. I wish I could help her more than offering her the use of a guitar that barely has strings, but short of stomping on her ex—which I'm not averse to—there isn't much I can do for her.

She disappears to get ready for her set. Other musicians arrive, and I take my cue to get up and find a spot out of the way while things get going. Someone lowers the lights. I check the brightness of the LED at the back of the stage and switch my static camera on. The first act on the stage is a white bloke with a set of maracas and the worst rendition of 'One Love' I've ever heard, but he looks good enough on screen that I can leave the static to do its work.

I spend the next few hours looping the bar with the gimbal. From time to time, I catch sight of Tanner through the camera lens. He's not supposed to be working, but it's a while before I see him find a stool to drop onto. He doesn't know I'm watching him, and he seems tired. He scrubs a hand down his face before his phone interrupts him.

Whatever he sees on the screen makes him smirk, and I like that. His features get lighter, and his eyes gleam. I forget there's a bar full of people I'm supposed to be filming, zero in on him, and everything seems so simple. There isn't a lifetime he won't talk to me about, and my heart doesn't jump in fear every time I contemplate how hard I'm falling for him. He's a just bloke who happens to be hotter than the goddamn sun, and I'm the idiot who can't stop staring.

I'm so caught up in him I nearly miss Molly taking to the stage. Cursing, I tear the camera away from Tanner and slip through the crowd to get to the front of the stage. Molly is already in position. She's wearing a hockey jersey as a dress, cowboy boots, and a Stetson. It's the strangest outfit I've ever seen, and Rainn doesn't seem to like it, if his scowl is anything to go by, but she makes it work.

She starts to sing, unaccompanied by a single thing except the snap of her fingers, and *man*, she's good. I sweep around the stage, catching her at every angle, then I crouch low and point the camera up at her face. The shot is on point. She's got killer cheekbones—only Tanner's are better.

Stop it.

I pin my mind to one spot, to Molly, and search for the tunnel vision I need out on the trails to focus on bobcats and squirrels when my feet are so cold I'm pretty sure they're about to drop off. Molly sings more songs, and by the third, I've found the zone where my camera is an extension of my arm.

It all comes together. Molly soars through her last song and beams at the audience who are lapping her up. For a girl often so quick to put herself down, it's fucking magic.

I'm grinning like an idiot as I turn the static cam off and lower the gimbal. Molly grins, and steps out of the spotlight just as a beer bottle soars over my head and crashes into the space she's left behind.

The world often moves slowly, and yet at a million miles an hour.

Glass shatters on the stage like daggers of ice. Molly screams. I lunge for her and drag her off-stage, tucking her under my arm to barrel through the panicked crowd. My elbow connects with anyone who gets in my way. I tap the code into the door to get to the stairwell and pull her to safety.

She's shaking. I fish Tanner's key from my pocket and press it into one hand, and my precious gimbal into the other. "Go to Tanner's apartment. Stay there until one of us comes up. Don't open the door for anyone else."

Molly nods and dashes upstairs. Her lack of protest leads me to believe she has a fair idea who in the usually chill crowd at V and V would throw bottles at her. Her ex? Someone else? Who-the-fuck knows. And actually, I don't give a shit, as long as anyone I care about is okay.

I dash back out to the bar. The chaos I left behind has dulled to a hum of anxious activity. The usually low lights are bright and fluorescent. It makes it easy to find Tanner in the midst of it all, furious as he marches through the crowd.

Rainn is sweeping up glass.

Satisfied that Tanner is okay, I help him, and move my static camera to a safer place. "What the fuck just happened?"

Rainn shrugs. "Fuck if I know. Whoever that was is gonna die when Tanner gets a hold of them, though. Did you get Molly out?"

"Yeah. She's in Tanner's apartment. I told her to stay there."

Tanner reaches us as I finish my sentence. He nods, absorbing the information. "Did you see anything?"

"Nope. And my cameras were both facing the stage. All I saw was the impact."

"I saw someone ducking out of the front door," Tanner growls. "But they were long gone by the time I got outside. Fucking asshole. I bet it's Brent."

"Her ex? You think he'd try and hurt her like that?"

"Not exactly. He's an attention-seeking dickstain. I think he threw it deliberately as she stepped away, because she blocked his number."

"She didn't tell me that earlier. Just that he stole all her stuff."

Tanner's dark gaze flares with empathy. He *knows* what that means to me even if the comparison isn't literal. "I want to go to his place and stomp on his head."

It's so close an echo to my earlier thoughts that I almost smile. But I don't. Because there's no humor to be found in a grown man hurling missiles at a young woman who kicked him to the curb. That shit is scary.

Tanner storms away to call the cops and calm the crowd. He bribes the patrons who've stayed with free wine, and it's not long before the charm he thinks he lacks brings a chilled hum back to the bar. He turns the lights low again, and Rainn flicks the music back on. Jazz fills the gaps conversation doesn't. It's business as usual, but adrenaline still courses through my veins. I keep busy packing my gear away. The footage on my static cam is epic. I watch it through on the tiny screen of the camera, then it occurs to me that the cops might want to review the footage on my handheld camera—they're already upstairs with Molly and Tanner.

I take my shit and knock on Tanner's front door. It swings open before I've retracted my hand, and he's right there.

He pulls me inside and brushes a fleeting kiss to my jaw. "You okay?"

"Course I am. I'm not the one who had a bottle chucked at my head."

"So?"

I don't have an answer for him. I set my tripod down in the hall and point at the living room. "Molly brought my Sony upstairs with her. There might be something in the footage the cops can use."

Tanner nods, his gaze still searching my face for who-the-fuck knows what. I push past and duck into his living space. Molly is sitting on the couch where I used to lay my head. She's wide-eyed and pale. A female cop is perched on the coffee table, just like Tanner does.

There's another officer by the window gazing out at the street. My gimbal is leaning against the wall beside him. I detach the camera from the frame and find the footage I've taken of the bar. It sucks me in. Distantly, I hear Tanner explaining to the cops who I am and what I'm doing, but their holstered guns are freaking me out enough that I don't look at them. That's right, even after all these years away from English bobbies and their batons, I'm still not used to how the rest of the world works.

The footage on the Sony is dark—at least it will be until I get it onto my laptop. Faces I'm not directly shooting are hard to make out. And I don't know who I'm looking for. Attuned to me as ever, Tanner peers over my shoulder. His solid body presses against mine, and I lean into him, absorbing his warmth. "There's two hours of footage here. I'm gonna speed it up, tell me if I need to stop."

He hums his agreement. I feel the low sound everywhere, but there are too many cops and guns in the room for my dick to respond, and I'm not sorry about that. I click the footage into a faster frame rate. Images flicker through the screen. It's too rapid for me to tell if I've done a good job tonight, so I focus on the people I don't know to see if anyone jumps out at me.

They don't, but I know the moment Tanner spots who we're searching for. His muscles tense like steel and a growl rumbles from his chest. "There he is."

I pause the footage on a shot that makes my heart thump. It's of Tanner, right before Molly hit the stage, and it captures my obsession with him so perfectly that it still takes me long slow seconds to spot the figure lurking at the end of the bar behind him —a gangly dude dressed head to toe in red.

Jesus. How did I miss him? I rewind the frames and hand the camera to Tanner so he can show the cops.

Molly looks too. "Wow. So it really was him, huh? I was hoping it was just kids."

"I don't let kids in my bar, Molls," Tanner says sharply. "If I'd been paying attention, he wouldn't have gotten in either."

Then what? He'd have waited for her outside instead? I don't like that thought any more than I do the reality of what's actually happened. Imagining Molly bloodied and hurt makes me want to puke. And kill someone.

Raging, I retreat to the kitchen. I can still hear every word exchanged in the living room, but I'm an expert at tuning the world out. I light the stove beneath Tanner's archaic kettle. It comes to the boil. I take it off and do nothing with it. Tanner comes up behind me. He says nothing, just kisses my neck, then he's gone again and I miss him.

Man, what a day. I'm battered by every emotion that's come my way since I dragged myself into Wildfoot HQ at arse o'clock this morning. Elation from the lynx footage. Angst from the past and for the future. Every fucking feeling that comes from being anywhere near Tanner. And now red-hot fury simmers in my veins too. I want to punch stuff. I want to lie down and sleep with Tanner stretched out beside me. I want to—

"Hey." Tanner is behind me again. "The cops want to take your memory card. Is that okay?"

I spin around. "What?"

"The memory card from your camera. They want to take it so they can upload the footage onto their computers at the station."

Giving up my memory card is like asking me for my kidney, and it must show on my face. Tanner speaks again before I can push it aside and acquiesce. "Never mind. Let me find my laptop. I must have a flash drive somewhere. We can make that work, right?"

Easier said than done. Tanner's laptop is older than mine and struggles to cope with the humongous video files from my camera. It takes an hour to transfer the information, and by then, the cops have already taken the call that Molly's ex has been picked up drink-driving his way out of Burlington.

Tanner's gaze is still mad as hell. "Dipshit got as far as Montpelier. Can you believe that?"

Molly cringes. "His other girlfriend lives there."

"His *what*?"

"Don't." She looks away. "I *know*, okay?"

Nothing about this is okay. And the sad reflection in her huge eyes breaks through the haze that's kept me silent up until now. I sit with her as Tanner accompanies the cops out of the building. "I'm sorry this happened to you. Toxic relationships are fucked up things."

"You don't think it's my fault for staying with him so long?"

"No. And no one else thinks that either. It's not like you married the dude and lived with him for half a decade after he hurt you the first time."

"Is that what happened to you?"

"I didn't marry a dude."

"Don't be cute. You're too British."

"It's the truth."

"Did you get divorced?"

It's my turn to cringe. "Nope. I ran away instead. Genius move. Don't be like me." I wrap a fraternal arm around her slender shoulders.

Molly sighs and leans against me. "I can think of worse things than being like you. Tanner gets all smiley when you're around. That's a freakin' superpower."

"Is it?"

"Yeah. He's happy when you're here."

I love Tanner's smile, but I don't see it anywhere near enough, so I can't claim Molly's theory as a win. Instead, I squeeze her tighter. "Are you going to stay here tonight?"

"Are you?"

"Very funny. Answer the question."

Molly shakes her head. "He said I could, but I'd rather go home. My friends are already there waiting for me. I'm going to get an Uber in a minute."

"Tanner won't drive you?"

"He's had three beers. He said he'd come with me, though."

There are two things wrong with that—first, it's a waste of money. Second, I'm not down with Tanner being away from me for however long it's going to take him to cab it back and forth from wherever the fuck Molly lives. "You don't need to get an Uber. I can drive Tanner's car."

As seems to be his skill today, Tanner returns to catch the end of the conversation. He nods and tosses me his keys. "Works for me."

He takes Molly downstairs to find the handful of belongings she brought with her to the bar. She's still wearing the hockey jersey. I give her my coat and we head out to the parking lot.

Tanner's car needs gas. I drive to the gas station, then follow his directions to Molly's place. I haven't driven in forever. Long enough that I've forgotten how much I like it, and because Tanner has a peep hole into my brain, after we've seen Molly safely into her dorm he points me the scenic route home. "It's only five minutes longer, but you can see more of the lake."

"It's dark," I point out. "And I've seen plenty of it already. I can see it from my bedroom window."

"Drive around in circles, then. Whatever you need, man."

It bothers me that he knows I need something unspecific when I don't have the first fucking clue what's going on in his head. Or that maybe I do and I don't trust myself. He doesn't hide his emotions—he just declines to explain them. I drive around in circles anyway, though, and he lets me, tipping his head back on the seat and watching the road through hooded eyes. Eventually, I feel bad enough for keeping him out so late that I head for home. But as we near the parking lot, my grip on the steering wheel tightens and my knuckles turn white. I can't explain it, but I'm fucking fuming.

"Hey." Tanner trails a light fingertip over my rigid hands. "You want to talk about it?"

"About what?"

"About whatever's got you ragin'."

"I'm not—" Fuck. What's the point? I'm good at keeping quiet, but I'm shit at hiding my feelings too. "I'm just worried about how this is gonna play out for Molly."

"She'll be okay tonight. They'll keep him locked up till they interview him in the morning."

"And then what? Even if they charge him, he can post bail and get out, right? So he can go after her again?"

"Not for a while. She won't be here. I'm going to book her a plane ticket when we get home so she can go back to her folks in Ohio."

"She didn't tell me that."

"She didn't know until I just texted her."

Somewhere behind the anger boiling out of me, I fall for him a little bit harder. He's so fucking *good*. It's so unfair that he doesn't seem to know it. "She can't stay in Ohio forever, unless she wants to give up her whole life to get away from him. And what if she doesn't? What if she doesn't even want to give *him* up and she goes back to him?"

"That won't happen—"

"You don't know that! He's a manipulative cunt. How else would she have been with him this long when she knew he was banging other people? He's got her thinking she's not worth any better. That everything she cares about is a waste of fucking time."

I'm shouting by the time I pull into the parking lot.

Tanner flinches. For the briefest moment, he misses a beat. Then he unbuckles his seatbelt and opens the door. "Come on. Let's get ice cream."

CHAPTER FIFTEEN

Tanner

Jax doesn't believe I can get him ice cream in the middle of the night, but I know the dude who lives above the ice cream store. He's a nocturnal stoner who's happy to slip me a double scoop of maple cookie dough at the back door.

I take it back to where I've left Jax on a bench outside V and V. He's pulled his hood up, hiding his face, but the tense set of his shoulders calls to me like a beacon. I pass him his dessert and drop my hands on him, manipulating his rigid muscles. "This was too close to home for you, huh?"

Jax sighs. "Not really. No one ever tried to hurt me like that."

"I don't mean the physical stuff." I mean the coercive control and manipulation Molly's lived through to get to this point. *Jax* has lived through that kind of abuse too. His anger seems to be draining away, but mine is just getting started. "You know we'll take care of her, don't you? Not just me, but my boss too. He's good people."

He must be for letting a clown like me run his bar, and the thought makes me smile, but Jax isn't smiling. Nowhere close. And he doesn't answer my vaguely rhetorical question. Either he doesn't believe we'll take care of Molly, or he absolutely does and this conversation is about something else.

I can't work it out. Jax is so often an open book I forget how impossible he is when he's not. And I'm tired too, mentally. This entire day has lasted a lifetime and my soul feels bruised. I need him to be okay. *I* need to be okay, so this night can just be over already.

It's hard to recall that I've spent most of it watching him zip around with his camera, forearms rippling as he moved the heavy gimbal up and down, shirt riding up to gift me a glimpse of the barest hint of his gorgeous skin. I was so enthralled by him that douchebag Brent slipped by me and put the entire bar in danger, Jax included. I need to sleep before my brain decides to dwell on that, preferably with him safe in my arms—if he wants to be.

Jax isn't eating his ice cream. His shoulders have softened under my attention, but he's still tense as hell.

I round the bench and crouch in front of him, my hands on his knees. He gazes at me from the shadows of his hood, his blue eyes dark pools that threaten emptiness. It's not a good look on Jax. I'm used to him being animated, even when he's quiet. I'm used to him laughing and grumbling and muttering under his breath. I'm used to his eyes shining when he's got something to say that he's not quite ready to share.

His ice cream is melting. I dig the bamboo spoon into it and scoop some up. Jax leans forward as I hold it out. "Nah," he says "You eat it."

Works for me. Our late lunch is a distant memory, and I'm a fool for ice cream. Like most good things in my life, there's no flavor I don't enjoy.

Jax watches me eat. His gaze gentles, then intensifies in a different way. He leans lower. I take a chance and slide the spoon into his mouth, parting his sinful lips and watching his tongue flicker out to catch the melting drips. "Wow, that's good," he says around a mouthful. "Almost as good as watching you eat it."

"Oh yeah?"

"Yeah."

The single syllable is laced with sudden heat.

At least, it's sudden to me. I spoon more ice cream, but Jax scoops it up with his finger and brings it to my waiting mouth. *Fuck yeah.* I got him the ice cream to calm him down, but as he slides his sweet finger into my mouth, I change my mind. I don't want him calm. I want him in my bed and *damn* if either one of us is gonna be sleeping anytime soon.

The ice cream hits my tongue. I swallow it down, not giving a single shit about brain freeze, and hold out my hand to him. "Come home with me."

My apartment is dark and still. I tug Jax inside and kick the door shut behind him.

He's vibrating. Or maybe it's me. His eyes are something else right now, but I trust him to tell me if he's not down for the inferno gathering pace between us.

We've kissed a hundred times. More. But as I shove him against my front door and crash my lips to his, it feels different this time. Hotter. Deeper. As if it means more.

I'm rough with him. He fights back, kissing me harder and spinning us, reversing our position and working his way along my jaw and down my neck. My jeans seem to undo themselves. Jax's wicked hands touch me everywhere.

He cups my ass and squeezes my length through my underwear. An inhuman groan escapes me and I set to work stripping his clothes too.

His hot skin waylays me. I roam every inch of it as if I've never touched him before. His strong chest and cut abs. His back. The scars that tread a path down to his thigh. I drag his T-shirt over his head so I can see him better, even in the murky night. Man, he's fucking ethereal. How is it possible that he's more beautiful than he was an hour ago?

I can't find an answer to that, so I stop trying. I toss his T-shirt Lord knows where and unbutton his jeans. Despite the fact that we've been naked together before, it feels like the last barrier. I ease them over his hips, taking his underwear along for the ride. He returns the favor, and it's time for a change of scenery.

He takes my hand and leads me to my bed. We tumble down, but in truth I've been falling since I met him. Lingering clothes disappear. His skin slides against mine like a dream. I'm so hard for him it fucking hurts.

I roll him onto his back and loom over him. "What do you want?"

He tilts his head. "What do you mean?"

I shrug and narrow the space between us, cupping a palm to his cheek. "I mean, how do you want to fuck? I can go either way."

His swallow is audible, and I know I've shocked him. The cogs turn in his brain, and I get the war he's waging *so fucking much*. I want it *all*, and it lights me on fire that he might too.

"I can go either way too," he says eventually. "But…I like to be fucked."

"You do, huh?"

The flush on his chest grows darker. "Yeah, I mean, it's been a minute, but I remember what I like."

"And that's to be fucked?"

"Yeah."

I don't need telling twice. Three times. What*ever*. We go back to kissing the hell out of each other. I'm in no hurry, but at the same time, I can't fucking wait. I want him. I *need* him.

And fortuitously, my nightstand is prepared enough that we don't have to dance that awkward dance to the bathroom. Every-thing we need is right here.

Condoms and lube appear like magic. Jax pulls me over him again and wraps his legs around me.

I hook my hand behind his neck and kiss him so hard I taste

blood, but he kisses me back harder, and the message is clear: *Bring it. I can handle it.*

But still. I draw back and push his damp hair out of his face. "Gonna ask this once so be sure of your answer. Do you need me to be gentle?"

Jax growls. "Don't you fucking dare."

Message received. I get on my knees and crawl between his spread legs, spellbound, as ever, by everything about him. He rolls a condom onto me, lubes me up, then watches as I start to ease inside him, holding his breath as he takes me in.

Despite the firepit in my blood, I go slow. But his eyes still water. "Bloody hell. You're a fucking beast."

I snicker. "You've seen your dick, right?"

"Fuck off."

I'm not going anywhere without him. I bury myself to the hilt and come to terms with the body-shaking pleasure of having him wrapped so tight around me. He is hot breaths and liquid heat. Teeth on my neck and blunt nails digging into my shoulders. I start to thrust, *slowly*, again, but he doesn't need my caution. He arches up and moves against me. Raw moans fall from his unhinged lips, and I'm so fucking gone. So lost in him I can't see a point where I'll ever be anything else.

Rhythm builds, deep and fast. Jax grips my ass again, urging me on, head flung back, throat exposed. Sweat slicks our skin. It's hard to look at him with my eyes in the back of my head, but god, I feel him in every millimeter of my red-hot veins.

I pull out and flip him over. Slide back in without the due care I took the first time.

Jax pushes back against me. His thighs hit mine. *Fuckyes.* But I'm scared too, of the most ridiculous thing. I've wanted this for so long, and in my dirtiest daydreams I've imagined tumbling Jax to this bed and fucking him all night, but the reality of being inside him is so consuming there's zero chance we'll get that far.

I don't want this to end.

But I can't stop. I move inside him again, finding the hypnotic rhythm that's already got me set to blow. Skin and friction. It's all we are. And I want more and more and more.

I drive deeper into him. He sinks to his forearms and a filthy curse spills out of him. My chest is fused to his back. I bury my face in his neck, hunching over him. His muscular body fits mine like a glove. A blood-pumping wave of pleasure rocks me and a hoarse groan bursts from my lungs. "I'm gonna come."

Jax flails a hand back and digs his fingers into my hips. "Me first."

I don't know if it's an order or a warning. Then he arches his back and his ragged cry consumes me in a heat so intense I don't recognize the sounds I make. I wrap my arm around him and fight hard, but I lose. Jax's head drops. He comes, and I press deeper into him and follow him off the edge.

For long moments after, there is no sound, save for my pulse banging against my eardrums. I'm fucking shell-shocked, or shell-shocked by fucking. Either way, I'm the best kind of mess I've been for a very long time. I withdraw, shaking, my nerves jumping with an energy that should've been sated.

Jax is wrecked. He rests his head on his forearm, breathing heavy, his strong back rippling with the effort to put himself back together. His skin has reddened patches all over where I've manhandled him, and I kind of feel bad for him.

Because this isn't over.

CHAPTER SIXTEEN

Jax

Tanner fucks me all night long. There isn't an inch of his mattress we don't cover, and by the time dawn breaks, I'm pretty sure the whole neighborhood has heard me come. And him, cos *fuck*, neither of us are quiet. And I love that. His easy passion lights me on fire, even now, hours after we first tumbled to his bed.

He rolls me onto my side and presses inside me again, his hands slipping on my sweat-sheened skin as he curves around me. His strong arms hold me tight as he fucks me hard enough to rattle my bones, but I'm so ready for it. Cos I love that too. I fist the sheets and punch his mattress. I've already shot my load too many times to count, but the orgasm barreling through me now is unreal.

Tanner's breathing grows ragged. He grasps the back of my neck with one hand and holds me down with the other. My hands fly back to grip his thighs, drawing him deeper. He hits every spot inside me, and I'm so fucking done. I come just as his dick starts to erupt in me.

He slips out of me and leaves the bed to get rid of the condom.

I hold out for the six seconds it takes him to come back, then we finally knock out.

At least, I do. It's daylight when I open my eyes again. Tanner's awake, of course. I wonder if he ever truly sleeps. He stares at me. I stare right back, and a stillness surrounds us that wasn't there before. As if the frantic nature of our attraction to each other was making everything cloudy.

Noisy.

My desire for him is far from sated, but I can breathe through it now, and I revel in the fact he hasn't spoken yet. That the spell is unbroken. Sometimes I'm so frustrated with his silence I could fucking shake him, but when he's like this I remember that none of it matters. That we have time. And I'm so blessed that a man so fucking sweet wants to be with me that I have no right to complain. About anything. Ever.

Tanner touches my face. "What are you thinking so hard about?"

"All kinds of nothing."

"Is that a lie?"

"No. It's the best I can do right now."

I say it with a smile and I get my reward in the form of his slow grin.

"Sounds fair," he says. "I'm gonna make some coffee. You want tea?"

I nod and he leaves me. I think about sitting up and hobbling to the bathroom, but his bed sucks me down deeper and I stay where I am. My head's in a good place, but my body is *sore*, a fact Tanner is quick to notice when he comes back with two mugs.

"Did I hurt you last night?"

"This morning, you mean. And no...not at the time anyway. I'm just tired, man."

It's the wrong thing to say to him, but for once he doesn't shutter and silently freak out. He finds his ancient laptop and puts a movie on. Then he plays with my hair while I doze in his lap. At some point, he gets up again and brings mugs of soup and grilled cheese sandwiches back to bed. I inhale them like a starving man.

He laughs and makes some more.

Until he goes to work, it's probably the best day I've ever had.

CHAPTER SEVENTEEN

Jax

Time blurs by in a haze of long cold days out on the trails, and hot sweaty nights in Tanner's bed. I'm not prepared for the intensity that comes with having sex with him. It's so consuming some nights I go home and sleep alone just to contemplate it.

He doesn't chase me. He lets me go and greets me whenever I come up for air as if we've been apart a few simple minutes. I love him for that.

I love him for a lot of reasons.

A couple of weeks after the violence at the bar, Thanksgiving creeps up on me. Eve's invited us both to spend it with her and some girlfriends, but before we can enjoy whatever feast she's prepared, we're going to fetch Molly's belongings from her ex's apartment.

He's not supposed to be there. He posted bail under the condition that he return to his parents' place somewhere I've never heard of and stay there until his next hearing. He's got friends in the apartment block he called home, though. Weed-soaked buddies who give me and Tanner hazy-eyed stares as we barge through the front door and rescue Molly's things.

"They want to fight us," Tanner says.

He sounds amused. I am too, until one of them emerges from the kitchen as we're leaving.

He sizes us up and picks me to square up to. I don't blame him. Tanner is…well, Tanner. But this idiot is a lifetime too late to land a punch on me.

He lunges.

I sidestep. "Fuck off, mate."

But he comes again, and I slam him into the wall. It's easy. *Too* easy. And he's on his arse before I stop to make sense of chinning someone in a cramped apartment doorway.

Brave dude spits blood. "Brent's gonna fuck you up when he finds you."

"Give a shit." I step over him and leave.

Tanner follows, chuckling. "You're a bruiser, huh?"

I snort and open the trunk of his car. "Nah. Just a pub brawler. You have to be where I come from to survive the townies every summer."

"That sounds familiar."

"Yeah, but Vermont is way more civilized than a British beach in high summer."

"For real? You don't all sip tea and play billiards?"

"No, we drink bad lager and fight about it."

Tanner makes the face I see most often when he's not sure if I'm taking the piss out of him. It's adorable, and I enjoy not confirming either way far too much.

We take Molly's stuff to her dorm. She's still in Ohio, but her Dutch roommate hasn't gone home for the holidays and lets us in. We put her stuff in her room and head back to the car.

Tanner tosses me his keys. "You drive."

"Why?"

"Because I want to ogle you while you mutter curse words at other drivers."

"I don't do that."

"You do."

Okay. Maybe I do. But it's worth it if it makes Tanner laugh. Most things are.

Eve's new place isn't far, but it's a long enough drive that I get to enjoy Tanner's quiet humor. It gets me pondering too. Thanksgiving doesn't mean much to me, but it's everything to all the Americans I've ever known, and I wonder what it is to him. So I ask and he thinks hard enough about his answer to stoke the curiosity I'm trying to contain.

"I guess it's nostalgia," he says eventually. "Cliché, but it's true. We weren't a family of four for long, and after my dad died, my mom worked every holiday in an all-night diner. But when I was a kid, I remember the turkey and the cranberry sauce from the can. My dad let me and Gabi drink beer too, the real stuff that made us giggle and fall over till my mom got mad."

"I can't imagine your brother giggling."

"Yeah, it's a reach these days, but it happened, I swear. What were the holidays like in your house?"

I park outside Eve's house and kill the engine. "We don't have Thanksgiving—it's all about Christmas, and we always went to my grandparents' place. Turkey, Christmas pudding, and my nan's decimated Brussel sprouts. Good times."

"Were they?"

"Yeah. It was the one day of the year we stayed in one place and stopped chasing ideals that don't exist."

"Do you miss them?"

"Who?"

"Your family."

"No. Well, maybe my sisters. They were pretty young when I left and I've missed everything important to them. I regret that. What about you and Gabriel? Eve says you're close, but you never talk about him."

"I just did."

I skewer him with a scowl that has him rolling his eyes. And I'm joking. Mostly. Almost. I think.

Tanner sighs. "We're as close as we can be with him gone so much. And I have regrets too."

"Like what?"

"Like not being stable enough to appreciate him last Thanksgiving when he was here."

"Stable? Were you sick?"

"Something like that."

It's the most I've ever drawn from him. If we were alone in his bed or mine, I might've pushed for more, but Eve's appearance outside the car gives me a reason to stop. I find his hand and squeeze. "Don't know about you, mate, but I'm fucking starving."

Tanner laughs and it meets his dark eyes. "Me too, but Jax?"

"Yeah?"

"I'm not your mate."

Tanner

Eve's place is a communal cave of boho rugs and incense. She cooks a huge turkey for me, Jax, and four of her yoga friends who haven't made it home for the holidays. Three chicks and one dude whose gaze flickers to Jax often enough for me to want to throat-punch him.

Jax doesn't notice.

Eve does. She drags me into the kitchen to help her lift the ostrich-sized bird out of the oven. "Stop giving Rumi that nasty glare."

"The fuck are you talking about?"

"Your stink-eye. Stop it. For starters, it's making me miss Gabriel too much, and second, it's not fair. Can you blame anyone for looking at Jax when he's as chill as he is right now?"

"Chill?"

"Yeah. Chill. It's almost like he got laid."

"How do you know what that looks like?"

"Not the same reason as you, I'd imagine." Eve tilts her head sideways, daring me to challenge her. I don't. But as her gleeful laughter rings out, I wish I had. If Jax hasn't told her he's sharing my bed, I'm not going to take that away from him.

"If I promise to stop scowling at your friend, will you shut the fuck up?" Eve quiets as though I've put tape over her mouth. Her eyes light up with real joy, but I shake my head at her. "Don't. Not yet."

I carve the turkey for her, and she carries it to the dining table. There's a million other dishes to go with it—mashed potatoes, green beans with almonds, sweet potatoes with brown sugar and cinnamon. Stuffing with Vermont apples and sage.

Grinning, I set the sweet potatoes near Jax. "Good guess," he says with a wry grin. "Fight you for them?"

"If you like."

His hot gaze has told me a dozen times what he likes, and I could easily forget every dish on the table in favor of another hour in bed with him, but he needs this, even if he doesn't know it. Maybe we both do.

We overeat and drink too much cider. Eve's friends are nice, Rumi included. We do the dishes together while everyone else falls asleep in front of a Lifetime movie. Jax is on the couch with his head on Eve's thigh. She's fiddling with his hair, and I'm jealous, but only because I love his hair.

"Are you two together?"

"Hmm?" I spin around, dish towel in hand.

Rumi is watching me gawk at Jax with a knowing grin. "You and Jax," he clarifies as if I need him to. "You seem super close."

I don't know how he's figured that when we've been in a room full of people all day, and we haven't touched. But I'm too stuffed with good food and softened by booze to deny anything. I shrug. "We're friends," I say, because it's the truth. Even without the fuck-hot sex, I feel closer to Jax than I ever dared dream. He doesn't know all of me, and I don't know all of him. But fuck, we're getting there.

Rumi lets it go and returns his attention to the sink. I study him to keep my mind off Jax. He's slim with shaggy hair. He looks like Klaus from *Umbrella Academy*, and in another world I might've thought about banging him, but this world was built for me and Jax. I just need to fix the shit that makes his eyes go tight when I don't give him enough words.

The realization threatens the lazy buzz in my veins. But Jax is my Patronus. He drifts into the kitchen and winds his arms around me, lips to my neck, not giving a single fuck who sees us. "Shh."

"I didn't say anything."

"You don't have to."

"What...ever?"

"Don't push it, Reid." He takes more cider from the refrigerator and disappears again.

Rumi snorts as he lets the water out of the sink. "I want to paint you two."

"Excuse me?"

"I'm a painter," he says in case it isn't obvious. "With my hands, not brushes, and you two are a fucking wet dream for me —artistically, not literally."

"Erm...thanks? I think?"

He laughs again. "You're welcome. Come find me when you've figured out your qi."

"What?"

"Trust me, you'll know."

I don't know much except I'm done with drying dishes and being away from Jax. Rumi knows Eve's kitchen better than me. He volunteers to put the last few dishes away, and I leave him to it. I follow the sound of gentle guitar-strumming through the living room and to the den where Eve and Jax have escaped to. Jax has an old guitar in his hands, and he's playing a quiet song I feel I should know, but I don't.

Eve is singing along and smiling at him. The way he grins back is so open that for a moment, I feel like an intruder. But his expression doesn't change when he sees me, save for the flicker of heat, and I soak in his lazy posture and cider-hazed eyes as I claim a seat at Eve's feet, facing her with my back to an old chair. "What are you playing?"

"'Live Forever'," he says. "You won't know it unless you're up to date on British rock from the nineties."

"How are *you* up to date on it? You weren't born till '94."

"Hey, this shit is modern to Jax," Eve says. "He has an old soul."

Jax flips her off as he shifts to a different tune, but it makes sense to me. My mom told me that no one ever walked this world just once. That who we are comes from the heartscape of every life we've lived before. I feel as if I've known Jax longer than the time I've been alive. Or maybe I'm just drunk and delirious on pumpkin pie.

Or high on the warmth in my chest every time I look at him. It occurs to me that the only way I'd feel more myself right now would be if my brother was sitting at Eve's feet, and she was rubbing his shoulders instead of mine. And I was on the arm of the couch beside Jax, dozing to him strumming 'Son of a Gun' and pretending I'm not on the cusp of falling ridiculously in love with him.

Eve leans down and whispers in my ear. "You guys want to stay here tonight? It's getting pretty wet out there and you've had way too much cider to drive."

I cast a bleary glance at the window. The old glass is rattling from the force of a downpour outside. Heavy winds lash the trees. Even with Jax for company, I don't relish the long, drunken walk home. Then it dawns on me that I've made a heavy assumption that he even wants to spend the night with me. He doesn't always. Some nights, something—perhaps everything—about him and me is too much for him, and I'm okay with that. How can I not be when most days I'm too much for myself?

Eve nudges me. I've taken too long to answer her question. Jax is still strumming the guitar, but he's staring at me as if whatever I say is important.

I got nothing.

He shrugs. "We'll stay. I spend enough time getting wet as it is."

It shouldn't excite me that he's made the decision for himself *and* for me.

But it does.

CHAPTER EIGHTEEN

Jax

The spare bedroom in Eve's communal house is downstairs, away from everyone else, and I can't say I'm sorry about it. Her friends are nice enough, and I love her more than life, but I want Tanner to myself.

More than that, I can tell he's done peopling for the day. He needs the peaceful quiet of the dark room that contains nothing but a king-size bed and a dozen houseplants. There isn't even a lamp, and I'm way too drunk and full and *Tanner* to deal with overhead lights.

Tanner drifts to the bed as I kick the door shut behind us. He sits on the edge and looks thoughtfully at his thick wool socks. Vermont socks. I didn't see the point of them until he rolled a pair onto my feet a few weeks ago. Now I can't live without them and the prospect of my heart imitating my sock obsession is ridiculous.

A slow chuckle escapes me.

Tanner raises his gaze. Our eyes lock. There is nothing else.

Nothing but him and his obvious amusement at whatever my face is doing.

I kick his foot. "What?"

"Nothing. You're just funny."

"Funny-looking, or bona fide hilarious?"

"The second one. There's nothing funny about how you look."

"No?"

"No." Tanner reaches out to grab me, but it's unnecessary. I'm already right there, straddling his waist.

I let the darkness of the unfamiliar room surround us and take a breath. Tanner doesn't blink and it feels like he's on the precipice of disappearing into the shadows or letting me lead him away from them. I kiss him hard. *Choose me.* He kisses me back with just as much force, then he slows it right down to a languid pace that's fiercely possessive. We're pretty much the same size, but his hands feel bigger than mine as they roam my back, his arms stronger. His dark beard rubs my scruffy jaw and every tiny sensation is a bond around my soul cut free. We grind together as if we have the rest of our lives to do this, right here. I'm so fucking hard it's making my stomach ache, but it's the kind of pain that makes my blood pump faster and my head spin, and I can't get enough.

Clothes disappear. Tanner's body is perfection even though I can't really see it, cos it's not about how he looks. Everything between us is the way he makes me feel. How his dark eyes blaze at me. The trembling in every limb, his and mine, as he lays me down on someone else's bed.

He covers me with his body, still kissing me as if he'll never stop, and I don't want him to stop. I want to sink into this moment and stay here forever.

I want to tell him I love him.

I reach for his cock instead and squeeze hard enough for him to break away with a rough groan.

He tips his head back. "I want to fuck you so bad."

"Don't let me stop you." I sink my teeth into his neck. "I'm never gonna say no to that."

Tanner groans again. "Slight problem with that...I think I have the world's oldest packet of lube in my wallet, but no condoms."

"We don't need them."

"What?" Tanner raises his head, instantly alert and sober. "What do you mean?"

"I mean I haven't slept with anyone since my wife, and that was four fucking years ago."

He blinks. "Wow. That's a long time."

"Yeah, well. Shark food didn't do it for her."

Tanner's fingertips instinctively skim my scars. Too many emotions to decipher flicker through his gaze. "She was a fucking fool."

"I don't want to talk about her. I'm just saying I'm good if you are."

He sucks in a long, slow breath. "It's been a while since I got tested, but I haven't slept with anyone since. I mean, I've done *stuff*, but not—" He waves his hand to finish the sentence.

I get the picture. "So…we're good?"

He licks his kiss-swollen lips. "I think so."

We go back to the slow grind of kissing each other dizzy until he remembers the lube in his wallet. He drops it somewhere on the bed, and then kisses me again. He's in no hurry, and I can dig it.

I roll us over so I'm above him again. Rain batters the windows, and lightning slashes the stormy night sky. The spooky darkness is almost Cornish. I gaze down at Tanner, at his inked chest as it rises and falls fast enough to let me know he's as sweetly tormented by this as I am. His cock is hard beneath me. I want to ride him, but…not yet. I want to do something else first.

His dick is in my mouth before the thought completes. I scoot down his body and swallow him whole, sucking him down my throat.

"Fuck!" Tanner arches from the bed, and his hands fly to my head, fingers sinking into my hair. He stops himself from ramming into my mouth, but I don't need him to. I'm ready for this. I'm ready for *him*.

I work him as slowly as he kissed me. The build of pleasure is another puzzle piece, and I soak up his low moans and full-body shudders. I need him inside me, but I hold off as long as I can.

Long enough that he can't take it.

He drags me off him and up the bed. "Ride me, or I'm gonna blow down your throat and roll you over for a second round."

I laugh, but it's cut off by his fingers slipping inside me, slicked with the lube he's claimed while I've been having my fun with his cock. Like a laser, he finds every spot I need him to. My body pulses around him and my composure abandons me as if it never existed.

Shaking, I fall forwards and rock on his hand. He kisses me, and I melt into him as he lays a careful fire in me, stick by fucking stick. I'm sunbaked tinder to a spark. For a brief moment, I thought I had him...thought I had hope of controlling this, but I don't. He's too fucking good at this.

Tanner plays me until I'm out of my mind. We scramble for the next step. He holds me tight as I sink down on him, and bends his legs to hold me up.

Every inch of him fills me. He's everywhere and it's different to the *many* other times we've fucked. He's gazing at me as if it's the first time, and I can't get enough of that. I can't get enough of every facet of him.

He flexes his powerful body, moving inside me, urging me on. I take the hint and ride him as slowly as the fire in my gut will let me. Pressure becomes pure pleasure. He meets me in the middle and we move together, lips fused, swallowing the desperate sounds that come from heat like this.

Sensation coalesces, gaining power. It's a gale that becomes a hurricane, and I couldn't stop it if I tried.

I don't try. I hitch a ride on the storm and press down harder, taking Tanner as deep he can go. He grips my hips and drives up into me. My dick is trapped between his abdomen and mine. I can't reach it, but I don't need to. He's gonna make me come without ever touching my cock.

"Jax."

I know. I slam my hand over his mouth as if I can keep his hoarse moans inside any more than I can my own. But it's a wild river running down a mountain. I come with a strangled shout, and Tanner comes too. Wet heat pulses everywhere. I can't stop moving until he stills me within the cage of his strong arms. He holds me so tight I can't breathe, but I don't need air. For this long, mind-fucking moment, I just need him.

Maybe I pass out. I'm not sure, but sometime later, the world solidifies enough for me to notice his embrace has loosened, and he's watching the rain batter the windows.

I raise my body from him, ignoring the sticky mess between us. "You're still here, aren't you?"

"Hmm?" His gaze is lazy, not distant, and I feel like an idiot.

But it's fleeting. Tanner makes me feel so many things, but never stupid. He helps me clamber off him and lie down, then he disappears and comes back with something warm and wet to clean us both up.

That done, he throws the bedsheets we've kicked to the floor back on the bed and stretches out beside me.

It's a cold night. I drop my head on his chest and he grips my knee to hook my leg over him. He cards the fingers of one hand through my hair, and splays his warm palm over the scars on my hip with the other. It's as close to perfect as I've ever known. I could sleep. But I don't, and neither does he. He takes slow, measured breaths. The silence is a cocoon I know he enjoys, so he surprises me when he speaks.

"What did Jerry tell you about what happened when I worked for him?"

I sit up, propping my head on my folded arm. "He told me a man died on an overnight camping trip and it wasn't your fault."

"What else?"

It's on the tip of my tongue to tell him that was it, but it's a lie. He deserves the truth. "He said it fucked you up, and he felt really guilty about it."

Tanner studies something beyond my shoulder before he looks

back at me with clearer eyes than I'm prepared for. "He has nothing to feel guilty for. I was fucked up before that."

"He said that too, kind of."

"Did he tell you what I did to Gabi?"

"What? No. He didn't say anything about Gabriel except that you both knew the trails better than him."

"Oh. I thought he told you everything. At least, I think I did. I blocked it out."

"Why?"

He shrugs. "I run out of bandwidth sometimes."

"Can relate."

"I know." Tanner shifts onto his side so we're nose to nose. We tumbled into bed drunk on cider and each other, but we're sober now. Life has caught up with us. "I'm a terrible brother."

"No, you're not. Eve told me you and Gabriel are as close as twins."

"That's why I'm a terrible brother. I didn't care that I'd hurt him."

"Hurt him? How?"

"After what happened last year, I got really sick." He taps his temple. "Up here. Or maybe I was sick before then. I don't know anymore. Whatever. I made a plan to kill myself, then I got blackout drunk and told Gabi all about it—told him I didn't care that I was his only family because he was a shitty brother anyway and I was tired of having to worry about him."

"Did you mean it?"

"Which part?"

"That he's a shitty brother." I don't need him to tell me he was serious about the first part. I know it in every fiber I have.

"Of course I didn't mean it. But I was so fucking sick, I just wanted him to leave me alone."

"I'm guessing he didn't, as you're still here."

Tanner lets a humorless chuckle fall from his lips. "He threw me in a mental health facility, and I stayed there until I could function well enough to come home."

"Where was home? It wasn't here, right? Your apartment came with the job, didn't it?"

"No, actually. I scored it before Harrison gave me a shot at the bar. Before that, me and Gabi had a cabin out on Black Claw, but we haven't been there since I told him I was gonna wait for him to pass out so I could put his gun in my mouth."

I search the mental maps I have in my head. There's a few abandoned cabins on Black Claw. Only one looks like it's been lived in any time in the last century. It has big windows and a cozy wooden porch that taunts me when I catch sight of it from the farthest lookout point. "Is it the one with the baby maple tree growing out of the old boot?"

"Yeah."

"And you haven't been back there at all?"

"Nope."

"Well, your tree is still alive, in case you were worried." *And so are you.*

Tanner smiles a little. "I'd forgotten about the tree. It's not mine. Eve planted it when Gabi kept forgetting to bring his boots inside."

"She's never mentioned the cabin. I thought your brother was absent enough that he just stayed with you when he's not with her."

"He never stays with me. I can't deal with him analyzing me all the time."

I process that, trying to match it with my sibling relationships, but there's no common ground. I'm the mysterious older brother who fucked off to America and never came back. "Can I ask you something?"

"If you like."

"What happened before you came back to work for Jerry? Did something happen in Alaska?"

Tanner breathes in and out, and it seems to take forever. "Nothing happened."

For the first time since we met, I don't believe him, and it must show on my face as he shakes his head. "I mean nothing specific," he clarifies. "Turns out I'm just not wired right for digging dead bodies out of avalanches week-in, week-out. It got to me before I could catch it, then a couple guys I worked with died in a winching accident, and I knew I'd had enough."

"So you came home?"

"Yeah, but I didn't do anything else...as in, I didn't fix anything. I'd had this burning need to come home that I'd never felt before...like, if I could just get here, everything would magically be okay. And I was naive enough to believe it. I got another job on another mountain, and, well, you know how that panned out."

I do, and though the knowledge has gouged a hole in my heart I can't see ever healing, a weight has shifted from my brain. Everything about him now makes sense—the nightmares, the irrational fear of me dying in my sleep, and his reluctance to set foot in the wilderness he once called home. "Did you have therapy?"

"For a while. They figured I was probably having some kind of depressive breakdown before I even went to Alaska. I kept asking them what triggered it, as though if they told me that it would all make sense. Took me a long time to realize the details weren't that important. Maybe I just wasn't built for that life."

"I don't think anyone's built for what you've lived through, mate."

"But I didn't live. That's the point. You know the old dude who died on the Gentle Deer trail? His wife climbed Kilimanjaro this summer. She didn't give up on the whole world like I did."

"You're not the same person. She didn't live your life up until that point."

Tanner makes a frustrated sound. "I know what you're saying. And some days I believe it, but I'm a wreck, Jax. You know that, right?"

He's not. But it's not me he needs to hear it from, it's himself. I touch his cheek, trailing a finger over the high bone, lost in his long, dark lashes. "I'm sorry."

"For what?"

"That it happened to you. All of it."

Tanner sighs. He's done talking, I can tell. He's breached his limits just to have this conversation, and I don't know why. As in, why *now*? And I'm not sure it matters. I lean in to kiss him.

He stops me. "Jax, I can't go out there with you. You know that, don't you? It's fucking stupid, and I know it, but every time I even think about it, I just—"

"Shh." I quiet him with a soft hand over his lips, so different to the palm I slapped across his face when we were fucking. "I know, I know. I shouldn't have asked you. Jerry told me not to, but I didn't know how deep this was for you. Or maybe I did, and I thought I could fix it. I'm so fucking sorry."

Tanner closes his eyes. When he opens them again, the despair in them rips me in two. He takes my hand from his mouth and kisses my knuckles. "You can't fix this. I've done all the healing I've got in me."

"But—"

He shakes his head, and it's his turn to silence me with gentle hands. "I know how to keep myself sane. You just gotta let me do it."

CHAPTER NINETEEN

Tanner

A nightmare kicks me out of bed. It's not the worst I've ever had, but it's enough to have me pacing my apartment as sweat cools on my skin and wishing I'd given into the soul-deep craving in my bones and followed Jax home after work. It's official: I don't like being alone anymore, and maybe I never did. But it's not a good enough reason to wake him up at two a.m., so I stayed home, and now here I am, playing chicken with old ghosts.

My heart pounds against my ribcage. I make the tea Jax says tastes like a muddy puddle and will it to stop. It doesn't, so I take a shower and switch the water temperature between hot and cold until I don't know which way is up.

Shivering, I pad from the bathroom and find my cooling tea. Heating it up again gives me something to do. I won't drink it, though. I know this as I take it to the couch and set it on the coffee table, but I do it anyway. Rituals, yo.

I flick the TV on. NHL highlights fill the screen. I think of Jax, but it reminds me of sleepwalking him to my bed, so I try and think of Rainn and his unreasonable hate of all things hockey instead. I fail, though, naturally. Sleepwalking isn't my best hook-up line, but I can't regret it. Sharing my bed with Jax is the best thing I've ever done. Purging my soul to him half-lit on Shipley cider? Yeah, I'm not so sure about that, but it's too late. I can't take it back.

Man, I miss him. I haven't seen him much since Thanksgiving. Actually, that's not true. I've seen him most days, but our time together has been limited by his campouts on the trails and the crazy hours I'm pulling at the bar. I haven't seen him awake since the weekend. I wish we lived together.

And I wish I had the balls to tell him so. I definitely don't want to think about the fact that his contract at Wildfoot is finite. That there's every chance he'll move on when it runs out. But it's ass o'clock in the morning, and I have zero control over my anxious brain, so I think about it every second till I pass out on the couch.

Buzzing wakes me in the morning. I lunge for my phone, thinking it's Jax. But it's not. It's a message from Kai Fletcher, of all fucking people. Why the hell do I still have his number in my phone?

Kai: *Sorry for getting up in your grill before the holidays. Meant it tho. Job here for you if you want it. We can take it slow, ease you back in. Or maybe you can help me train new guys? Whatever man. Call me.*

I delete the message on impulse, my stomach in my throat. Then second thoughts hit me like a train, and I don't know what the fuck is going on in my head. I don't want to work mountain rescue in Vermont. I never did, or I wouldn't have gone to Alaska in the fucking first place.

But why did you go to Alaska?

It's not a question Jax has ever asked, but I hear it in his voice all the same. And for once I know the answer. I went to Alaska because my arrogant self had decided Vermont was boring. That the terrain wasn't dangerous and exciting enough to draw me out of the storm already brewing in my depressed brain. *Wow*, I was an idiot back then. I'm still an idiot now. I've learned to love my job at V and V, but the sense of wasting time creeps up on me some days until I remind myself the wilderness holds no place for me.

Not even with Jax out there with me.

I spend my morning working out and making my best attempt at grocery shopping. Jax talks in his sleep. The last whole night we spent together he told me all about some cookies he used to eat as a kid—something to do with wheels, wagons, and jam. That boy and his jam. I find something fitting the description in the global foods section at the grocery, and buy him some actual jam too, because he's run out and we're domesticated as fuck right now.

Then I go home and dump it all in my apartment before I head down to work.

I have a busy day. Payroll and staff schedules keep me occupied right up until the bar opens for happy hour. I'm not in the mood for people, or faking a sunny disposition. I dodge the bar and roam around, restless, checking my phone every ten minutes to see when Jax is coming home, and where he's planning on laying his head for the night. I rarely ask him to stay with me, I let him choose, but tonight I just need him close. I don't know why, I just do.

So tell him.

No. Because that would mean missing out on hours of yearning for something he'd willingly give me if I'd just fucking ask, and where's the "fun" in that?

Happy hour has passed by the time my phone buzzes in my pocket. I'm on the bar, covering staff breaks, and I don't get a moment to reach for it. Resentment seeps out of me, and I struggle to keep up the facade of caring what the whole damn world wants to drink. My bland smiles start to hurt.

Rainn gives me a look. He's better at this than I am. Dude can charm the birds from the trees when he wants to, and I gladly let him take my place.

Away from the bar, the tension in my chest fades. I finally find my phone and read the three messages Jax has sent me in the last hour.

Jax: *Back at HQ. Might be a while*
Jax: *Leaving now*

Jax: *You're busy. I'll be next door for a bit*

Next door. It takes a minute to compute that he means the Veritas side of V and V, the bookstore I rarely have cause to visit. I give Rainn the signal that I'm stepping out, then I follow the pull in my chest out of the bar and into the cozy space where it all began for V and V. Even without spotting Jax at one of the tables by the window, I get hit with an instant wave of calm. I'm not a book person, but this place has good vibes, man.

Then I do spot him and I feel like I've swallowed a fucking benzo.

I weave my way through the shelves and tables to where Jax is folded into an armchair, ear buds jammed into his ears as he glowers at his laptop on the thick wooden desk in front of him. The scene is all kinds of cute. I wonder if he's watching the lynx footage for the thousandth time. I take a peek over his shoulder and see a freeze frame of my own face. Awesome. That'll teach me.

Jax hasn't noticed me. I lay a careful hand on his shoulder and slide it up to cup his neck, my fingers tangling naturally into his hair. He closes his eyes and leans back. "That'd better be you, or I'm about to deck someone."

"It's me." I bend down and kiss his cheek. Someone nearby lets out a low whistle, but I don't follow the sound. I get it: Jax is hot. I'd whistle too if I was a complete fucking douche hound. "Whatcha working on?"

"The open-mic-night footage. The cops said I can use it now if I cut Brent Dicksplash out of it."

Truth be told, the mic-night footage has slipped my mind. Or at least, the reason Jax was shooting it in the first place. I haven't even paid him yet. I peer at the screen again. At my face, twisted in my natural scowl. "You must have better shit than that to work with."

Jax grins. "I have plenty of frames with your face in. Can't think why."

Neither can I. I tap the screen. "What else have you got? Or am I not allowed to see it till it's done?"

"It is done. I just need to grade it so the footage from both cameras fits together."

"Show me?"

Jax taps a few keys, and thankfully the close-up of my face disappears. I'm replaced by Molly. Two frames split the screen, one with her Stetson-topped auburn curls dulled by the moody shadows of the bar, the other with them cast in warm glow that makes her wide smile shine bright.

I lean closer. Jax smells of the earth. "These are from different cameras?"

"Yup. I haven't graded the static footage yet. See the difference?" He clicks through a few more frames and sticks one of his earbuds into my ear. Molly's live performance filters out and mingles with the footage Jax has captured. It flows like goddamn honey and even my mean mug in the background doesn't ruin it.

I do whistle this time. "Wow. That's incredible. I don't remember that night being like this. My bar is kicking, huh?"

"Of course it is. Where do you think you work?"

I shake my head slowly. "Not there. I must see the world in fucking grayscale half the time."

"No one sees *you* like that."

"How do you know how people see me?"

"Because I listen." Jax flashes me another grin. "That's how I know your boss wants to up the mic nights to every second Sunday, starting this weekend, and that you're definitely gonna have to work because Rainn is off."

I blink. "Damn. You're good."

"Everyone needs a skill, mate."

I cast a pointed glance at the easy charm he's created from the chaotic shitshow the last open-mic night turned out to be. I think about every ounce of magic he's collected from Mother Nature in places most people see nothing but mud, trees, and a long walk home. If he thinks listening is his only skill, maybe he is as fucked up as me after all. "Harrison's gonna wet himself when he sees this. You might have yourself a regular gig."

Jax snorts. "I wouldn't say no to getting paid to hang around wherever you are, but I can't do it this weekend. I'm taking a group of environmentalists up to Lynx Point for an overnight. I won't be back until Monday."

"Lynx Point. That's the official name now?"

"Sure is. Jerry's restricting access, though. You'll need a permit to go up that far."

"He's coming on the overnight with you, right?"

"Actually, no. He's gone away for a few days. Won't be back until Monday night, but I don't need him to babysit me. I've been up those trails a thousand times by now."

I know that. And I know Jax has his shit together. But I can't help the lick of fear that spreads through me. Swallowing, I try hard to contain it. Fail, and straighten up instead so Jax can't take one look at me and know exactly where my brain has gone.

"You know it's been pretty wet these last few weeks. You gotta watch out for rockfall."

"You told me that yesterday," Jax says softly. "And you told me what to do if it happens. I listen, remember? I'll be safe, I promise."

"I need to get back to work."

"Okay." Jax shuts his laptop. "You mind if I steal your couch for a while? I don't feel like hoofing it home just yet."

"You know you don't have to hoof it home at all. You could just, I don't know, stay?"

Jax stands. His hands fall on my hips and he tugs me close enough that his lips are an inch from mine. "You want me to?"

I always want him to stay. More than that, I want *him* to want it too. I settle for a shrug. "Yeah. But don't wait up if you're tired. I'll get you in the morning."

"Counting on it." Jax kisses my jaw, and we part ways on a promise.

CHAPTER TWENTY

Jax

The rest of the week passes so fast I can't distinguish one day from the next. I spend my time helping the Wildfoot marketing team weave the material we've gathered into something coherent, and every other minute with Tanner. I've stopped worrying about the gut-deep cravings I have for him when we're not together. It's hard to be afraid when being with him makes me feel so damn good.

Thanksgiving plays on my mind, though, and I regret the shedload of cider I put away after dinner. I remember every second of rolling around in an unfamiliar bed with Tanner, but the desperate conversation we had afterwards, not so much. Or maybe I do remember it, and I wish I didn't. All this time I've been obsessed with puzzle pieces, but now I have enough to hold in my hand, the sum of them is a picture I'm not ready for.

The Wagon Wheel biscuits Tanner's bought me help. I eat them all and fold the wrappers into tiny triangles that I leave in a neat pile by the coffee machine. The sight of them makes him laugh every morning, and I cling tightly to the deep rumbling sound every time I wake up to it.

Sunday morning dawns. I'm not ready for that either, but

Tanner is ready for me. He's been awake long enough to brew tea and make coffee, and he's come back to bed…naked.

We fuck. Shower together. Then I offer Tanner my limited kitchen skills and scramble eggs for breakfast while he toasts the bread. Somehow he knows I'll burn it. We eat standing up, leaning against the counter. Then I kiss him, and it's time to go.

Tanner takes a breath. I know he's about to tell me to be careful and safe and all the other things he worries about. But he stops himself. "Have fun," he says instead. "Let me know when you're back?"

"I'll send smoke signals from my bedroom."

"I'll come running."

"I hope so. It's about time you fucked me in *my* bed."

He smirks. "That right?"

I shrug, because it's whatever. He can fuck me anywhere he likes. Regardless, I have to *go.*

One more kiss, then I leave him standing in his kitchen, and head out, hiking out to HQ to claim the Wildfoot truck.

HQ is bustling when I arrive. The brace of excited environmentalists are waiting for me, loaded down with rucksacks far too heavy for the hike we're going to make when we reach the bottom of the trails.

It takes me half the morning to negotiate their loads down to a reasonable weight. By then, we're running short on time. I drive out to Black Claw and leave the truck in the spot I think of as Jerry's. The day is closing in on us. We have limited time to hike to our campsite, but I still linger a moment where the cell service works and send Tanner a final text.

Jax: *Heading out. Wish you were here. Gonna tell you I love you when I get back.*

I hit sent before my brain can reel my heart in. The message barrels free into the ether, and as hard as I try, I regret nothing.

Tanner

Jax loves me. It shouldn't surprise me, but it does. I read his message a thousand times, searching for a reality check. The punchline that lets me know I've misunderstood. But it's not there. Jax doesn't bullshit. He loves me, and he's gonna tell me to my face the next time I see him.

Deep breaths rattle my lungs. I pocket my phone. Get it out again and reread the message. I haven't replied. Yet. But only because I don't want the first time I return the sentiment times a million to be on fucking WhatsApp. Also, he won't see it. Black Claw has zero cell service on a good day, especially where he's headed.

Without Jerry.

Worry gnaws my heart. I dampen it with a shot of Vermont cider-brandy. Molly, back from Ohio, watches me, her eyes even rounder than usual.

"Don't start," I warn her. "It's gonna be a long couple days."

"Not even that long," she retorts. "He'll be back tomorrow."

"Who will?"

"Jax, dummy. Don't pretend you're freaking out over tonight. You don't get shook by busy shifts and chaotic karaoke."

"It's not karaoke. It's open-mic night, and you're the star. How do you feel about that?"

"Nice deflection." Molly slumps onto a barstool. "I'll let you have it, though. I've got all night to needle you."

"Gee, thanks."

"You're welcome. And to answer your question, I feel pretty damn good. Brent is miles away, and no one saw me screaming like a banshee last time because Jax pulled me off stage so fast. He's such a doll."

I beg to differ. I've seen Jax naked and doing things that dolls don't do, but I keep that shit to myself. "I'm glad you're not nervous. I'd be pissed as hell if that asshat had fucked your confidence."

"He hasn't. I mean, I'm gonna be terrified of dating for the rest

173

of my life, but I've been making a show of myself on stage since I was a little girl. No one can take that away from me."

"You shouldn't be scared of dating either. Most guys aren't Brent."

"Yeah, but some of them are. How do I tell the difference?"

"You date them for the right reasons, and get the fuck out as soon as they show you their ass."

Molly sighs. "It sounds like common sense when *you* say it. I like Jax better."

"Me too, kiddo. Me too."

I retreat to my office and check the YouTube link I uploaded to Facebook this morning, as per Jax's instructions, is doing its job. As predicted, my boss was beside himself after seeing Jax's work and wants him back for every event V and V ever hosts from here on out. I'm not gonna complain about that, and given the hefty tip Harrison has added to Jax's paycheck, I'd imagine he won't either.

The link is working perfectly. The views are rising by the hour, and the buzz about the repeat event tonight is enough that I'm fairly sure I'm in for the shift from hell, even if we get through it without disgruntled ex-boyfriends throwing bottles around.

It's my cue to go back downstairs. I shove Jax's check into an envelope and take it to my apartment for safekeeping for no reason whatsoever, as no one is going to take it from my office. But wasting time feels necessary, as if simple tasks need to take three times as long as they should to stop me obsessing over the fact that despite weather reports that forecast the opposite, it's raining and raining and raining outside, and I'm worried about all kinds of ridiculous things.

They're not ridiculous things. If they were, Jax wouldn't have known all about them without your bellyaching. But still. Worrying about Jax doesn't make him safer, or make me any less of a basket case for him to come back to, so I give chilling the fuck out a good college try and go back to work.

Open-mic night runs like a dream. It's the busiest Sunday night we've ever banked, and even without Rainn, my crew is a well-oiled machine. Molly smashes her performance too, and the crowds that have come from all over the state to see her hoot their appreciation.

Harrison claps me on the back as she floats off stage. "This is perfection, Tanner. It's everything I wanted this place to be. *Thank you.*"

He's gone before I can appreciate the irony of *him* thanking *me* for just about anything. But his praise makes my chest warm. This night really was perfection. The only thing missing is Jax.

I shut my bar down, buy my team drinks, and see them all safely home before driving Molly back to her dorm.

The weather is still wet as hell. I think about Jax in a tent with two strangers and tighten my grip on the steering wheel. She gives me an odd look as she exits my car, and I don't blame her. I am odd, and I need to try harder to fix it.

My brain is percolating as I drive away. My phone chirps in my pocket, and I force myself to ignore it. It won't be Jax, and there's no one else I want to talk to.

But the noise is insistent. I pull over with a heavy sigh and answer the phone without checking the screen. "What?"

A deep chuckle rumbles back at me. "A nine-hour delay, followed by eight hours on two planes, and *that's* how you're answering the phone to me?"

"Shit. Gabi?"

"It's me, bro. Who were you expecting to call from my phone? Pablo Escobar?"

"At this time of night? Maybe. Where are you? Where did you fly to?"

"Vermont, dumbass. I asked you to pick me up, like eight hours ago. Sorry I'm late."

I open my mouth. Shut it again. I haven't checked my phone since the last time I reread Jax's goodbye message. Barack Obama could've texted me, and I wouldn't have known about it. "Fuck. Sorry, I'd have let you down. It's been crazy at the bar. Did you call Eve?"

"Nope. I'm calling you. Figured you'd be up, but I can get a room at the airport if you're, uh, otherwise engaged."

"I'm not. Jax is away," I blurt before I catch myself.

Gabriel laughs again. "So you'll pick me up?"

"Of course."

"Awesome. I'll be outside with my cigarettes."

My brother hangs up. I check my messages and find that he's been texting me all day.

Gabi: *catching a flight out of houston today. can u pick me up?*

Gabi: *delayed. bad weather. might be late. that cool?*

Gabi: *connection delayed too. call u when i land.*

Gabi: *answer your damn phone*

Oops. I turn my car around and point it in the direction of the airport. It isn't the first time my brother has come home out of the blue, but I'm still flummoxed by his sudden appearance. Or, more accurately, by my ability to forget the fact that he'd told me his job was coming to an end earlier than he'd anticipated. Maybe I hadn't believed him. He's been wrong about that shit before.

But whatever. He's home, and I'm glad of it. I've missed him, and with Jax in my life now too, worrying about him has spread my mother hen disposition too fucking thin.

I hit the gas, driving as fast as I can without attracting the cops. I've seen enough of them in recent weeks, and luckily for me and anyone else on the roads, the airport isn't that far. Even better, true to his word, Gabi is waiting outside, a cigarette jammed in his mouth and a bag on his back.

For a moment, he looks so like me that I think his broad grin is mine. Or maybe it is, and he's returning whatever he sees on my face. I stop the car and jump out. He drops his bag and hugs me, and the long months he's been gone fade away.

I lean back to check him out. He's bearded and needs a haircut, but his eyes are bright. Whatever he's been doing has panned out, and more than that, he's happy to be home. "How long?" I ask him. "Are you here till after Christmas now?"

"Maybe. I need to talk to Eve first."

"That sounds…promising?"

"*Maybe*," he repeats. "Can you give me a ride to yoga town?"

I let it go. Gabi is a man who talks when he's good and ready, unlike me who swallows it all down until it bursts out after the hottest sex of my life. Damn, even thinking about that night in a negative light makes my blood heat, my heart turn over, and blows all thoughts of my long-lost brother from my mind.

Gabriel shakes me. "Earth to Tanner? Did you light up before you got here?"

"What?"

"You left me, and not in the bad way you used to. What are you thinking about that's got you grinning like an idiot?"

I'm close to my brother, but not that close. I shake him off and take his bag from his back. "Nothing. Let's go."

He doesn't believe me, I can tell, but I couldn't give less of a fuck. As I drive us back into Burlington, the rain fades away. The sky is bright and clear and full of stars, and maybe for the first time in as long as I can remember, they're starting to align.

CHAPTER TWENTY-ONE

Tanner

Eve's house is dark and quiet. It dawns on me that she's not expecting Gabi either, and I'm glad I'm here. I want to see her face when she opens the door to him.

But my brother has other plans, apparently. Plans for me. And him. A brotherly bonding session on a damp porch over his horrible cigarettes and a can of Pepsi I find in the back of my car.

I don't even drink soda. And I don't fucking smoke, but here we are.

Gabriel sits his ass down on a soggy wooden step and motions for me to do the same.

I roll my eyes and find a drier spot.

He laughs. "You've gotten soft. What happened to the man who'd sit happily in a thunderstorm and drink his beer?"

"I got struck by lightning. And you didn't bring beer, so…"

"Stop whining."

I stop and take a moment to revel in my brother's company. The last time we were alone together like this was two weeks before he left. We got drunk and he lectured me on taking care of myself. I lectured him on his hypocrisy, and we parted ways a few days later with mutual frustration. Back then, it had felt as if nothing would ever change, but it doesn't feel like that anymore. Gabi might be the same man, but I'm not. The earth has moved for me, and not just in bed with Jax. I'm different. I wonder if Jax knows. Then I wonder how he could *not* know. If Gabi can see my shadows so clearly, surely he can see the light too.

Or, maybe Eve's told him I'm getting laid. Yeah. That makes more sense.

While these thoughts meander through my brain, Gabi watches me, smoking his Marlboro Lights. I eye the box. It's nearly empty. "Are you trying to smoke them all before Eve wakes up?"

"Yup."

"Then what?"

"Then I drink green tea and eat egg-white omelets or whatever."

"She feeds me cider and macaroni."

"Maybe you don't annoy her as much."

"You can fix that, though, right? Annoying her, I mean. All you gotta do is stick around."

Gabriel blows smoke in my face. "Are you still banging your roommate?"

"I don't have a roommate."

"Answer the correct version of that question, then."

"Why?"

"Why not?"

I don't know the answer. Gabi's my brother and my best friend, when we're not stuck in a perpetual loop of bad communication, but I don't want to talk about Jax like he's a notch on my bedpost. Fucking him is incredible, but I'd give it up to just be with him.

"Wow." Gabi lets out a low whistle. "So it's true."

"What is?"

"That you've got it bad, brother."

The only person on earth who could've told him that is Eve. And after Thanksgiving, I can hardly blame her. She walked in on us the morning after. Jax was still asleep, naked and splayed out on my chest, and despite drunkenly vomiting my soul to him before we'd passed out, I was the happiest I've been in, like, ever. That I can remember, at least.

Wrong word. It wasn't despite *having a difficult conversation. It was* because *you did. Wake the fuck up.*

My subconscious kicks me in the dick. I slow-blink while Gabi watches, his expression an infuriating mix of concern and amusement. A whoosh of air escapes me, and it's ridiculous. It's hardly an epiphany to realize that talking to Jax is good for me. That talking to anyone or anything that isn't the depressive devil on my shoulder can only be positive. But the connection between that and the warmth in my gut feels brand new. As if I'm seeing it for the first time now I have my sardonic asshole of a brother for an audience.

Words bubble up my throat and fall out of me before I can stop them. "I don't have anything bad. I fucking love that dude."

Gabi nods, expecting the confession. "Have you told him?"

"Not yet."

"Well, get on with it," he says. "Don't be me. Don't wake up in another fucking state and realize you've only got one chance left to make shit right."

"Is that why you're here? To make shit right?"

He shrugs. "Ask me tomorrow."

I wake to clear skies. I'm alone, but it doesn't feel that way. Gabi is across town in Eve's yoga house—unless he's pissed her off already—and Jax is coming home this afternoon. At least, I hope he is. His cell isn't connecting yet. I know it because I woke in the early hours of this morning and finally replied to his message.

Tanner: *tell me you love me. so I can say it back*

I don't send it, and I won't until Jax comes down from high ground. But it doesn't matter. I can wait, even if I do have the whole day to myself to endure it. I usually spend Mondays in the office, catching up on paperwork, or in the bar while it's closed, cleaning stuff that didn't get cleaned over the weekend, but Harrison is there today, and he's banned me from showing my face until tomorrow morning. *"Take a day, Tanner. Please. I need to sit and revel in the amazing space you've built for me."*

He gives me too much credit, but I'll take the day off. I haven't been grocery shopping in forever, and when Jax gets back, if he's game, I don't plan on going out. I wanna eat dinner in bed with him, and breakfast too.

I want to tell him I love him for real.

An energy I don't recognize fills me. I roll out of bed, dress in clothes Jax wears too, and leave the apartment. I drive to a grocery store instead of walking to the one I can see from my bedroom, just to kill time. I load my cart with breakfast foods and a big bag of Vermont apples. By the register, I spot more British candy bars I've heard Jax talk about. They're weirder than the wheel things with the jam, and they were gross as fuck.

Doesn't stop me buying them, though. I might not want to eat them, but the smile they put on Jax's face is worth just about anything. I'm hooked on finding the wrappers by my coffee machine. I keep them there, in a mug. Or maybe I'm the mug, and I don't give a single fuck.

I'm back in my car when Gabi calls. Though I'm expecting it, the sound of his voice still brings a warm wave of surprise. "I was half convinced I dreamed last night."

"Still having nightmares, huh?"

"Not about you."

"Good to know. *Are* you still having them? We talked a lot last night, but not about that."

"I still have them," I say before I can check myself and be flippant and vague. "Not as much as before, though."

"What about the other stuff?"

"Yup. It's all still there, but it's…better, I guess."

"You guess?"

"Don't be a dick."

"I'm not. Eve told me to talk to you about something that doesn't involve who we're having sex with, so here we are."

"Are you having sex with someone who isn't Eve?"

"What do you think?"

"I think I'm trying to deflect the conversation away from my mental health because I'm super bad at talking about it, especially with you."

A mutual brood stretches between us. I've never seen Gabi in Eve's new place, but I still picture him on her mandala rug, lying flat on the floor like he owns the joint, probably in sweatpants and nothing else. His eyes are closed, but his brain is working a million miles an hour like it always does. He's trying to find words that won't upset me, but he doesn't have to do that anymore. Somehow in the last twenty-four hours I've made peace with myself. I was sick, maybe I still am, but I'm not broken.

I no longer feel weak.

"Listen." I slide my key into the ignition and tuck my phone between my ear and my shoulder. "I know I've been a pain in the ass since forever, but I'm trying real hard not to be like that anymore. You don't have to second guess everything you say to me."

Gabi sighs. "I don't think I ever did. I just got in the habit of doing it because it was easier in the moment. Avoidance—we're good at it, huh? It started when Mom pretended Dad hadn't really died so we spent a year waiting for him to come back from the store even though we both knew she was lying."

"We're not good at it, Gabs. It's fucked us up."

"Wow. That's a heavy reality check right there. Now I know you're feeling better. What's next?"

"What do you mean?"

"I mean what's gonna change in your life to keep this moving? It's not enough to say it, bro. You gotta live it."

I roll my eyes. I know he's right, but I'm not taking life advice from him. Every bad habit I have is his too. Most of them, anyway.

Intrusive, morbid thoughts are all mine, unless he's super good at hiding them. "All right, you got me. I haven't put much into practice yet. I've talked to Jax some, but I know it's not enough."

"It's a start, though."

"Is it?" It's my turn to sigh. "I don't want to unload all my crap onto him."

"You'd better start unboxing it by yourself, then. Huh. Maybe you could go to the cabin and sweep up that coffee pot you threw at my head."

"That didn't happen."

"Didn't it?"

Fuck, I have no idea. All I know is that this conversation, combined with the one we had last night, is the most real talk we've shared since the night I apparently threw a coffee pot at my brother.

"I'm sorry."

Gabi snorts. "You only get to say that if I do, and you've told me a thousand times it wasn't my fault you got so sick without me noticing."

"It wasn't your fault."

"It wasn't yours either, so why don't we nix the apologies and move on?"

I blow out another long breath. Moving on sounds good, but I'm out of practice. And I'm out of words too. Gabi has given me so much to think about that I can't form another coherent sentence.

So I grunt and hang up. It's a thing we do.

But I don't stop thinking. I start my car and drive out of the grocery store's parking lot. Ten minutes ago, I had every intention of going home and waiting out Jax's camping trip, but Gabi is right: I can talk to Jax every day for as long as he'll listen, but some boxes of shit I have to face by myself.

I point my car out of Burlington and drive, following Jax out into the hills. But it's not his steps I'm retracing, it's my own.

The Black Claw trails are forty-five minutes away. The drive is an old friend and seems to pass in the blink of an eye. Habit sees me bypass the obvious parking spots and stop instead at the foot of a trail I doubt even Jax has walked. Why would he? It doesn't go anywhere except the cabin that's apparently overdue for some housekeeping.

I'm not dressed for hiking, but I make it work for the ten minutes it takes to reach the cabin. And you know what? Nothing happens. No one dies. Not even me.

Idiot.

The cabin's key is under the boot implanted with the baby maple tree. I scoop up the key and scan the horizon, wondering how near Jax has been to the cabin in order to spot it. It feels good that he's been close, as if he's with me. But at the same time, I'm glad he's not. I don't want him to look at me and see whatever scrunched-up face I'm making as I unlock the cabin door, or put his hand on my chest and know my heart is racing for all the wrong reasons.

One foot inside and I feel sick as hell. I keep my gaze low, taking in the bare wooden floor and the scent of leather and oak. It smells like V and V, but stronger. Deeper. Like home, but it's not home, because I'm not the same man I was the last time I was here. *But do you wanna be the dude you were then? Drunk, selfish, and so fucking lost you wanted to die?*

Of course I don't. And maybe facing where rock bottom finally hit will do me good.

I raise my head, expecting carnage, but it's not there. The cabin is spotless, no broken glass or upturned furniture. No empty liquor bottles. At first glance, it's as if the month-long meltdown I had after Vic died never happened. Then I step closer to the old leather chair that's Gabi's favorite. On the weathered arm is a streak of blood, and I know it's mine. I can tell by the sickening churn in my belly. I'm good with other people's gore. My own, not so much.

Dazed, I move through the cabin to the tiny kitchen. Clean dishtowels are stacked by the sink. I crank the faucet and soak one. The water is unearthly cold, underlining where I am. I let it run over my fingers until they're numb, then I take the dishtowel back to the chair and scrub the blood Gabi somehow missed—it's how I know it was him and not Eve who cleaned up this place—until it's as clean as it's going to get after all this time.

I don't look at the stain it leaves on the cloth. I fold the dishtowel as small as it will go and dump it into the empty trash can. It seems symbolic, though I can't say why. It's not as if I haven't junked over my entire life twice to get to this point. But something about today, about *me*, feels different. My lungs move as if set free and as I cast my gaze toward the floor to ceiling windows at the cabin's rear, the colors I see in the wilderness are the brightest I've ever seen.

It's a seismic shift, and Jax is the catalyst. He hasn't fixed me, and he never will, but he's made me want to fix myself better than the Band-Aids I've been slapping over my heart until now.

I pull out my phone to check if my WhatsApp messages have gone through yet, but of course it's me that has no cell service now. And no battery. My phone dies as I'm poking at it. I need to go home. Hell, Jax is probably half way to Burlington by now and I'm not fucking there.

The prospect of missing a moment with him drives me out of the cabin. I lock the door and set the key back in place beneath the maple sapling. Raindrops cover my hands. I straighten as light drizzle begins to fall and turn toward the trail that will take me back to my car.

Movement catches my eye. A lone figure is approaching the cabin in a coat emblazoned with *Wildfoot Adventure*. For a moment, my heart leaps. *Jax*. But it's not Jax, it's Jerry, and the anxiety creasing his weathered face kills the cautious optimism blooming in my soul.

I jump down from the porch. My boots crunch the ice and slip a little, reminding me they're the wrong fucking shoes to be on my feet right now. Jerry is two yards away, and I know that frown. Something's wrong. "What is it?"

"Is Jax with you?"

My heart turns over. "No. Why? Didn't he come down from the campsite yet?"

Jerry shakes his head. "Not yet. And we've had no contact either. I'm sure it's fine, but I came up to check it out and saw your car by the ridge. I thought he might've brought the group here for a pit stop."

"He's never been here."

"Shame. It would've helped him out these past few months."

There's no accusation in Jerry's words, but I feel the guilt all the same. This whole time Jax could've stayed right here, avoiding the forty-five minute drive to Burlington every damn day, and I never said a fucking word. It wasn't a conscious decision, but wow, I really am a dick. "I never even thought of it. I haven't been here since—"

"I know," Jerry says. "It's why I didn't mention it either, but if it's any consolation, I think Jax is pretty happy with how things have worked out."

"But he's not back yet."

Jerry's ghost-like grin fades. "No. I'm sure he's fine, but we've been getting more rain than snow this year, and I'm worried about—"

"Rockfall," I finish for him. Black Claw is known for unstable ground. Jax and Jerry have spent the past few months marking out safe routes up and down the trails, but Mother Nature is unpredictable. Anything can happen, anytime, anywhere. Ask me how I know.

Actually, don't. I don't need those images right now. I need to know Jax is safe.

It takes me a split second to make a decision, and thirty more to reclaim the key from beneath the maple tree and go back into the cabin.

The closet is in the hall. It's stuffed full of every kind of outdoor gear a man could ever need, some Gabi's, some mine. I find waterproof pants, a thick coat, and some gloves. I throw them on and stamp into snow boots that have seen better days.

Jerry nods as I hurry outside. "I've got the satellite phone. Sure you wanna do this? I'm probably worrying about nothing."

"Shut the fuck up."

He accepts my answer, and we set off up the trail, taking the route Jax had preplanned, tracking him and the conservationists to Lynx Point. It's a long hike, and the terrain is tough. After more than a year kicking it in the city, my legs feel it, but it's a good pain. The best. My lungs breathe the clean Vermont air and relief wars with the building worry in my heart for Jax. We traverse a steep ridge. I sweep the landscape I once knew like the back of my hand. There are patches of loose ground everywhere, not enough on their own to cause a serious problem, but, put them together, and it's enough to cause big trouble.

Jerry waits as I scale a rough notch to get a better look. "This is new," I call down. "Some of this has slipped in the last twenty-four hours."

"Damn." Jerry grimaces. "I shoulda told him not to go."

I don't answer until we're level again. Then I shake my head. "This is a risk all year round. What he needed was for the dumb-fuck local to go with him and have his back."

"Are we talking about me or you?"

There's no time to give Jerry the withering glare he doesn't deserve. We walk on, both of us ignoring the fact that it's the first time we've been in each other's company since he came to see me last fall, and I didn't speak to him for the entire two hours he sat with me. I need to tell him I'm an asshole, and he was the best boss I could've asked for. That what happened to Vic was even less his fault than it was mine. But we keep moving instead. I steady him over harsh ground and meet his gaze with my whole self and hope that by the time I get around to saying that shit, he'll already know.

The site where Jax made camp overnight is still a mile away and we're running out of time to reach it before we lose light. So far we've found no trace of Jax's group, and there's every chance he changed the route of their descent when the unexpected rain hit last night. He's likely already back at the Wildfoot truck and speeding home to Burlington. But the *what-if* monster in my brain is loud. If there's loose ground on this route, there'll be loose ground everywhere. What if it's already slipped? What if it slipped *last night* and Jax is hurt? Trapped? What if—

Jerry squeezes my shoulder and points into the distance. "Let's keep going to the ridge over there. We'll be able to see as far up as we're going to at this level. If we don't see nothing, we gotta go back. Ain't no use to anyone, least of all Jax, stumbling around in the dark. I already let Kai know we might need him tomorrow."

It's a sensible plan. I know it in my head, my gut, and my heart, but there's zero part of me that can truly contemplate leaving Jax out here another night. I stride on, pushing for the ridge. Jerry's a heartbeat behind me. The incline is steep and littered with boulders big enough to kill a man if they rolled over one, but I try not to think about that. I focus on the clearing sky, and the faint strains of winter sun fighting the rain clouds. It reminds me of Jax smiling at me when I'm so sure I want to be miserable. When he's stumbling sleepily around my kitchen, cracking eggs into a pan and somehow missing the goddamn pan, and it's the funniest thing in the world. It's him laughing at everything and nothing, and me absorbing every sound he makes to wrap around my fucking soul. His light to my dark. Sunshine and storms make rainbows, right?

"Tanner."

Jerry says my name as a low rumble breaks through the Jax-centric meanderings in my brain. His hand is on my back, and I follow his gaze to the ground above us. At first, I see nothing, then the rumble grows louder, and the ground beneath us shakes, reacting to the rocks and boulders barreling down the hillside.

It's heavy and fast-moving, picking up speed and debris. With the tough terrain below us, we have zero chance of outrunning it. Whatever we do, it's going to hit us, and it's gonna hit hard.

My brain snaps into autopilot. I rip the pack from Jerry's back, open it, and hurl it as far down the hill as I can. His belongings spill out, leaving a trail that will hopefully lead whoever comes looking for him close to wherever we land after this. The satellite phone is in his coat pocket. For it to be of any use to us, he needs to survive this hit too, but there's no fucking time. I shove him sideways and hope for the best, then the rockfall hits, and the world spins out of control.

Earth and sky fight for dominance.

Tumbling.

Falling.

Stone clatters into my head, and the sky wins.

CHAPTER TWENTY-TWO

Jax

The ground shudders. Mother Nature is pissed, but thankfully not with us.

I've lived through earthquakes in California. Tectonic shifts that anger the ocean and sway buildings like branches in the wind. Rockfall is something else. It's energy that grows and swells and surges, crushing anything that gets in its way. Unpredictable. Changeable. I knew the second I set foot on Black Claw yesterday that the routes I'd planned to Lynx Point and back were already unsafe.

I plotted new ones as we went, marking them on the map, avoiding loose, sketchy rock and soft ground, stuck in the cycle of constant evaluation. And now our final descent stretches out before us, and I can't wait for it to be over. As much as I've come to love this wild land, there's an urgency in my bones I can't explain. I need to get home.

The earth finally stills. I straighten from the crouch I dropped into when the rumbling struck, and look out over the horizon. At first glance, the landscape seems the same. Nothing has changed. Then it solidifies, and I see the clumps of rock and boulder that have shifted downhill, taking trees and one of my static cameras with it.

My heart mourns the lost footage, but I know better than to traverse the unstable ground to retrieve it. If more landslip doesn't kill me, Tanner will.

Tanner. My heart flips from disappointment to longing. Old me wants to be nervous about the text I sent him and his response. But the man I've become on these trails, the same man who shares Tanner's bed, dinner, breakfast, and more bottles of cider than I can count, feels nothing but peace. He might love me back; he might not. It doesn't matter. I'm gonna tell him anyway.

You already did, idiot. You blew your load too soon.

Guilty as charged, but I have no regrets. Only a yearning in my soul that won't quit until this long-arse day comes to an end.

We tiptoe down the trail, dodging suspect ground. Perhaps we're overcautious, but if Tanner and Jerry have taught me anything, it's that there's no such thing. I force myself to move far slower than my heart wants, my companions at my back as silent and obedient as they've been since they got into the Wildfoot truck yesterday. In the distance, I spot what I now know to be Tanner's cabin, and hope surges, bright and free, then movement on the lower ground distracts me.

I stop and zero in on the lone figure in a heap at the bottom of the trail. At least, it looks like the bottom of the trail, then I realize it's not. The landscape has altered even more than I first thought. The trail as I know it no longer exists, and worse, it's taken someone down with it. "Fuck. We need to get down there."

"That way." The conservationist closest to me points over my shoulder. "The other guy looks worse off."

"What?"

Gloved hands grip my shoulders and turn me. My gaze swivels from the body at the bottom of the hill to one I haven't noticed further up. It's half hidden by rocks and rubble, only the red of the man's coat stands out against the unruly earth. "Shit. Okay. I'll go to him. You two head for the other guy and try and catch some cell service. And Jesus-fucking-Christ remind me next time we do this to bring a satellite phone."

I part ways with my companions. They're capable outdoorsmen and I don't worry about them picking their way across the unstable ground any more than I worry about myself. I focus on the flash of red in the distance and on not dying before I get there. The red consumes me. For long minutes I forget it's attached to a broken body. I move like the lynx we've been watching on camera, wide-footed and light, but I'm not a fucking wildcat. Eventually, the ground wins, and I tumble the last few feet to the injured walker.

Dazed, I land in a heap, searching for the red fabric that's guided me this far. But I can't find it. Red surrounds me, but it's not solid, it's soft and wet and viscous.

It's *blood*, and it's seeping from the arm impaled on the daggered branch of an unrooted tree.

Fuckfuckfuck. I lurch forward, searching for the source. Icy rock buries the body attached to the arm. I dig through it, keeping a sharp ear out for further rockfall as I sling debris over my shoulder. Blood stains my gloves. I feel sick, but I keep digging, revealing the body of a man who's tall and strong. His legs are long and well-muscled, and clad in waterproof trousers that are the same as mine, except mine are blue and his are black.

He moans. The sound is quiet, but it rattles my bones. Urgency turns to panic. I fight to uncover the man's face, brushing earth, dirt, and crushed rubble away. His features reveal themselves, one by one. His dark beard, cut cheekbones, and inky hair.

No. My heart drops like the stone that's buried him. The man is conscious. Barely. And the coal eyes flecked with gold staring back at me aren't those of a stranger.

It's Tanner.

No. This can't be real. I shake my head to clear it. It's not Tanner. It can't be. I left him in Burlington, tending bar in the safest, nicest drinking establishment in the entire fucking world. There's no logical reason for him to be out on Black Claw. He *told me* himself he'd never come out here again. More than once. *It's not him. You're seeing things.*

But as hard as I fight to regain my sanity, every instinct I have fights back. The man moans again, jerking the arm that's caught on the tree. His dark eyes flash, then flutter closed. And I fucking miss him enough to know it's true. It's him, and the what-the-actual-*fuck*-is-happening-right-now ceases to matter.

"Tanner. *Tanner.*" I shake his chest with one hand and grip his shoulder with the other, keeping his injured arm still. "Wake up. It's Jax."

There's no response. I shake him harder, raw fear building in my gut. I'm covered in his blood. He's *still* bleeding and his face is deathly pale. I'm no fucking doctor, but I don't need to be to know he's badly hurt. That whatever's happened to him is going to kill him if I can't keep him awake and get help to him fast.

I shake him again, harder, still gripping his injured arm.

He doesn't answer me, and his eyes stay closed.

"Fuck! Goddamit, Tanner." I cast a desperate glance down the trail. One of the environmentalists—Steven—is headed my way. He jumps over a displaced tree trunk and lands beside me. "It's Jerry," he blurts. "He came looking for us when we were late back. The fall hit him and Tanner Reid. He said to tell you it's Tanner."

"I know it's Tanner," I growl. "He's lost a ton of blood, and I can't wake him up. We need help. Did you get cell service down there?"

"No. But Jerry brought a satellite phone. We've called it in. Help's coming."

Relief floods me, but as I turn back to Tanner, it's a hollow victory. He's getting paler by the second. His lips are turning blue. If help doesn't come soon, he'll die on the trails he swore blind he'd never tread again. A vow he broke to come looking for me. *No.* I can't let that happen. Tanner's not dying for me.

I'm still gripping his shoulder, holding his injured arm in place. The blood flow has slowed, but it's enough to make me weak at the knees. "Get my bag from my back," I bark at Steven. "We need to cut his coat off his arm and anchor that branch."

Steven moves fast and retrieves the Swiss Army knife I have in my bag. He deftly cuts Tanner's coat free and the blood-soaked strips fall away.

The branch is stuck in his arm, right where his artery is. Blood oozes from the wound. I can only pray the branch is slowing the flow enough to keep him alive. We wrap the arm, securing the branch. Then Steven holds it still while I squeeze Tanner's good hand in mine and call his name over and over, as if I can will him awake.

Time passes. I'm not sure how much or how fast. Tanner doesn't move or speak. I'm scared he's already gone. That he's died on the icy ground. Then I hear the shouts of rescuers and feel the beat of activity on the hillside.

Somehow Tanner hears it too. He groans and his eyes wrench open. He stares at me, and there's a spark in his deep gaze, a fear that matches mine. He rips his hand free and makes a clumsy swipe for my knee. "I'm gonna be sick."

I grip his face and hold it firm. "You're going into shock. Do whatever you need to do. I've got you."

CHAPTER TWENTY-THREE

Jax

Tanner doesn't throw up. He falls unconscious and stays that way, so he doesn't see the men who scale the hillside to rescue him, or feel my hands slip from him as they push me out of their way.

The next two hours are a blur. Vermont becomes a haze. Black Claw becomes a busy ER, and loose rock has turned into a hard plastic chair.

I'm alone. I have no idea what happened to Steven and the other environmentalist. Or Jerry, though he was conscious when they took him. I heard him shouting Tanner's name. Or maybe it was me shouting.

Damn.

My head throbs. Time ticks by. Numbness wars with a fear I've never felt before. It's paralyzing. Consuming. I'm frozen in place, as if I so much as move my eyeballs, I'll shatter into a million pieces.

All I've done is call Eve. She didn't answer. Her voicemail kicked in, but I didn't leave a message. Couldn't. At some point, I'll have to resurrect myself and call her again, but...not yet.

Maybe I won't have to. Gabriel is Tanner's next of kin. He'll call her when the hospital reaches him.

Yeah, in fucking Texas, or wherever the hell he is. It's gonna take him forever to get here and the doctors aren't going to tell you shit until he does.

More fear licks my heart. Logic tells me Tanner was taken straight to the OR to free his arm from the impaled branch and repair the damage it's left behind—the seeping hole that was leaking his blood into the earth. So much blood. I close my eyes and try to picture my own instead. Reclaim the gory photos my ex thrust into my face like a fucking trophy from whatever pit of my soul I've buried them.

It's a poor attempt at comfort. I survived because a British Army medic plugged my artery with his goddamn fingers. I found out later he was a trauma consultant in the NHS and it was inexplicable luck he'd been on the same beach as me on the wrong side of the Atlantic Ocean. Tanner hadn't had luck on his side, he'd only had me and the rudimentary straps I'd wound around the branch that was trying to kill him. My flailing hands and blind panic. As if it wasn't enough that he'd only been out there in the first place to come looking for me.

Shivering, I bury my face in my cold hands. I need to call Eve again. I need to take my boots off and change out of my wet clothes before I get fucking pneumonia. But I don't move. I keep my eyes squeezed shut, breathe in and out, and pray Tanner is doing the same.

A heavy hand lands on my shoulder sometime later. Perhaps I did fall asleep, cos there's no way the bearded dude staring down at me is real. Broad shoulders. Dark hair and molten eyes. For a moment, my heart leaps, then the lack of sensation where the hand clasps me registers. No tingling. No warmth. No live-wire connection running between us.

It's not Tanner, real or otherwise. It's Gabriel.

"Fuck." I lurch upright, new terror seizing my gut. If Gabriel's here, then *hours* have passed. Hours that Tanner has been sick, injured, and alone, if he even made it through the fucking surgery. For all I know, he didn't, and Gabriel has come to tell me. "I—"

Gabriel pushes me down. "Easy. No news. He's still in surgery."

"What? How? I mean, how the fuck is that true if you're here? I thought you were in Texas."

"I was. But I came home yesterday. Chill, Jax. Take a breath."

I take his advice, and shake my head to clear it, but I'm so cold, nothing happens. Gabriel says something I don't hear, then he drops into the chair beside me and wraps a strong arm around my shoulders.

"Jesus. You're in shock. Didn't anyone bring you a fucking blanket?"

"I don't need a blanket."

"You need something," Gabriel counters. "Hang on. I'll get you a candy bar."

He disappears as abruptly as he arrived. I'm pretty certain I've imagined the whole encounter, then he's back, brandishing a generic protein bar from the vending machine I walked past a lifetime ago. I want to eat it about as much as I want to sit on a chainsaw, and chewing it feels about the same, but I need to know whatever Gabriel knows, and he won't tell me shit if I'm a jabbering wreck.

I eat the bar. Gabriel watches, then passes me a bottle of water. He doesn't speak until I've drained half of it.

"It's not good," he says. "He lost a shit ton of blood and he's got a contusion on his head they're pretty worried about. They're going to scan him after the surgery."

"When will that be?"

"I don't know, man. Depends how long it takes to repair the artery. That goddamn tree sticking out of him was the only thing stopping him from bleeding to death. How fucked up is that?"

"Have you seen him?"

"No. They'd already taken him to the OR when I got here."

"Do they think he's going to die?"

Gabriel's gaze slid away from me. "The nurse I spoke to couldn't answer that question. They'll know more after the surgery and the CT."

Silence stretches between us. I'm a jittery mess of fear and misplaced energy. Gabriel is calm—*too* calm. As if he's been here before, and I remember that he kind of has, except last time, it was a threat, not a reality.

As if that makes any difference.

But it was different. Back then, Tanner wanted to die. He doesn't now. He's never told me that, but I know it like I know water is wet and Vermont is as beautiful as he is.

I want to tell Gabriel that. But when I open my mouth, something else comes out. "He was awake when I found him."

"Was he talking?"

"He said he was going to be sick. He wasn't, but I think all the blood got to him."

I regret the words as soon as I say them. Gabriel doesn't need the gory details of his only brother gravely injured in the wilderness. He needs the doctors to come out and tell him that everything's gonna be okay. That Tanner lost a lot of blood, but they fixed him, so he doesn't need to worry about it, or spend the rest of his life imagining what it looked like.

He doesn't need the flash of pain that crumples the sharp features that are so like Tanner's. He doesn't need the shuddery breath that rattles his bones.

"Fuck, I'm sorry."

Gabriel sighs. "Don't be. He'd still be out there if it wasn't for you."

"You're wrong. He wouldn't have been out there at all if it wasn't for me."

"How do you figure that?"

"We were late back. Him and Jerry came looking for us."

Gabriel shakes his head. "That's on them, and the fucking weather. The way Jerry tells it, you did everything right, and he and Tanner got caught in the wrong place at the wrong time.

That's how it goes out there. Tanner knows that better than anyone."

"I know. Wait, you spoke to Jerry? Is he okay?"

"Yeah. Dislocated wrist and some stitches in his head. He's gonna be fine."

"I should go see him."

"All right, then. I'll come with you."

Gabriel helps me to my feet and we navigate the ER to where Jerry is. He's sitting on the edge of his bed, banged-up and bandaged, his face twisted in the same worry that claws my heart with every breath.

He grabs for Gabriel with his good hand and pulls him in while I linger in the doorway. "Any news?"

"Nope. We're gonna head upstairs in a minute and wait closer to the OR."

It's news to me, but it makes sense, and I want to go right now. I need to be near Tanner, even if there's sweet fuck all I can do for him. But I have to get through this first. I have to see for myself that Jerry's okay, cos somehow I know it's the first thing Tanner will ask when he's back with us.

Jerry and Gabriel murmur to each other, then Jerry calls my name. "You saved us," he says. "I couldn't press the buttons on that damn phone, and Lord knew where Tanner had landed. I couldn't find him, Jax. He was right there, pushing me out of the way, then he was just gone."

His words skewer me. I force my heavy legs forward and clasp his outstretched hand as Gabriel moves aside. "What the fuck was he even doing out there? He should've been at the bar."

"He was at the cabin. I don't know what he was doing there, he never said."

My gaze flickers to Gabriel. "He told me he hadn't been back to the cabin since last year."

Gabriel shrugs. "We talked about it yesterday. Maybe he got the urge to check on my housekeeping."

I'm missing something, but in the grand scheme of things it

doesn't matter. Jerry's okay, and that's all I need to know right now. I squeeze his hand and back up. Gabriel takes the hint and we leave Jerry at the mercy of his wife and the hordes of young kids she's brought with her to the hospital.

We take the elevator upstairs. The OR waiting room is practically empty. We find a quiet corner and take root in chairs with more cushioning than the ones in the ER. I'm wrecked with fatigue, but I can't sleep because I'm petrified the only man I've ever loved is dying somewhere beyond the double doors at the front of the room.

I'm terrified, and it hurts. I can't lose Tanner now. We haven't been happy.

The surgical resident is the blandest motherfucker in the entire world, but I'm glad of it. By the time he appears several hours later, I'm no longer able to deal in anything more than cold, hard facts.

"It was touch and go for a while, but we've repaired the artery and stabilized the hypovolemia with transfusions and platelets."

He says other words, but they wash over me. I already know how injuries like Tanner's are treated. "What about his head? Did you scan it?"

"We did. The neuro attending reviewed it and couldn't see any bleeding or swelling. Mr. Reid is going to have quite a headache when he wakes up, and perhaps some minor concussive symptoms, but we're not worried about it. Overall, his status is as positive as we could hope for right now. Whoever strapped that tree branch in place saved his life."

"Tell him twice," Gabriel says, nudging me. "Jax is having a hard time believing his own heroics."

The doctor doesn't smile. Just nods and turns to go.

I lean forward. "Wait. Can we see him?"

"Soon. I'll send a nurse to come and get you when we're ready."

He leaves. I sit back in my seat and remember Gabriel beside me. "Sorry. You'll want to see him first. You're family."

Gabriel snorts. "As if he'll be pleased to see my mean mug if you're not right there with me. He'll probably punch me in the face."

I stare at him. "What?"

"He loves you, man."

"How'd you figure that?"

"He told me."

"When?"

"Yesterday. And let me tell you, it was the first time I've seen that fucker smile like that in years, so can it with the guilt bullshit, okay? He's alive because of you, and something tells me it's because of you he wants to stay that way too."

By the time I've processed his words, he's tipped his head back and closed his eyes. He's not asleep, but I sense the worry draining from him as he makes his own peace with what the doctor told us. I study him and measure the man I've judged him to be against the kindness he's shown me in the last few hours. The easy acceptance of the man his brother apparently loves. I've done Gabriel Reid wrong. Just like his brother, he's the nicest guy in the world.

The thought keeps me company while I wait for the elusive nurse to come back. My phone buzzes in my pocket.

It's Molly.

It's Rainn.

It's Oz, and Auden, and every other bartender under the sun who has somehow got my cell number and decided I'm their person on this craptastic situation. But I have nothing to say. I can't tell them their fearless leader is going to be okay because whatever the doc says, I haven't *seen* it. I haven't seen *him*.

I ignore them, for now, and open the last message from Eve.

Eve: *I'm so sorry, J. I'm at V and V fetching Tanner some things. Tell me what you need. I'll go to your place too.*

Jax: *I don't need anything*

Eve: *Liar. Unless you're planning on leaving that boy and coming home at any point before he does*

She's got me there, but for the life of me, I can't think of a single thing I need beyond knowing for certain that Tanner's okay. I can't remember a point in time when I've ever needed anything else.

Jax: *I don't know. I can't think.*

Eve: *I can't figure out which clothes are yours and which are Tanner's anyway. I'll bring enough for two. Is Gabriel okay?*

She's not asking me about Tanner, which tells me Gabriel has already told her what the doctor said. She needs to know her one true love is okay as much as I do mine. And I owe her that. Fuck, I owe her so much more.

Jax: *He's dealing. I'd be fucked without him. Think he'll feel better when we see Tanner tho*

Eve: *Tell them both I love them.*

Jax: *I will, I promise.*

Eve: *See you in the morning x*

Jax: *You're not coming tonight?*

Eve: *I can't, honey. Only two family members are allowed in at night. Be good. I'll see you soon, and don't forget I love you too x*

My phone dies before I can return the sentiment. I'd kept it switched off out on the trails, but it's old and ill-equipped to deal with thirty-six hours without a charging point. Fucking Apple. Her messages play on a loop in my tired brain, though. *Family*. It's not a word I've thought about much since I came to Vermont. The disconnect I feel for my own is as strong as ever. It never occurred to me I'd find another, but as I sit beside Tanner's stoic brother, and picture Eve mothering his crew at V and V, I realize how badly I needed one.

And perhaps that I wanted one too.

The nurse takes forever to come and find us. I'm still wide awake when she appears, but Gabriel has dozed off.

I nudge him awake, and this time it's me who helps him to his feet and steers him through the hospital until we come to the room where Tanner is.

Gabriel's awake by the time we get there, but he hangs back and pushes me forward. "Go on. It's you he'll want to see."

But as sweet as that is, I already know Tanner's not conscious yet.

I slip into the sterile room. The bed and the dozen wires and tubes don't shock me. I'm expecting it all. I'm even prepared for the heavy bandaging on Tanner's arm and the hospital gown covering his strong body.

It's the pallor of his face that gets me. Somehow, I'd convinced myself he'd have color in his cheeks again. That the ash tone of his skin when I dug him out could be consigned to my nightmares.

But it's still there. I sink into yet another chair and take his good hand in mine, knowing I'll get no response. Tanner is beyond asleep. He isn't going to wake up any time soon or be capable of holding coherent conversation. I know this. I've lived it. I know that even when he does wake up, he's going to feel so sick he'll wonder if he's actually died. That he won't know which way is up. That he might not even care. But as Gabriel takes his place on Tanner's other side, I know we stand a good chance of persuading him he does.

CHAPTER TWENTY-FOUR

Tanner

Ouch.

No, scrap that. It's a childlike word that doesn't fit the jack-hammer in my head, or the thousand knives some motherfucker is stabbing into my arm. It hurts like a bitch. That shit travels and hits me everywhere. Even my toes throb. I have zero interest in being awake right now, but there's an asshole squeezing my hand who has other ideas. And what do you know? He's a big enough asshole to tap my face, laughing, until a fucking angel tells him to stop.

The angel has a melodic voice. It's lilting on syllables that should be harsh, and the soft, gruff tone wraps around me like a spell. I still don't want to be awake, but that voice. Man, there's nowhere I won't go to hear it speak, even if opening my eyes feels like death.

A snort comes from the first voice. "See? Told you it wasn't me he wanted to wake up to."

I don't want to wake up at all, but the answering chuckle shifts the weight a whole other fucker has parked on my eyelids.

Bracing myself, I force my eyes open. Two things hit me at once. First, that Jax looks like he's been dragged through a Shipley orchard backwards. Second, everything hurts and spins so much I'm gonna puke.

Hard.

There's no stopping it.

I lurch sideways and get sick over the side of the bed. It's vicious, and painful, and the groan that escapes me sounds like a dying animal.

It's a while before my surroundings catch up with me. I'm breathing as though I've run a marathon. There's something on my face and a warm palm is rubbing my chest.

Jax. The other voice was Gabi. I don't know when that manifested in my brain, but it has, along with the fact that wherever I am, he's no longer here. It's just me and Jax.

My eyes find their way open again. I'm in a hospital bed and Jax is leaning so far forward he's practically horizontal. He's watching me with eyes that haven't slept and he's still rubbing my chest. It feels nice—*so fucking nice*—but I can't work out why he's doing it. "Are you okay?"

The words are hoarse. Scratchy, like I haven't spoken for days and days and days, and they're hampered by the mask on my face. I make a clumsy swipe for it with the arm that doesn't feel like it's on fire.

I miss.

Jax has my back. He lifts the mask free and cups my face with his magic palm. "I'm okay, and so is your brother, and Eve, and Jerry, and anyone else you haven't asked about yet. I promise. You don't have to worry about anything except feeling better, all right?"

I believe him. Jax is a part of me I can't let go. He's truth and trust and honesty, but for the fucking life of me I can't remember already having this conversation. All I remember is puking. A lot. On boots that aren't his or mine.

Gabriel.

Oops.

I fade out again. The next time I'm conscious, Jax is gone, but

Gabi is there before I can panic. His hands aren't magic like Jax's, but they calm me enough to figure I can stay right here in this bed.

"He finally went home to take a shower," Gabi says before I can ask. "That dude has only left your side to take a piss for three days straight, so if you were fretting over whether he really loves you, stop."

"I'm not fretting."

Gabriel's eyes widen and grow wet. I think my words have surprised him, then he shakes his head. "That's the first coherent sentence you've said to me. Damn. Are you really back, or are you fucking with me?"

"The fuck are you talking about?"

A heavy whoosh of air escapes my brother. He sinks heavily into a nearby chair and shakes his head. "You're back. Jesus-fuck-ing-Christ."

That's a lot of fucks for such a short conversation. I let Gabi recover from whatever meltdown he's having and make a shaky attempt to anchor myself. Without Jax, it's a marathon, but I try. I don't want to be in whatever state I'm in right now when he comes back. I don't want him to look at me the way my brother is.

My head pulsates with bone-deep pain. There's a bruise on my temple, I can feel it, and my limbs ache with more scrapes and wounds, and the strain of inactivity. Nausea rattles my belly, but it's distant now, not a gathering storm. I ignore it and focus on the one thing I don't understand—the searing pain in my arm. "What happened?"

Gabriel leans over me. "You don't remember anything?"

"I remember the landslide. What did it do to me?"

"Threw you a quarter mile down Black Claw. You banged your head pretty good and impaled your arm on a tree. It got your artery. You're lucky Jax strapped it so well when he found you, or you'd have bled out right there."

It's everything I need to know, but it takes me a moment to collect it into coherent thoughts. I take a breath to ask about Jerry, but my brain buzzes. I already know he's okay. "How did Jax find me? We were looking for him…I think, right?"

"You're right," Gabi says. "He took those conservationists up to the new point on the trails. It was an overnight, but the rain came in harder than forecast, so he took a longer route back. No contact, so Jerry freaked and went looking for him. He found you at the cabin on the way and you went up with him. Quite the way to break your self-imposed city quarantine, huh?"

It's too much. I pick out the information I need right now and let the rest go. "But Jax is okay?"

"Yes. He always was. Turns out my worry-wart older brother had already told him a million different ways to get back if the ground shifted too much for plan A."

"You're being a dick."

"I know. It's my coping mechanism. Sound familiar?"

"I'm sorry."

"Don't be. Just be okay, Tanner. We love you."

"We?"

"Yeah. Me. Eve. Jax. That crazy chick with the curly hair who keeps wiping her eyes on my favorite shirt."

Molly. A laugh bubbles somewhere inside me. It can't get out just yet, but I cling to the feeling until Gabi's bitching sends me back to sleep.

Jax

Tanner is so fucking strong. He handles every debilitating symptom his injuries throw at him, and even the concussion that made him so sick when he first woke up doesn't keep him down for long. After four days of sketchy consciousness, I come to the hospital at the arsecrack of dawn to find him sitting up in bed, wide awake and waiting for me.

"Hey." I slip through the door and cross the room in two strides. "You're awake."

"I am," he agrees. "I missed you."

"I missed you too."

I almost choke on the words, and he hears me. He reaches his good arm for me and pulls me into the closest thing to a hug he can manage right now. He doesn't tell me everything's okay, that *he's* okay, he just holds me as long as he can, which isn't all that long.

He wavers. I help him ease back against the pillows and take a seat on his bed. It's a far better view than the one I've had from the uncomfortable chairs beside him. Fuck those bastards.

I stroke Tanner's face, enjoying the alertness in his hooded eyes. "How long you been up?"

"Dunno." He leans into my touch. "I was thinking about you and here you are."

He doesn't make as much sense as his bright gaze has led me to hope, but it's cute as fuck, and I've never thought of Tanner as cute. Beautiful, kind, funny, and hotter than the earth's core. But never cute.

I like it.

"What are you grinning about?" Tanner's hand is on my face too. He's rubbing my cheekbone with his rough thumb, and it feels so fucking amazing I close my eyes to it. I've missed his voice, and his arms around me, but perhaps it's moments like these that I've missed the most. Tanner might not make a habit of being cute, but he's tactile and sweet, and I've grown way too dependent on his touch.

"Hey." Tanner's thumb stops moving. "Whatever you're think-ing, try and flip it, okay? Nothing else bad is going to happen."

"What? Like, ever?"

"Can't promise that, but everything about this, about you and me? Yeah. It's all good, Jax. I love you."

I already knew it. Gabriel blew the whistle four days ago— four *long* days that have felt like a year. But hearing Tanner say it is something else. It blasts through the angst, making my eyes feel scratchy, and I take a sharp breath to catch it. "You love me?"

"Yeah. Does that scare you?"

"No." I shake my head slowly. "It didn't scare me when I realized I love you too. Then this happened, and I had to think about what it would be like if I never got the chance to tell you…properly, I mean, not in a garbled text message I was too dumb to say in person before I left."

"You're not dumb."

"I am sometimes. Maybe if I wasn't, we'd have had this conversation a month ago, and I wouldn't have to live with the fact that I've pushed you away so many times."

"You never pushed me away. There's no shame in needing space, Jax. Fuck, man, I know that feeling."

"It wasn't you I needed space from. It was myself. It's always myself."

"Can relate." Tanner throws a phrase he's picked up from me right back in my face.

I laugh, and it feels good. "I really do love you. And it doesn't scare me anymore. I didn't even need you to say it back to know that."

Tanner takes my hand from his face. He twines it with his and I gaze at our tangled fingers like I have so many times before. That feels good too, but it's different, perhaps because I've had to face a reality when the fingers wrapped around mine were cold and blue, and the breaths in his chest were raspy and shallow, not deep and soothing like they are now. I'm never going to take this feeling for granted. He is my most precious thing.

"So…" Tanner says after a few beats of silence. "I talked to a shrink yesterday."

"You did? When?"

"After they tried to make me eat the worst grilled cheese in the history of grilled cheese." Tanner shivers. "Apparently my insurance covers therapy after near-death experiences. Ironic, huh? They sure didn't give a shit when I was actually sick enough to need it."

"Are you going to have it? The therapy?"

"Yes." There's zero hesitation as Tanner speaks. "I don't think I need it because of what happened out there this time—if anything, that bang on the head has brought me back to life—but there's a lot of old shit floating around that I need to deal with, so I'm gonna deal with it, and who the fuck knows? Maybe next time we're out on those trails, we'll be out there together."

The thought fills me with more hope than I've ever dared dream. I've thought of Tanner every day out on those trails since I learned the connection between him and Vermont's sacred wilderness. I've dreamed of treading the earth together. Of watching the seasons change with him at my side. "That would be fucking amazing, but more than that, I want you to be well, in every sense, so if there's anything I can do to help you, you've gotta let me."

"Back atcha, sunshine."

"Are we making some kind of deal on our future happiness?"

"Maybe. Ask me when I'm not stoned on whatever sorcery they put in my IV."

I have no idea what's in Tanner's IV. Gabriel asks the doctors the questions and listens to the answers. I watch Tanner. And listen. And wait. But I'm not waiting anymore, he's right here and smiling, and, apparently, hungry.

Another first. I leave him for as long as I can stand and fetch him a bagel filled with cream cheese. He eats like a starving man. Then his grin grows wider and the color in his cheeks deepens.

A doctor comes to talk to him. The details pass me by until the young resident speaks the magic words. "We can start talking about your discharge tomorrow."

Tanner gives me a long, piercing look. It's warm and penetrating, and I see the cogs of his brain turning as he formulates his response.

He shifts his attention back to the doctor and gives her a firm shake of his head. "Fuck that. I'm going home today."

CHAPTER TWENTY-FIVE

Tanner

Evidently, I'm pretty persuasive. Who knew? I can't stand up without wobbling like a drunk person, but the doctor comes back that afternoon and signs me out. I'm going home. At least, I think I am, but Jax doesn't drive my car to V and V. He takes me to the parking lot by his apartment instead. "Your brother told me to. He said you'd be cleaning glasses by the weekend if I took you to the bar."

"How would I do that, when I can't walk in a straight line?"

"I don't know, mate. But I believe him."

I grunt, but I'm not all that annoyed. I've come to realize that I only really like my apartment when Jax is in it, and his place is basically one room, so even if I can't get up, he'll never be far away from me.

He takes the win and parks the car. The doors open and shut before I can blink and he's right there. "Come on."

"What?"

He rolls his eyes. "I know you only let Gabriel help you to the car because he's your brother, but if you want to actually come home with me, you're gonna have to let *me* help you."

"Thanks, but I'd rather stay here forever."

"I'm glad the concussion gave you a sense of humor. Now give me your good arm."

"Are you saying I wasn't funny before?"

"You were hilarious. Arm."

I like bossy Jax. It makes me feel things my body isn't quite ready to feel again, and it makes accepting his help to hobble from the car to his apartment easier to take.

I'm done with the world by the time we get there, though. I'm spinning, and I can't see how I'll ever stop.

Jax sits me on his bed and stands between my legs. He holds my head to his chest and rubs my back. "You won't feel like this forever. It passes, honest."

"You remember, don't you?"

"I do." He pulls back so I can see his face. "But I was alone, so I fell over a lot." He points to a tiny scar splicing his fair eyebrow —*How have I never seen that before?*—"That's not going to happen to you. You're not going to fall, Tanner, I promise."

We're talking about more than my terminal motion sickness, but I don't have the equilibrium to dissect it. So I don't try. I wrap myself in clothes that could be mine, or they could be Jax's, and crawl into his bed. He moves around his apartment for a few minutes, then he slips in beside me and flips the TV on. "This is us for the next few days. No aggro, got it?"

Aggro? The fuck does that mean? I don't dissect that either.

Recovery is harder than I'm prepared for, but I don't need to be battle-ready, because Jax has done this shit before. He knows how I feel before I feel it, and true to his word, he catches me every time I fear I might fall.

I don't fall anywhere except more in love with him. And I get to know him better too. Jerry's given him paid vacation time, so he only leaves the apartment to buy groceries and give me and Gabriel the occasional privacy to bicker about everything and nothing. As the pain fades, it's a good place to be. I learn more about Jax than I have in the entire time we've known each other.

Like he doesn't give a shit about movies unless they're wildlife documentaries. And he can cook three things: scrambled eggs, sandwiches made from bacon and ketchup, and some kind of a pasty with potatoes and beef that heals me from the inside out. With Eve filling the gaps with regular food drops, I have nothing to complain about.

I also learn that his taste in music extends beyond British indie rock I've never heard of. He plays Black Keys albums through his Bluetooth speaker, and strums Scar Tissue for me on his beat-up guitar with all the irony I need to make me laugh.

He kisses me too. A lot. And my body responds, but he won't let me wrestle him out of his clothes, or slide his hands beneath mine. "Not yet," he whispers.

It's the only thing about him I'll ever dislike.

Because I *want* him. Perhaps now, more than ever.

He's probably right that we shouldn't, though. Not if I want to stay awake longer than the full six minutes I've likely got in me right now.

I've been kicking it at home for two weeks when Eve and Gabi arrive one afternoon to break us up.

"I'm taking Jax out," Eve announces. "He's getting pale with all this indoors time. Not everyone's a vampire like you, Tanner."

"Vampires don't sleep eighteen hours a day," I retort, but I nod when Jax sends me a questioning stare. She's right: he needs to get out.

They leave and I resign myself to an extended sit-in with my brother, a prospect I could only have dreamed of a month ago. He's brought me coffee. I all but snatch it from him and take a sip. "Damn. You spiked it?"

"Bourbon," he confirms. "It's medicinal."

"Since when has liquor cured balance issues?"

"Since today. And I figured if it made you wobble, you could just climb right back into Jax's bed."

I'm sitting cross-legged on said bed, dressed as ever in sweats and a thick sweatshirt, so I don't have a million miles to fall, but I scowl at Gabi all the same. It's a luxury I've enjoyed since he told me he has no plans to leave Burlington any time soon. And I drink the bourbon-laced coffee. Fuck it. Maybe the caffeine will counter any horrible effects from the alcohol.

"You look good," Gabi remarks when I'm done with his magic potion. "I meant to say it when I walked in. Do you feel better?"

"Better than what?" I say around a wide yawn. "I'm so fucking tired."

"I know, but you don't look so green anymore."

"Are you still mad at me for puking on you?"

"Yes."

"Thanks for sharing, bro."

"You're welcome, but I was trying to be nice, so fuck you right back."

Gabriel snickers into his coffee, and I feel sixteen again. We've stolen booze from our mother's tiny stash and snuck out to the woods to drink it. Later, we'll stumble home to find her already asleep in bed and wonder why we hiked so far to drink her cheap whisky, but there you have it.

I let the nostalgia take me for a while, leaving Gabi to shout at the hockey game he's put on, but eventually, he shuts it off and gives me his full attention. "I was serious about you looking better. I thought you'd died again when I saw you a few days ago."

"I never died in the first place."

"Yeah, but it was the closest you've come that I can remember, so let me be dramatic."

"You're always dramatic."

"And you're always—" He stops himself before this descends into the kind of conversation two men pushing thirty have no business having. "Whatever. Let me in and I'll stop being so annoying."

"You're not annoying. I am. I'm sorry, it's a bad habit to be evasive. I'm trying to be better."

"You *are* better. That's my point. You're in good shape, in every sense. Has Jax really changed things so much for you?"

I think about it for moment, then shake my head. "Jax only changed things in the sense that I totally fucking love him. He didn't fix me—no one could do that."

"Not even me?

"Not even you, Gabs."

He sighs. "It's a real bitch you had to nearly die for us to have this epiphany."

"Speak for yourself. I knew it all along."

"Love you, bro."

"I love you too. Did you bring more bourbon?"

Gabriel leaves before Jax comes home, and it's the first time I've been alone since I walked out of the cabin to find Jerry on the doorstep.

I don't like it, and not just because I miss Jax more than his three-hour absence truly warrants. My thoughts have been calm since the accident, as if my subconscious knows my brain has all it can handle right now. But Gabi was right about me feeling better. I *do*. I can sit up without the room tilting, and stand without swaying. I don't feel sick after a five-stride trip to the bathroom, and I'm pretty sure I could make it downstairs and outside without needing a nap.

It's…something. But with my renewed wellbeing, my mind finds the time to wander to a reality that demands more of me than simply putting one foot in front of the other. Or maybe it doesn't, and the concept isn't as literal as I think. I've found a new place to swim, but I still need to keep swimming.

The analogy makes me think of sharks trying to eat Jax. I don't like those thoughts. I get up to escape them and shuffle into the tiny kitchen area of Jax's apartment. It's spotlessly clean, naturally, and his refrigerator actually has food in it. I open the door and ponder the contents. We've eaten our supply of Eve's mac and cheese, and I'm alert enough by now to the fact that cooking is the bane of Jax's life. He hates it almost as much as he loves me. Which is a lot. I know it even though he hasn't said it since he told me in the hospital.

I haven't said it, either. Jax doesn't need more heavy conversations. He needs me to get back on my feet, so I can be more to him than someone who lies in his bed and stares at his profile while he gets pissed at the camera angles in *Planet Earth*. And I need—

Fuck. I don't know. I need to make him dinner. I need to make a therapy appointment. And I need to turn my phone on and reply to the eleventy thousand messages Molly has sent me over the past several weeks.

I start with dinner. Jax has enough random vegetables and leftover ham in his refrigerator to make soup. I hack everything up one-handed, let it simmer, and return to the bed to find my phone. It's hidden under a stack of clean laundry I have no memory of anyone doing. Was it Jax? Eve? Definitely not Gabi. He makes me look house-proud. At least, that's what I'd always figured until I discovered he'd cleaned up the cabin. Now I don't know what to think, and turning my phone on is more important than ever.

It needs charging. I plug it in and sit on the floor with it while it buzzes to life. More messages flood in: Molly, Rainn, Harrison, Finn. Too many to contemplate until I do the one thing I turned my phone on for. Distraction is killer, and I don't want to die.

Not anymore.

Jax has left the business card the hospital shrink gave me on the nightstand by the side of the bed. I don't know if he meant to, but I'm glad I don't have to go looking for it. I punch the number into my phone and make the call. It's less painful than I anticipate. And the therapist has space for me starting next week.

Damn. I'm ready. I hope she is too. It's a call I should've made a long time ago, whether I could afford it or not, and the weight in my chest shifts as I hang up and stare at the blank phone screen Dr. Canon leaves behind. I'm not the same person I was before I made the call, but whoever I am, I need a shower, and I finally feel stable enough to take one without Jax.

After, I turn the soup off and pace his apartment, sporadically replying to the gazillion unread texts on my phone. Molly pings straight back with a bunch of new ones.

Molly: *OMG. You texted me back. How are you? Are you okay? We miss you! xxx*

Molly: *Like, seriously. Rainn is super grouchy without you to out grouch him. Help me! xxx*

Molly: *When can we see you? We made you things. We miss you! Are you coming back to work soon? We miss you! We miss you! Xxx*

I don't want to know what she means by *"we made you things,"* if it's anything she expects me to eat or drink. Her coffee is murderous and she can't tip potato chips out of a bag without spilling them all over the floor. But...I miss her wide eyes and infectious smile. I miss all my guys. But not enough to crawl back across town and behind that bar. Not yet. Even without the cloud of fatigue hanging over me, I'm not done being alone with Jax. I don't know why—what else I could possibly want?—but as a new, healthy agitation sweeps over me, I start to get an idea.

CHAPTER TWENTY-SIX

Jax

Eve keeps me out most of the day. It's dark by the time I skin out of her car and run up the stairs to my apartment. I expect to find Tanner in bed, or at the very least on it, but he's nowhere in sight as I let myself into my place. The bed is as neatly made as he's ever going to make it, and something that I haven't cooked is scenting the air from the kitchen area I can't see from the hallway.

I bend to untie my boots. Footsteps come up on me and Tanner's socked feet appear in my peripheral vision. "Hey."

"Hey," he says. His feet keep moving. Pacing. And I raise a brow as I straighten up.

Up until this point, he's slept a lot. If I don't think about what had to happen to get us here, it's been kind of nice. I've never really seen him rest. But he's not asleep now—he's wide awake and prowling. He needs something, but what?

I watch him fidget as I take off my coat and boots. He's agitated, I can tell, but it's not the same as the anxious energy I've seen in him before. The accident has temporarily knocked it out of him. It'll be back, I *know* that, but I'm enjoying its absence. *And* having Tanner all to myself in the weeks it's going to take before he can work again.

Selfish? Without doubt. But I love him. I'm never gonna feel bad about that. "Everything okay?"

"Yeah."

"Sure about that? You seem kinda buzzed."

"Gabi gave me some medicinal bourbon, but that was a while ago."

"Medicinal?"

"Didn't you know he's a fucking doctor?"

"He never said."

Tanner smirks. "That's because he's full of shit, but...I don't know. It sure did something to me."

"I can tell."

"Can you?"

I insert myself into his personal space. He's practically vibrating, and the heat in his piercing stare goes straight to my dick. "Yeah, I think so."

Tanner kisses me. It's soft at first, and he runs a gentle hand under my clothes and up my spine. He cups the back of my head and pulls me closer. Our bodies collide, melding together, and my bones turn to liquid as he slips his tongue into my mouth. The heat between us is raging, volatile after weeks of light touches, sweet kisses, and not much else. I want to be careful with him, like he was with me for so long, but I didn't need that then, and he doesn't need it now. Tanner's a big boy. He's still living life without the use of his injured arm, but the rest of him works just fine.

More than that, he *wants* this. He tugs me to the bed and topples us down, then he pulls me over him and splays his arms, as submissive as I've ever seen him. His eyes blaze. "Whatever you want. Take it."

"What do *you* want, Tanner?"

"Everything."

"Don't say it if you don't mean it."

"You think I'd do that?"

"No."

He smirks and stretches his good arm over his head to find the lube in my bedside table. He throws it at me. "Do your worst. I can take it."

I remember his words the first time we ever fucked. *"...I can go either way."* Hotter flames lick the inferno already tearing through my blood. I drop my head to kiss him and it's not gentle this time. Lips bruise. Teeth clash. Until I pull back and grip his face. "You want me to fuck you?"

Tanner licks his lips. "Yeah. I think I do."

I don't need telling twice, and something shifts between us, as if we've dropped gloves in a hockey game, but we're not going to fight, we're going to fuck. We wrestle each other out of our clothes and Tanner rolls onto his belly, holding his injured arm out of harm's way. I fit behind him like a dream, and ease inside with every intention of fucking him slowly, of making it last, but the gravelly sound of pleasure he makes obliterates my sweet resolve.

His back is everything. I lie over him and pump my body, building and building, until I'm fucking him hard enough for him to growl and fist the blue pillow he's buried his face in. I bite his neck. He pushes back against me, demanding more, and I give it to him, blinded by the sweat that runs down my face and into my eyes.

We've skipped a few steps—no foreplay, just kissing and then fucking at a million miles an hour. It's ridiculous, but I can't stop. I can't slow down and savor this moment. It's as if the worry and heartache we've been through to get to this point need exorcising. I'm shouting as I drive into him, and he answers me with soul-deep groans of satisfaction. His body flexes, and it's beautiful. *He's* beautiful, and I'm spellbound. Lost. I don't know how I'm gonna wait for him to come before my entire body explodes.

The bed starts to shift with the force of how we're moving together. Tanner braces himself with his good arm and raises his body from the bed, leaving his chest low, his legs spread wide. The change in angle blows my mind. I dig my fingers into his hips and they slip on his sweat-damp, inked skin. I press my face between his shoulder blades and groan. "I'm gonna come."

Tanner lets out a choked laugh. "Me first."

The echo of our first time together warms my bones, but I'm too far gone to enjoy the sentiment for long. Tanner arches his back, and any rhythm we had when we began this rowdy dance abandons us. Fucking him becomes clawing and desperate. I wait for him, clinging to my release, and I make it by a split second.

Tanner comes. His muscular body seizes up, clamping down on me, and he drags me into the fire. My cock erupts inside him. A plaintive noise escapes me, and my toes curl so hard I get fucking cramps in my feet. "Fuckfuck*fuck*."

I can't stop moving. And then I can't move at all. I'm frozen in place inside him and there's nowhere else I ever want to be.

Tanner collapses in a heap. I fall with him, briefly, then I remember he's still fragile and quickly roll off him, reclaiming my spent dick.

I ease Tanner onto his back and check him out, searching for signs of actual discomfort.

He shakes his head. "I'm fine. Don't freak out."

My chest is still heaving. It takes me a minute to speak. "I'm not freaking out. I just fucking love you."

Tanner beams. "That's lucky, because I fucking love you too."

His smile latches onto my soul. If he didn't have my entire heart already, I'd have handed it to him on a platter in this moment. Warmth fills the space the retreating heat of our half-crazed encounter leaves behind. I lean over him and touch his face, tracing his rough cheekbones and long lashes as if I've never seen them before. He grins at me some more, but his lids grow heavy as he clutches my hand to his chest. Whatever rejuvenation he's been through today is fading fast. I watch him go, and it's nice. Peaceful.

And despite his coma-like tendencies of the past few weeks, he's not gone for long.

I'm still naked when he wakes a half hour later. His eyes open, and they're still bright and unworried. Lively, even. Apparently my dick wasn't magic enough to calm the restlessness jumping in his restored blood. "Can we go to the bar?"

I pause in the action of bending over to retrieve the clothes we scattered all over the floor earlier. "You want to go to work?"

"Not to actually work. I need to see my guys. I miss them."

Of course he does. Before the accident, he saw them on a daily basis, and every single one of them had him on speed dial. V and V is his home. His family. He needs them as much they need him.

As much as he needs me. "For sure. You up to the walk? Or you want me to drive?"

"I can walk. I'm not wasting gas on a three-block stroll."

He hasn't walked further than the bathroom since he came home from the hospital, but I take him at his word, cos I know he'd do the same for me. I coax him into eating the soup he's made first, though, and load him up with the hydration he's lost through fucking.

Then we leave, hand-in-hand, and amble the short distance to V and V in the brisk chill of the evening. It's late when we get there and slip inside unnoticed, but the bar is still kicking. It's chaotic, too, without Tanner's efficient leadership. There are more glasses stacked on the tables than usual, and no one has restocked the shelves in a while.

"Don't," I say to Tanner as his gaze flickers around the carnage. "That's not why we're here."

As I speak the words, Molly looks up from clearing glasses and lays eyes on Tanner. Her excited shriek pierces the air. She drops a tray onto the table and blurs across the bar, stopping only milliseconds before she crashes into him. "Oh my gosh! You're here!"

The commotion alerts the rest of the staff to his presence, and he's soon surrounded, customers forgotten. I move aside and take a seat at the bar, watching it play out. Molly cries. I'm sure she's not the only one, and after a while, I feel like an intruder on a private moment. I avert my gaze and fish my phone from my pocket. I haven't checked my email in days. My inbox is stacked with bullshit. Most of it I ignore, all but two. One is from a lawyer's office in California with divorce papers attached, the other is from Jerry. He's offering me a permanent job at Wildfoot Adventure under the condition no one ever leaves the office without a satellite phone ever again.

I blink at my phone screen. The two emails seem to bookend my life so entirely I have no idea what to do with it.

A large frame folds into the stool beside me. For a moment I'm so convinced it's Tanner I hold out my phone to my new companion.

I realize too late that it's Gabriel. He scans the emails with a frown, and it doesn't occur to me to stop him. Or object when he opens the attachments.

He studies the divorce petition, then the contract Jerry has sent. Nodding as though it's a done deal, he hands the phone back. "Do you need a pen?"

"Wouldn't do me much good. They're electronic documents."

"A hypothetical pen, dude. I'm just trying to tell you we all want you to stick around."

"We?"

"Eve. Tanner. And whatever makes them happy makes me happy too."

Contracts and divorces be damned, I have no intention of going anywhere. I'm not the one who works out of state. "I'm sticking around. What about you? I love Eve and Tanner too, and they need you, man."

"I know." Gabriel reaches over the bar and pours himself a glass of red from the nearest bottle. He holds it up to the light and frowns at it. "Is this the good stuff? I only drink beer and soda."

"I don't know. Ask Tanner."

Gabriel snorts. "He doesn't know either. But to answer your question, I'm sticking around. I'm tired of being snarled up in a job that nearly gets me killed for no good fucking reason. If I was saving the world, I could live with it, but all I've done the last few years is line the pockets of rich oil dudes and miss the fuck out of my girl and my brother."

"So we're both staying?"

"Yup. Which is just as well. I don't think your boy is of the mind to let either of us leave."

Tanner is with us before I can respond. I can't tell if he knows Gabriel is staying yet, because their relationship is still a mystery to me. They communicate in grunts and intense stares, or they bicker like schoolgirls. There's no in-between, but god, they love each other.

I snag Gabriel's stolen wine and sip it. It's rich and red and tastes like Christmas, another fast approaching holiday I've done nothing about. I think about Thanksgiving and the warmth and contentment that surrounded us then. It has nothing on how I feel right now and I'm almost scared of what the future holds. Of how much my heart can expand before it explodes.

It's quite the image, and I laugh at myself as Tanner wraps his arms around me from behind and leans heavily against me. He buries his face in my neck and breathes me in.

I reach for him and find his bare hip beneath his T-shirt. "All right back there?"

He nods, then grips my shoulders and spins me around, ignoring his brother entirely. "I really fucking love you."

I take his good hand and squeeze it. "I know, mate. I love you too."

CHAPTER TWENTY-SEVEN

Six months later…

Tanner

Jax is setting up the tent with one hand; the other is still pointing his camera at the squirrels playing in the trees above us. I want to tell him to pay attention to what he's doing, but I swallow it down and park my ass in the sun instead.

I tip my face to the sky, absorbing the kind of warmth that only Jax can match. Then I open my eyes and soak up my surroundings. We're at the highest point of Black Claw, and my heart still thumps as if it's the first moment I've been outside since the accident. But it's not. We come up here all the time, and I've learned to accept the sporadic anxiety that still haunts me. My biggest problem is hating myself for letting it control me for as long as it did. For the impact it had on the people I love too.

Deep breaths cleanse my soul. Guilt remains my nemesis, but I've learned new tools to deal with that too. Therapy is a drag, but it's working, so I go every week and continue my quest to be the best man I can be.

"I'm glad we waited until we'd known each other a while to do this shit together." Jax drops down beside me, without his camera *and* his shirt. *Awesome.*

"Oh yeah? Why's that?"

"Cos I can't fucking cope with how hot you are in mountain-man mode. It's, like, six levels up from sexy bartender."

"I'm still a bartender."

"Yeah, but you gave me time to build up to peak mountain man."

By "doing this" he means spending every free day we have out here together. I never took the job Kai Fletcher offered me—I love the bar too much—but Jax took his job with Jerry, and I help him as much as I can. And he helps me just by existing, so it's a win-win. When the weather's bad, we sleep at the cabin, but on days like this when there's not a cloud in the sky, we sleep under the stars with only canvas between us and the big wide world. "I dig that you like the way we live now," I say, punctuating my words by pulling him on top of me. "I'm just sad we weren't living this way all along."

"I'm not." Jax finds his own punctuation in rough kisses and snatched breaths. "Humans don't appreciate the stuff that comes easily."

"True story. I'm pretty pumped Jerry decided not to open Black Claw after all. Humans wreck everything."

Jax hums vaguely enough that I can't tell if he agrees or not, but it doesn't matter. We don't have to agree on everything. Life would be boring if we did. And trust me, life with Jax isn't boring, whether we're up here doing his job in the great outdoors, or huddled in my apartment above V and V. It works because we want it to.

I kiss Jax again, taking control of what he started, and rolling him over on the blanket I laid out while he was messing with the tent we'll sleep in later. It's summer, so he's wearing cargo shorts. The sun has lightened his hair enough that he really does look like the surfer dude he once was, and it's longer now too. Wavier. I grip the golden strands as I plunder his mouth, then I groan as he takes advantage of my distraction to unbutton my shorts.

He has calloused hands from his time in the Vermont wilderness. They feel amazing on my dick, and it doesn't take me long to strip us both of the rest of our clothes. We brought lube, obviously. We don't camp without it.

I dig it out of my discarded shorts and pop the cap. Jax doesn't ask where I plan to put it, and I don't ask him what he wants. Being happily versatile works for us, but I can't deny there's something special about fucking him up here. It's the other benefit of Black Claw staying closed to the public—we can fool around out in the open without worrying about being caught. The spot we've picked only has one approach route, and I can see it clearly every time I glance up, which admittedly isn't as often as I should. With Jax naked beneath me, tearing my gaze from him is impossible.

I fuck him slowly, rocking into him with deep, steady thrusts that make his eyes roll. I'm on my knees, body curved around him, and his legs are bent to his chest, one knee hooked over my shoulder. There isn't an inch between us, and no sound in the air that isn't completely fucking natural. No bar patrons or friendly bosses calling our names. Just him, me, and the squirrels who are totally watching us fuck.

Jax shudders through his orgasm. I screw him a little harder, pumping my hips, chasing the ultimate pleasure that's twisting his handsome face. It's not far from my grasp. Sensation overwhelms me. I bury my face in Jax's cut chest and come with a deep groan.

After, we lie together, panting and sweating, and then drowsing as we look out over the land and run lazy hands over each other. Jax tells me Molly's asshole ex-boyfriend has moved to Seattle, which still isn't far enough in my opinion, after a douchebag lawyer got the charges against him dropped. I tell him Eve's friend Rumi still wants to paint us, and he wants us to be naked.

Jax laughs, and it really is as magical as the fucking sun. "I'll do it if you will."

"For real?"

"Sure. I mean, it's finger painting, right? How the hell is he gonna capture fucking teeth marks with his pinky? Or all your ink? How bad could it be?"

I snort, and then shiver as he runs a finger down the jagged scar on my wrist. It's pretty tidy compared to the scars Jax has, and mostly hidden by ink, but some days it seems starker than others.

Today I've forgotten it's there. I'm as Zen as I ever feel, and even Jax talking about his finalized divorce doesn't piss me off. "It never bothered me that you were still married, but I'm glad you're not anymore."

"I was never sure you even knew until after her lawyers found me. You never asked."

"It didn't matter to me. Only bad feelings I have about it is that it made you feel so shitty about yourself."

"It's over now."

"I know." And it's true in more ways than one. The pain Jax has endured to get to this point is more subtle than mine, but he's a different man than the one I found on his ass last winter. He's sharper, stronger, and has no problem telling me or anyone else exactly what he wants. Choices no longer faze him. And he's not scared of being happy. Neither of us are.

We talk about Gabi's new job with a local PI agency, and how hilarious it is that he's still living with Eve at her yoga commune. We talk about the poker game I play with Jerry on Monday nights. Then we fall silent. My heart is still banging against my ribcage, but it's no longer anxiety making my pulse jump. It's Jax's arms around me, his head on my shoulder, and his soft breaths in my ear. It's the box he still keeps behind the couch in my apartment, and his hand in mine when he sits outside my therapist's office with me.

It's everything we never knew we needed.

It's Jax.

It's me.

It's the heartscape we'll leave behind when we're gone.

THE
END

Made in the USA
Monee, IL
16 May 2021